The Rake's Game

Lady Mary could not believe this was happening, that she was actually being kissed by the Marquess of Pemerton. Oh, he had always flirted with her, to be sure, but it meant nothing. She had almost gone mad the night at the Opera when he had toyed with her hand throughout the last act, and even brushed his lips against her neck. But she knew it was merely his way with women, just a game he played.

And yet this was no game, she thought, moaning lightly as his lips and tongue tantalized her neck, his silky black hair tickling her cheek.

Or if it was a game, it was one of which she had no experience, no understanding of the rules.

It was a game in which she had so much to lose . . . and so much to gain. . . .

A Change of Heart

by

Candice Hern

A SIGNET BOOK

SIGNET
Published by the Penguin Group
Penguin Books USA Inc., 375 Hudson Street,
New York, New York 10014, U.S.A.
Penguin Books Ltd, 27 Wrights Lane,
London W8 5TZ, England
Penguin Books Australia Ltd, Ringwood,
Victoria, Australia
Penguin Books Canada Ltd, 10 Alcorn Avenue,
Toronto, Ontario, Canada M4V 3B2
Penguin Books (N.Z.) Ltd, 182–190 Wairau Road,
Auckland 10, New Zealand

Penguin Books Ltd, Registered Offices:
Harmondsworth, Middlesex, England

First published by Signet, an imprint of Dutton Signet,
a division of Penguin Books USA Inc.

First Printing, December, 1995
10 9 8 7 6 5 4 3 2 1

To Greg
for his constant support and encouragement,
great advice (some of it taken), tireless
reading and re-reading,
and for giving me the idea to write
in the first place

Chapter 1

Jack Raeburn, Marquess of Pemerton, raised his quizzing glass and studied the young girl dancing with Lord Grayston. He leaned negligently against a pillar, half hidden by an extravagant floral arrangement, as he eyed the girl up and down. Miss Pettibone was very fair with masses of blond ringlets and huge blue eyes that gazed up in awe at her noble partner. She was a pretty little thing, Jack decided, as she shyly smiled up at Grayston. He was enjoying a clear view of her full, white bosom rising up and down with the exertion of the country dance when he suddenly felt a presence at his side.

Dropping his quizzing glass, he looked over and then down at the tiny woman who stood next to him. How long had she been there, he wondered? She was also looking intently at Miss Pettibone. But then she turned to look up at Jack, wrinkled her nose behind the screen of her open fan, and shook her head. Jack glared down at her and quirked a brow.

"Too young," she whispered, still shaking her head.

Jack choked on a hastily suppressed snort of laughter as he watched her eyes move back toward the dance floor. Who was this woman? She looked vaguely familiar, but he couldn't place her. She was not young, but not precisely old either. Though small, she was nicely rounded in all the right places, he was quick to note. She had ordinary brown hair, a too wide mouth, and a slightly crooked nose; but the eyes that had looked up at him had been enormous pools of hazel. Other than the eyes, her face was quite unremarkable. That was probably why he could not place her. She was not the sort of woman who normally piqued Jack's interest.

He dragged his eyes from his unknown companion and once again raised his quizzing glass as he surveyed the ballroom. This time his gaze fell upon a lovely young redhead standing along the opposite wall, flirting with a circle of admirers. She brought her fan to her lips as she giggled at some remark, then snapped it shut and slapped it down on the wrist of her nearest gallant, batting her eyes coquettishly. Her hair was absolutely glorious, with one long fiery curl hanging over a creamy white shoulder. By God, no one was going to tell him that there was anything wrong with *this* young beauty. Nevertheless, tearing himself away after one last admiring gaze, he reluctantly turned his glass upon the woman at his side and raised his brows in question. She hunched a shoulder and raised her fan to partially cover her face. Jack's greater height gave him a clear view behind the fan, and he watched as her mouth twisted in distaste. She leaned toward him in a conspiratorial manner without taking her eyes off the girl.

"Too silly," she whispered.

Jack grinned down at this impertinent unknown who nevertheless intrigued him. What was her game? Well, whatever it was, he was just bored enough to play along and find out.

This time he raised his glass to study Lady Amanda Palmer, Egerton's eldest daughter, as she was partnered by Lord Ainsley. She was a glowing beauty with glossy dark brown curls and amber-colored eyes. Her face was lit up with a spectacular smile, and her cheeks were slightly flushed from the dance. Jack's glass followed the line of her graceful neck down over the rounded shoulders to the full swell of bosom revealed by her rather daring neckline. He knew this to be at least her third Season, and her manners were open though modest. Surely there could be no objection to this young lady, he thought as he looked down at his tiny confederate.

She sighed and looked up with a resigned shake of her head.

"Of course, it is up to you, my lord," she said in a husky whisper, "but Lady Amanda has an unfortunate tendency toward plumpness. Only look at her mother." She cocked her head in the direction of the corner of the room reserved for dowagers and chaperones.

Jack's glass followed her gaze toward the sea of plumed turbans in the corner. It was hard to miss Lady Egerton whose bulk took up almost an entire settee. One of the spindly-legged chairs used by the other matrons would have surely collapsed under the woman's tremendous girth. Jack bit back a smile.

He dropped his quizzing glass, which, attached to its black ribbon, fell against his white brocade waistcoat. He heaved a dramatic sigh.

"Well, madam," he said in a bored tone, "I seem to be foiled at every turn. Perhaps you have a candidate of your own to recommend?" Most likely the woman had a daughter or niece or some other charge under her wing, with hopes of securing an advantageous match. Well, thought Jack, so long as the chit came with a plump dowry, he was willing to entertain any and all suggestions.

"Not at the moment," the woman replied, smiling brightly up at him. "But I would be happy to help you in your search, Lord Pemerton."

Jack pulled away from the pillar, straightened up, and peered down at the woman, furrowing his brow in puzzlement. Still, he could not place her, though she obviously knew him. Of course, there was nothing particularly distinctive about her that would have kept her in his memory; although he thought he might have remembered that intriguingly husky voice, surprising in such a small woman.

"I beg your pardon, madam," he said, "but you seem to have the advantage of me. You apparently know who I am and yet I don't—"

"Oh, but we *have* met, my lord," she interrupted.

"Indeed? I must apologize, then, for I am afraid I don't recall—"

"No need to apologize, my lord," she interrupted again, this time with a wave of dismissal. "I do not expect you would remember since you were thoroughly foxed at the time."

"Oh, good Lord," Jack mumbled as he raked a hand through his hair and dropped his eyes to the ground. What transgression had he committed in this lady's presence? Before he could ponder the countless possibilities, his attention was firmly snatched back to the present by the sound of a rich, throaty chuckle. He looked over to find the lady's head thrown back as she abandoned herself to laughter. The sound was so delightful, almost like a rusty gate, that he could not help but smile.

"Lady Mary Haviland," she said at last, offering her hand.

"Your servant, Lady Mary," said Jack as he took her hand and bowed over it. "Haviland? That would make you Assheton's—"

"The late earl was my father," she said, somewhat abruptly. "You and I were introduced at Lord and Lady Bradleigh's wedding last year," she continued in a brighter tone.

"Ah," Jack said, nodding his head, "that explains why I don't remember you, Lady Mary. I don't remember much of anything about that day. I'm afraid I was too busy drowning my sorrow at losing a longtime companion in dissipation to the dreaded state of matrimony."

"And yet you are now contemplating that same dreaded state for yourself."

Jack reached once again for his quizzing glass, narrowing his eyes as he glared through it at Lady Mary. "How is it that you know so much of my business, madam?" he asked in a chilling tone. What was this tiny vixen up to? Since she was no matron after all, then she must be looking to feather her own nest. Ha! On a cold day in hell, if she was lucky. She was not at all his type.

"Oh, do put that thing down, my lord," Lady Mary said, playfully swatting away the quizzing glass with her fan. "No need to get haughty with *me*. The fact is, all the world knows that you are looking for a bride."

"Do they, indeed?"

"Well, of course," she continued. "It is only to be expected after—" She stopped abruptly, brought her hand to her mouth, and gave him a stricken look. "Oh, dear. Please forgive my wayward tongue, my lord," she said in a tight voice, her eyes bright with . . . what? Tears?

Damnation! He was sick to death of Society's endless intrusive sympathy. It had been just a year since the tragic boating accident had claimed not only his father, but his two older brothers and his only nephew as well. That dreadful day had elevated Jack, a younger son with no expectations beyond the small estate his father had granted him upon his majority, into the unwanted position of Marquess of Pemerton and head of the family. The care-for-nothing rakehell had been thrust headlong into a mountain of unimaginable responsibilities. Having no opportunity to face his own grief, he certainly had had no time or inclination to deal with the egregious, meddlesome condolences of the *ton*.

"How awful it must have been for you," Lady Mary was saying in a low, raspy voice. "Well," she said, suddenly brightening, "let us not dwell on that painful subject. Nothing can change what has happened, after all, and so you must get on with your life. Is that not so?"

"Yes," Jack said absently as he looked at Lady Mary in astonishment. He had been attempting to live by those very sentiments for the last year, but no one seemed to understand. He was constantly made to dwell on the multiple tragedy by his grieving mother, his sisters-in-law, his nieces, and most of his acquaintances. It had been such a freak accident that everyone seemed to want to discuss it—constantly, and at length.

All he wanted to do was to forget and move on. And oddly enough, this stranger, Lady Mary, seemed to understand what most of his friends and family could not. He studied her face as she gazed up at him, an honest, open expression in her hazel eyes. The errant thought crossed his mind that here was a woman he could trust, who could be a friend. A friend? As Jack had never before had a woman for a friend—indeed, he had rather scorned the entire female species as being unworthy of any consideration outside the bedroom—he was at a loss to understand this entirely foreign notion.

"Am I not correct in assuming that, now you are the marquess, you must find a bride and ensure the succession?" she asked.

Jack sighed and glared at Lady Mary. "Yes."

"Well, then," she said cheerfully, "since I know you to be a rake and a rogue—and rogues are among my favorite people in the world—I would be happy to stand your friend and assist you in your search."

"You honor me, Lady Mary," Jack said as he sketched a bow.

"Only, you must promise, my lord," she said, "not to become stuffy in your new position. You must retain *some* measure of your roguish ways else I shall become bored and disgusted with you. I have no patience with sober, dull pattern cards of propriety. Rogues, on the other hand, I find delightfully entertaining."

Jack reached for her hand and brought it to his lips. "I shall endeavor always to keep you entertained, my lady," he said in his most seductive tone. "And since you are so fond of . . . rogues . . . perhaps the best plan would be to marry me yourself. It would save me a great deal of trouble."

Lady Mary threw back her head and laughed. Jack was once again charmed by the husky, rusty sound of her laughter. His own laughter soon joined hers, and before long he felt several curious pairs of eyes on them. Not wishing to bring any unnecessary attention to Lady Mary, whom he decided he quite liked, he took her by the elbow and led her deeper into the shadows behind the floral arrangement. Of course, Jack thought with wicked amusement, being tugged into the shadows of a ballroom by the notorious Black Jack Raeburn could be even more damaging to her reputation. She turned to look up at him.

"You may rest easy on that score, my lord," she said, still smiling broadly, apparently unconcerned with what wagging tongues might make of her skulking in the shadows with a gazetted rake. "I am definitely *not* in the market for a husband. I am not at all interested in marriage. Nor," she added when Jack cast her a lecherous leer, "am I interested in dalliance, my lord."

Jack gave a sigh of mock despair.

"But I *am* interested in friendship," she continued. "One can never have too many friends. May I hope that *we* can become friends, my lord?"

"I believe we are already friends, Lady Mary," Jack said. "Indeed, I am certain we have been friends this last half hour or more."

"In that case," she said, "I am ready to help you find an appropriate bride. Although it is somewhat late in the Season and certain young ladies have already formed attachments, I believe there are still many admirable ladies available. I can think of several off the top of my head. But we must find someone who will appreciate your . . . er . . . more interesting qualities. And of course, a man in your position must always be mindful of the honor and dignity due his title. Unfortunately," she said, tapping her closed fan absently against her cheek, "that title will have the matchmakers beating a path to your door with their daughters in tow."

Jack gave a resigned shrug. "Yes," he said, "I have already had some experience in that respect. 'Tis a curious thing. A year ago most of those women would drag their precious daughters from the room in a panic if I so much as showed my face. Now, they dog my tail at every turn."

Lady Mary nodded in understanding. "All the more reason to accept my assistance," she said. "I can help you to sort out the eligible misses thrown in your path. Though I have no doubt your experience with females is vast," she said as a huge grin split her face, "unless I am much mistaken, I suspect that none of those females is precisely the sort you would want as your bride."

"N-no, not exactly," Jack sputtered. Was he truly having such a conversation with a gently bred, unmarried female? He shook his head in disbelief and grinned. He could not remember when he had been so vastly entertained by a woman—outside of the usual ways, of course—and such a plain little thing at that. And to think he had actually considered not coming to Lady Pigeon's ball!

"As it happens," Lady Mary continued, "I have been about a great deal these last few years and have, I am happy to say, a very wide acquaintance among respectable Society. I can easily introduce you to dozens of perfectly delightful, eminently acceptable young women. I will also be able to warn you against those who ought to be avoided for various reasons. Fortune hunters, for example."

"I begin to understand," Jack said. "I can see where your superior knowledge might be useful."

"Well, of course!" she said with an exasperated wave of her hands. "But first, you must give me your list of requirements."

"My what?"

"You know," she said with some impatience, "those qualities you are searching for in a bride. It will help me to identify the proper candidate."

"I haven't given it much thought," Jack lied. He would be damned before he would enlighten this perfect stranger, delightful though she may be, to his true motives.

"Don't be ridiculous! Of course you have. Let us start with the obvious. I presume she must be a beauty?"

Jack shrugged. He really would prefer to change the subject.

"Well, naturally she must be beautiful," Lady Mary said. "She will be your marchioness, after all. And it is only fitting, since you are quite good-looking yourself," she said with a teasing grin.

"Are your flirting with me, Lady Mary?"

"Don't be absurd," she said and then once again gave that throaty chuckle. "And so what else, my lord? Besides beauty?"

"You have already warned me against the too young, the too silly, and the too plump. I obviously do not have your discriminating tastes, my Lady. I shall leave the choice to your better judgment."

"Good heavens, Lord Pemerton, I did not mean to make the selection *for* you. Only to help steer you through the rocky shoals of the Marriage Mart. To help you from running aground upon the first sandbar you encounter. 'Tis a tricky business, you know. Dangerous waters, indeed."

"Since you seem to know so much about it," Jack said, arching a significant brow, "then why, if I may ask, have *you* never married, Lady Mary?"

The husky laugh once again disarmed him.

"As I have said, it is tricky business," she said. "Too tricky to be of interest to me. Besides, I am much too old for such nonsense."

"Too old for games of the heart?" Jack said, lowering his voice seductively. "Come now, my lady. Where is your sense of adventure?"

"Let us just say, my lord," she replied, matching Jack's tone with her own hoarse whisper, "that I am content to be a spectator in this particular game. I am quite happily and comfortably on the shelf, if you must know."

"Then why are you so anxious to thrust *me* into the dangerous waters of the Marriage Mart?"

"I believe I shall find it excessively diverting, my lord!" The broad grin once again split her face, and her eyes twinked with merriment. "Besides, you have already plunged into the water. I am merely offering to help you stay afloat. Anyway, now that we are friends, I want you to be happy. I want all my friends to be happy."

"You are very generous, my lady. And do you make yourself happy by ensuring the happiness of your friends?"

"I do indeed. It gives me a great deal of satisfaction. But in your case, I believe I shall find a great deal of amusement as well. I do so hate to be bored."

"So you have said," Jack replied. "Well, Lady Mary, during the last year I have been, if not precisely bored, then certainly not entertained. Like you, my dear, I detest boredom and have in fact spent most of my life in search of diversion. It shall give me the greatest pleasure to have you transform my current task into something more amusing."

"Ha!" she shouted, clapping her hands together and practically bouncing with glee. "I knew I would like you!"

"Well, then," he said spreading his arms wide, "what are you waiting for? Let the parade begin!"

Chapter 2

"Lord Pemerton? Good heavens, Mary, have you lost your mind?"

Mary could not hold back her smile, despite the look of horror on her companion's face. Olivia Bannister, hands frozen in mid-stitch as she looked up from her embroidery, had been in Mary's employ for over three years now, and yet apparently Mary still had the ability to shock the woman. Poor dear, thought Mary as she considered that she had likely been responsible for more than a few of those gray hairs sprinkled among Olivia's auburn curls. But she really ought to be accustomed to Mary's somewhat unconventional ways by now.

"Come now, Olivia," Mary said as she swung her feet up onto the sofa, tucking them under her in an unladylike position, which had more than once brought a disapproving frown to her companion's face. "There is no need to get into such a pelter. I assure you, the situation is quite harmless."

Olivia glared at her with a look of such outrage that Mary burst out laughing. At last, Olivia cast her eyes toward the heavens, as if seeking guidance from Above, bundled her embroidery into her sewing bag, heaved a resigned sigh, and fixed Mary with a stern look.

"My dear," she said, "as long as we have been acquainted, have you ever known me to cavil at any behavior of yours?"

"Well, you *do* have a certain look—the one you are giving me just now, in fact—which can quite put one off. But, no, Olivia, you have never to my knowledge openly questioned any action of mine."

"As is only proper," Olivia said with a sniff. "As your employee I am not in a position to object. But . . . as a friend . . ."

"A very dear friend."

"As your friend," Olivia continued, "I believe I must take exception this time." She rose from her chair and joined Mary on the sofa. "My dear, I sometimes think you forget that you are an unmarried woman and therefore bound by certain rules of Society."

"Fustian!" Mary said, brushing away those concerns with a wave of her hand. "Those rules were made for the protection of pretty young innocents straight out of the schoolroom. I am neither pretty nor young, and have no one to answer to but myself. And I have never done anything of which I am ashamed. I *do* have some scruples, you must know."

"I know, Mary. But—"

"And I would never do anything to hurt another human soul."

"No, of course you would not," Olivia said as she reached out to lay her hand over Mary's. "You are the kindest, most generous person I have every known."

"Thank you, my dear. Well then, what have I ever done, after all, that was so very shocking?"

"Well," Olivia said as the corners of her mouth began to curl almost imperceptibly upward, "there was the time you disappeared at Lady Dunholm's rout for over an hour with Lord Erskine."

"We were playing a private game of piquet in one of the back parlors, as you well know. Anyone could have found us if they had wanted to."

"And there was the time you blithely waltzed into Harriet Wilson's box at the opera."

"I simply wanted to meet her," Mary said, shrugging her shoulders nonchalantly. "And she was every bit as fascinating as I had expected. Well, she would have to be, would she not? I found her quite charming."

"And there was the time you went strolling in the gardens at Hatfield on a moonless night with that rake, Sir Rodney Lattimer. And returned with a very interesting tear in your dress."

It was Mary's turn to roll her eyes heavenward. "Sir Rodney

and I were having a very interesting discussion about modern composers," she said in an exasperated tone. "I simply was not paying attention to my surroundings and happened to catch my sleeve on one of the holly bushes. Perfectly harmless."

"Except," Olivia said in a tone worthy of a starchy governess, "to your reputation."

"Olivia! When will you get it through your head that people like me do not have reputations? No one cares what a twenty-nine-year-old, ugly, insignificant, unmarried woman does. No one pays me the least attention, I assure you. Society does not care tuppence for women like me. I am perfectly safe, Olivia, even if I *do* prefer to associate with rakes, rogues, and the occasional courtesan. I only want to make interesting new friends, you know."

"But you already have so many friends, my dear . . ."

"Yes," Mary said wistfully. "It is quite wonderful, is it not? How fortunate I am!"

"Yes, but . . . Lord Pemerton, Mary?"

"Oh!" Mary said, excited to discuss her newest friend. "Wait 'til you meet him, Olivia. I am persuaded you cannot dislike him. He is most amusing—and quite handsome."

"Mary!"

"Well, one can look, cannot one?" As long as one doesn't dream, thought Mary as she recalled the darkly handsome marquess. He did not have the fresh good looks of youth, nor the classical perfection of someone like Lord Bradleigh, the stunningly handsome husband of her friend Emily. And, to be sure, there were certain signs of dissipation in the lines about Lord Pemerton's mouth and eyes. But for all that, his face had a character that appealed to Mary more than many others. Yes, she could look. But she must take care that the piercing blue eyes, unruly black hair, and sensuous smile of the marquess did not too often invade her thoughts.

But then, Mary had always been very sensible about such matters. She accepted her situation without complaint, and almost never dared to cherish foolish dreams. She had certainly been around her fair share of attractive men, and even called some of them friend. Why, then, should this particular man give her cause to worry?

"But he is a rake!" Olivia exclaimed, drawing Mary's attention back to their conversation.

"So I am told," Mary said as she arched a teasing brow.

"But, my dear, I am sure you know that he is quite . . . well . . . notorious. A shameless womanizer. Why, I believe I have heard that he has fought several duels. The man is dangerous, Mary!"

"I promise you," Mary said with a grin, "that Lord Pemerton and I will not resort to pistols at dawn."

"But—"

"Olivia, I like him," Mary said. And she meant it. She really did like him. Quite a lot, actually. "You know that I have a soft spot in my heart for rakes," she continued. "They are so much more honest in their approach to life than the usual paragons of propriety. Those sober, proper gentlemen more often than not harbor cold hearts and dark secrets."

Only consider my own father, Mary added silently to herself.

"And most of those fine, upstanding fellows," she continued, "routinely deceive their wives with a string of ladybirds on the sly. I have no patience with such hypocrisy, Olivia. I much prefer the man who is open and straightforward in his dealings with people, even if he does not often stay strictly within the rules of Society. You can trust a man like that."

"That is all well and good," Olivia said, "and might have something to say to the matter . . . *if* you were another man. But as an unmarried female—"

"Oh, bother!" Mary said. "Must we go over this again and again? I hold no interest *in that way* for such a man. They can be comfortable with me. That is why we can be friends. And I am convinced Lord Pemerton and I will become great friends. I liked him at once. He has such a way with a quizzing glass! I wonder if he could teach me how to wield one with such aplomb?"

Olivia let out a long, slow breath and gazed at Mary with furrowed brows. "And so you are to help him find a bride?" she asked.

"Yes! Imagine, helping to select a bride for a notorious rake! This will be such fun!"

"But why you? Why can he not find his own bride?"

"Because the poor man has no idea how to go about it properly," Mary said. "He would settle for just about anyone, you must know, just to get the thing over with. I could not stand by and watch such a fascinating man tie himself to some giggly young fool, just for the sake of the succession. She would either lead him a merry dance or bore him to death. In either case, he would probably ignore her completely or abandon her at the first opportunity, and then two lives would have been made miserable. How much more preferable to find a woman who could accept him for what he is, and with whom he could be comfortable. I can think of many such women. In fact, I have been making a list."

"You haven't!"

"I have." Mary pulled a folded piece of foolscap out of her pocket. "Perhaps you would like to review it with me? I might have overlooked someone."

"Good Lord," Olivia groaned as she reached for the list.

Jack was stretched out comfortably on the bed. Hands propped behind his head, he stared up at the elaborate tented canopy while running numbers through his brain. He was mentally calculating how the rents from Pemworth might be used to offset the cost of draining the west pasture at Crutchley. Such thoughts were never far from his mind at any time these days. Was it only a year ago that his only concern, aside from the constant search for new pleasures to be experienced, had been the smooth running of his small estate in Herefordshire? Indeed, Broadhurst had never been a cause for much concern, as Jack had a very competent steward who ensured that the estate was run efficiently and profitably.

Yet now, here he was, saddled with no fewer than six large estates inherited from his father and brothers, and not a one of them profitable. In fact, not a one of them was free of debt. Jack had always understood that his father, though a charming raconteur and sportsman, had no head for business. Never, however, in his wildest imaginings would he have expected the man's affairs—now Jack's affairs—to be in such disarray. And all a result, as far as Jack was able to determine, of gross mismanagement.

He mentally ticked off rows of figures until he was convinced that by taking a bit from here and putting a bit over there that he could somehow finance the required drainage project. He breathed a sigh of relief. He must remember to contact Godolphin, his man of business, first thing in the morning to review the plan.

Good Lord, but he seemed to be spending all his waking hours dealing with his blasted, unwanted, unsought inheritance. Well, maybe not *all* his waking hours, he thought as his eyes drifted to the soft, white, naked body curled up at his side. As he watched her sleep, Jack decided that although Phoebe was deliciously voluptuous and incredibly responsive—but of course she was an actress, so one could never be sure about those things—that he really ought to let her go. She was already an expense he could ill afford; and lately she had been tossing out hints about diamond bracelets and high-perch phaetons that caused him to break out in a cold sweat.

Perhaps tomorrow he would buy her some small bauble as a parting gift, and give her her *congé*. He doubted she would have difficulty finding another protector. Dalrymple had frequently shown an interest. Perhaps he would take her on.

Jack wasn't going to waste any time worrying about her. Phoebe, he thought as he brushed a hand lightly along her hip, would take care of herself. She made a small purring sound and curled up closer against his side. He never gave a second thought to what became of women such as Phoebe.

The sounds of movement in the adjoining dressing room alerted him to the presence of Jessop, his valet. For a moment he had forgotten that he was not comfortably ensconced in his love nest on Half Moon Street. The small town house—the scene of many wild and passionate evenings over the years—had been sold some months ago. He could no longer afford the luxury of a separate house kept solely for the purpose of assignations. It galled him to have to bring his ladybirds to his own town house. It was simply not done. The fourth marquess, his grandfather, who had built the spacious Hanover Square house, was probably turning over in his grave at the thought of such women being brought into his home.

Jack gave Phoebe one last lingering look and slipped carefully out of bed. She stirred and made a soft whimpering sound before curling more tightly around the down pillow. He padded across the room and silently entered the dressing room, leaving the bedroom door slightly ajar. Jessop was busy tidying up the various garments strewn about the room. He looked up when he heard Jack enter, stopped what he was doing, and quickly retrieved a dressing gown from a hook on the wardrobe door. He held it out for Jack, who shrugged into it and sank down into a nearby wing chair.

"I will need you in a few hours, Jessop, to get Phoebe out of here before the household wakens."

"Of course, my lord."

"God, how I hate bringing them here." Jack nestled his head back into a corner of the chair and sighed deeply. He had no qualms about speaking so frankly to Jessop. They had known one another for years. Jessop was the son of the head gamekeeper at Pemworth, the seat of the Marquess of Pemerton. Less than a year separated them in age, and as a somewhat ignored younger son, Jack had found a friend in the young Tom Jessop. The two boys had spent many years romping the grou...ds and shoreline of Pemworth together, getting into all manner of scrapes.

Jack had lost touch with his young friend when he had left home to attend Eton and then Cambridge. It wasn't until many years later that their boyhood bond had been resurrected. Jack had returned to Pemworth for a visit when, one evening, the local prevention men showed up at the Hall looking for Jessop, whom they claimed had been involved that evening with a group of smugglers who had received a shipment of illegal goods in one of the nearby sheltered coves. Jack's father had begun to make some concerned remark when, almost without thinking, Jack had piped up, "Not Tom Jessop."

Suddenly, all eyes had turned to him. Remembering how many times young Tom had taken the blame for some mischief or other, Jack quickly equivocated that Jessop had been with him all evening, playing cards. Jack's father's steely glare had dared the prevention men to question the word of his son, and they had been forced to leave. Later that evening Jessop had presented himself to Jack, pledging his eternal thanks and placing himself entirely at Jack's service. As it happened, Jack had been in need of a valet, and thus a new chapter of their strange companionship had begun.

It had not been long before Jack had discovered that his boyhood friend had become an equally mischievous young man, always game for new adventures, new schemes, or new women. Since Jack had himself, by then, already fallen into a somewhat dissipated way of life, Jessop suited his needs precisely. Yet, through all the years of fast living, gaming, drinking, and womanizing, Jessop had remained steadfast, loyal—and extremely useful.

Jack stretched his arms and shoulders like a cat and burrowed deeper into the chair. "After I let this one go," he said, arching a thumb in the direction of the bedroom door, "perhaps I should take to patronizing Covent Garden nunneries instead of bringing them home."

Jessop, who had resumed brushing and folding the discarded clothing, stopped in midfold and raised his brows in question.

"I know, I know," Jack said. "It has been years since I have frequented such places. I honestly do not think I am up to it. I much prefer to be in full control of the situation—the surroundings, the timing, everything. Can't do that in someone else's establishment."

"That's a fact, my lord."

"Nevertheless," said Jack, "I cannot go on like this forever. And I do not even want to think about what I will do after I am married. I cannot exactly sneak girls up the back stairs with my wife in the next room."

"It wouldn't be right, my lord," said Jessop, shaking his head.

Jack laughed at his valet's serious expression. "No," he said, "it would not." He stretched his legs out in front of him and slid down further in the chair. "But perhaps if I find the right sort of bride . . ."

"If you find the right sort of bride," said Jessop in response to a significant glance from Jack, "you will be able to buy another place like the one on Half Moon Street."

"Right you are, Jessop," said Jack, flashing a grin at his altogether too clever valet. "By the way," he continued, "did you have any luck this evening?"

"Depends on your point of view, my lord," Jessop replied. "Daisy, that sweet little housemaid over at Lord Fairfax's, was most accommodating. Only she didn't seem to have any of the information you requested."

"Damn!" said Jack, slapping his hand on the arm of the chair.

"Sorry, my lord."

"Oh, it's all right, Jessop. Something, or someone, else will turn up. Speaking of which," said Jack as he made to rise from the chair, "I am shortly to have a whole new group of candidates to choose from. I met the most unusual woman, Lady Mary Haviland, who has taken a liking to me and is determined to help find me a suitable bride."

"A matchmaker?" said Jessop with a look of horror on his face.

"No," said Jack, laughing, "I don't think so. I don't believe this is her usual game. She is merely looking for some new kind of amusement. In any case, she could prove to be useful," he said as he walked toward the bedroom door.

"I hope so," said Jessop, though he sounded doubtful.

"Go on to bed, Jessop. I will wake you when it's time for Phoebe to leave."

"Yes, my lord."

Jack entered the bedroom once again and closed the door behind him. He tossed his dressing gown on a chair and slid between the sheets, gathering the sleeping Phoebe close to his side. His thoughts were still on Lady Mary. She was a curious little thing, but really quite delightful. He could certainly understand her search for new amusements. And although it was unlikely he and Lady Mary sought out diversion in precisely the same ways, he thought as he buried his nose in the sweetness of Phoebe's hair, he nevertheless felt she was in some ways a kindred spirit. He liked her.

They had agreed to meet once again at Lady Kenilworth's rout tomorrow evening, at which time Lady Mary promised to bring along her first candidates. He was curious to see what type of woman she thought would suit him. He seriously doubted that she had any understanding of his particular tastes. He nuzzled Phoebe's neck as he felt her foot inching its way up his leg. Perhaps he ought to have been more specific in providing Lady Mary with his requirements, he thought wickedly as he pulled Phoebe on top of him.

Chapter 3

"What do you think, Olivia? Do they not look well together?" Mary and her companion had paused in their perambulation of the ballroom to watch as Lord Pemerton danced a cotillion with Miss Lillian Carstairs. The dark good looks of the marquess contrasted nicely with the blond prettiness of Miss Carstairs. Mary was quite proud of this particular candidate, the third she had presented to Lord Pemerton this evening. Miss Carstairs, the granddaughter of an earl, was a particular favorite of Mary's. Though already three and twenty, this was only her second Season—her debut having been delayed first by illness and then by consecutive years of mourning. But her maturity was a mark in her favor as regards to Lord Pemerton. A blushing schoolgirl miss would never do for such a man.

"Hmph!" Olivia snorted and then tugged on Mary's arm to continued their stroll. "I do not understand how you could have presented that sweet young woman to that scoundrel."

"Yes, she is sweet, is she not?" Mary replied, ignoring Olivia's aspersion on Lord Pemerton's character. "It is most unfortunate that some have taken exception—quite wrongly!—to her passion for antiquities and labeled her a bluestocking. I am of the opinion that it enhances her character and conversation to have interests outside the latest fashions or the current *on-dits*. I am certain Lord Pemerton will also appreciate her wit and cleverness." She turned once again to watch the couple as they moved through the intricate steps of the dance. Lord Pemerton was smiling at something Miss Carstairs was saying.

"Oh, do look at them, Olivia," Mary said, smiling and squeezing her companion's arm. "I tell you, this could be the one! And to think, we are not yet even halfway down my list."

"Oh, but you are wicked, Mary," Olivia said in a hoarse whisper. "To act as accomplice to that . . . that *libertine*. Actually providing him with a list of potential victims! It has pained me to watch you these past few evenings, using your influence to convince decent, gently bred young women to be presented to that man. Marquess or no, the man is a cad!"

Mary laughed, amused as always by her companion's righteous outrage. "Victims, Olivia?" she said, still chuckling. "Miss Carstairs appears as unlikely a victim as I have ever seen. Just look at her. She seems to be thoroughly enjoying herself." It was true. As she watched, Miss Carstairs was now laughing at something Lord Pemerton had said. This was indeed promising.

"I do not like it," Olivia said, tugging Mary along once again. "What possible interest can he have in a decent young woman like that, except . . . well, except . . . you know."

"Olivia!"

"Well, it is true. Only consider what happened to that poor Miss Kingston."

"It was never proved that Lord Pemerton was the father, Olivia. And you know as well as I do that Miss Kingston was no better than she should be. Besides, Lord Pemerton told me himself that the girl had to have been increasing before he even met her. He can count as well as the next person, you know."

Mary stumbled when her companion came to an abrupt halt.

"He *told* you?" said Olivia, eyes wide with disbelief.

"Yes, of course."

Olivia stared at Mary in openmouthed astonishment. Mary chuckled and took her friend's arm once again and led her forward.

"I asked him," she said. Olivia's jaw dropped even further, if that was possible. "Well, I was curious," Mary said, shrugging nonchalantly. She wondered why this should be a matter of such concern. She and Lord Pemerton were friends, after all, and she had always felt that one should be able to speak openly with one's friends. Because Lord Pemerton had such an outrageous notoriety, she was sure most of the tales associated with him must be apocryphal. So she had asked, and had been shocked and delighted with the candor of his response.

Olivia's head snapped forward, and the rustle of stiff bombazine increased as she set a new pace to their leisurely stroll. Mary knew without looking that her friend's pleasant countenance was distorted by the tart pucker that had become more and more common since Mary's association with Lord Pemerton. For some reason, of all her supposedly unsuitable friends, Olivia had taken a particular dislike to Lord Pemerton. It was really most peculiar for Mary found him to be quite the most likable gentleman of her acquaintance.

Mary trailed along in silence, the polished wood floor echoing the fast clicking of her raised heels—always worn, though unfashionable, to provide her with extra height. The slightly narrow skirt of her pale blue silk gown—not to mention her shorter legs—caused some difficulty in keeping up with Olivia's long stride. After a few moments Olivia began to speak again and at the same time moderated her pace, to Mary's great relief.

"I know you say he is looking for a bride," Olivia said, "and for some unexplainable reason you have agreed to help him find one. But you know as well as I do that a man of his rank and fortune—despite his unspeakable reputation—can have his pick of Society misses. He does not need your help. I do not trust the man, and I believe he is simply using you and your list to add to his own list of conquests. Besides, he is well known for favoring more . . . more . . . well, more full-blown beauties than Miss Carstairs. Why should he single her out, if not for some illicit purpose?"

"I think she is quite pretty," Mary said. "She has a lovely, sweet face and all those glorious blond curls."

"Yes, a lovely, sweet and very round face," Olivia said. "Honestly, Mary, that man could not possibly favor her. Why, she is as plump as a guinea hen."

"Now, Olivia, I would not say she is precisely plump."

"Well, on her way there, in any case."

Mary cocked a brow at her elegantly slender companion, who ate like a bird because that was what ladies were supposed to do. Many a time Mary had noted Olivia's furrowed brow as she finished off a cream cake or other such delicacy, while Olivia left all but a single bite on her plate. And yet Mary's own tendency toward plumpness had never elicited a single disparaging remark from her companion. Mary knew that Olivia would rather cut out her tongue than criticize the physical imperfections of her employer. She knew that Olivia, like most people, felt sorry for her, for her plainness. She wished they would not. Mary did not feel sorry for herself, so why should anyone else?

Olivia caught Mary's eyes, blushed, and flashed a contrite look at her employer before lowering her eyes. "I beg your pardon, Mary," she said softly. "It is really none of my business why that man chooses to single out Miss Carstairs."

"He does it," Mary said, smiling and squeezing Olivia's hand, "because I asked him to." Their progress was interrupted by a sudden onrush of people—the music had ended and dancers were making their way from the dance floor. Unable for the moment to continue their stroll, Mary stopped and turned toward Olivia. "I told him," she continued, "I thought they might suit, and he trusts my judgment."

"Well," Olivia said, "I hope you know what you are doing. But I still do not like it!"

"Do not like what, Mrs. Bannister?"

The deep voice coming suddenly from behind her caused Olivia to jump.

"I beg your pardon ladies," Lord Pemerton said, smiling wickedly and looking terribly elegant in his all-black evening clothes. "I did not mean to startle you."

"I thought you were with Miss Carstairs, my lord," Mary said.

Lord Pemerton extended his hand, and Mary placed her own in it and allowed him to tuck it into the crook of his arm. It was amazing how comfortable they had become with one another after so short an acquaintance.

Olivia did not accept the support of his other arm.

"I deposited Miss Carstairs with her chaperone," Lord Pemerton said, guiding Mary toward the refreshment table. "After such a lively dance I am feeling quite parched. Will you ladies join me in a glass of champagne?"

"That would be lovely," Mary said, smiling up at the marquess. "Mrs. Bannister?"

"I would prefer punch, my lord."

"Of course." Lord Pemerton's eye caught Mary's, and he gave her a roguish wink. "If you will sit here," he said, indicating a recently vacated gilt bench, "I will only be a moment."

Mary and Olivia seated themselves and only had time to arrange their skirts before Lord Pemerton had returned. He handed a glass of chilled champagne to Mary and a cup of arrack punch to Olivia. He leaned negligently against the arm of the bench, supporting himself with a hand on its back. Mary could feel his hand brush against the curls at the nape of her neck as she turned to speak to him, causing a momentary tingle that she was quick to ignore.

"I was pleased to see you and Miss Carstairs getting along so well," she said. "You made a very handsome couple on the dance floor. She is quite lovely, is she not?"

"Miss Carstairs is all that is pleasing, my dear," he said, "but none can hold a candle to you this evening in that frothy blue confection." His fingers softly dragged along the neck of her gown for the briefest instant.

Mary was fascinated at how many ways he could touch a woman without anyone noticing. He was always doing it. Even Olivia was unaware of it, so adept was he at surreptitious contact. But then, he *was* a rake of some renown, after all. Such behavior was no doubt second nature to him, even with a woman such as herself. She grinned up at him, and he leered in return. Mary threw back her head and laughed.

Jack held his arms out for Jessop to remove his evening coat. He looked toward the door to his bedroom, standing slightly ajar, and caught a brief glimpse of ankle as Monique undressed. She was new to Drury Lane, and Jack had wasted no time in engaging her for the evening. He had settled with Phoebe a few nights earlier.

But there was business to attend to before pleasure.

"I need you to do another special job for me, Jessop," he said as the valet brushed out the evening coat.

"Yes, my lord?"

"Do you know anyone in the Carstairs household?" Jack asked.

"Carstairs . . . Carstairs . . . let me think," Jessop said as he hung up the coat in the open wardrobe. "Over on Portman Square?"

"Yes, I believe so," Jack said.

"I think I can manage something," Jessop said. "The usual information?"

"Yes, yes," Jack said, impatiently eyeing the bedroom door as he heard the unmistakable creaking of his bed. "Miss Lillian Carstairs. How much will she bring? Cash, mind you. No restrictions. No protected trust funds out of reach of a future husband. And not tied up in property or other investments that would need to be disposed of."

"I *know* the routine, my lord," Jessop said with no little indignation.

It was not the first time Jack had used his resourceful valet to unearth pertinent information about a prospective bride. Jessop, too handsome for his own good, was able to charm his way into almost any housemaid's affections. It was never long before he knew all there was to know about the private lives of his paramour's employers. In fact, it had often occurred to Jack that he had enough salacious information to blackmail more than a few members of the *ton*, if it ever came to that. But even Jack would never sink to such tactics. After all, it would certainly be a case of the pot calling the kettle black.

No, he was more inclined to repair his miserable fortune in the time-honored manner: by marrying a rich woman. But he would be damned before he made his motives known. He could not bear the notion of being labeled a fortune hunter—the sort of pitiful, contemptible creature he and his friends had often made fun of over the years. He would rather die than know he was the object of such ridicule. The very idea sent an involuntary shudder through his body. So he used the wily Jessop to ferret out the information he needed. He did not have time to waste courting the wrong woman.

"I know I can trust you to do the job, Jessop," Jack said, clapping his valet on the back. "Heaven help us both if anything ever happens to that pretty face of yours."

Jessop snorted with such disgust that Jack burst out laughing. The poor man hated to be reminded of his almost feminine looks. His pale skin and fair curly hair gave him a cherubic quality that women found irresistible. The face of an angel and the heart of a scoundrel, thought Jack. Much like himself—though he was, of course, no longer as handsome as he had once been. Nevertheless, that Jessop was cut from the same cloth as Jack had made him the perfect valet. They understood one another.

"There is also a Miss Dorothea Langley-Howe I would be interested in knowing a bit more about," Jack said in an offhanded way as he removed his brocaded waistcoat.

"Oh, I've heard of her, my lord," Jessop said. "Quite a beauty, I'm told. You'll have a bit of competition for that one."

"No doubt," Jack said. "All the more reason to determine the lay of the land before I waste any time on her."

"I'll see what I can do," Jessop said as he picked up the waistcoat that Jack had tossed on the floor.

"Thank you, Jessop." A look of understanding passed between Jack and his valet. Jessop gave a nod and returned to his work.

"I'll just be off to the King's Head, then," Jessop said as he hung Jack's waistcoat in the wardrobe. "One of m' chums in Portman Square owes me a favor. I assume you won't be needing me any longer this evening?" he asked as he cocked his head toward the bedroom door.

"Go on, Jessop," Jack said as he sat down to remove his stockings. "Get out of here."

"Yes, my lord. But I'll be back before dawn to escort the lady out." Jessop carefully folded the hastily discarded satin breeches and placed them in a drawer. In addition to his other useful qualities, the man was obsessively neat, a convenient counterpoint to his employer's somewhat untidy nature. Apparently satisfied that all was in order, he closed the wardrobe door, gave a sharp nod to Jack, and left the dressing room.

"At last!" Jack muttered as he turned toward the bedroom. Standing in the middle of the dressing room, wearing only his shirt, he yawned hugely and stretched like a cat. He wondered if he could pretend that the voluptuous, red-haired Monique was the very rich (he hoped), very plump Miss Carstairs.

He sighed. Not a chance.

He pulled his shirt over his head, tossed it in a corner, and flung open the bedroom door.

Chapter 4

"Alone at last!" the marquess said as he moved to sit beside Mary. He balanced his teacup in one hand as he gracefully eased himself onto the silk brocade sofa. Mary bit back a grin as she noted the scowl on Olivia's face, wondering if it was because Jack had already stayed well beyond the acceptable half hour and was obviously not ready to leave, or because he chose to sit close to Mary rather than the opposite end of the sofa. She nodded toward his cup, and he passed it to her. She deftly dumped its remains in the slop dish, poured a precise amount of milk into the cup, and then reached for the teapot.

"Not quite alone, my lord," she said as she poured. "After all, Olivia is still with us." She slanted a look toward her companion before returning her attention to the tea. She held out the steaming cup to Lord Pemerton, raising her brows at the smoldering look he offered.

"Indeed, my dear," he said as he gazed at Mary, a flicker of amusement in his blue eyes, "I could not forget the estimable Mrs. Bannister." He turned toward that lady and raised his teacup in salute. "And," he said, turning back to face Mary, "I thought you had agreed to stop 'my lording' me." He cocked a questioning brow.

Mary shrugged and reached across the tea table for Olivia's cup. It was true, they had lately dispensed with formalities, at least in private. Considering the nature of their joint project, it hadn't seemed appropriate to continue addressing each other as "my lord" and "my lady"; particularly as much of their conversation was at best immodest, and at worst downright improper. It was no wonder Olivia wore an almost permanent scowl—poor woman. Mary was certain that scarce a day went by when Olivia's exquisite sensibilities were not offended.

"I simply meant," Jack continued, "that it is a relief to be alone with you two ladies—to be free at last of that stream of gaggling females. Good Lord, Mary! How do you stand it—all those insufferable, meddlesome old biddies? Why did you invite me for today, knowing I would be forced to suffer through such an ordeal? I had hoped to find you—and Mrs. Bannister, of course—alone. Instead, I walk into a room full of prattling females whose inane yammering created such a din that my head began to ache."

"I am sorry, Jack," Mary said, grinning at his mock outrage. "I thought you knew that I am at home to visitors on Tuesday afternoons. But I *did* tell you to come late, knowing you would wish to avoid the usual crush. It is not my fault if you instead chose to show up earlier."

"No lectures, please, Mary," he said after taking a long swallow of tea. "My head still aches. Consider me properly chastised. *Never* again will I clutter your doorway on a Tuesday afternoon. What about the other six days of the week? Is it safe to drop by? No literary salons? Reform committee meetings? Charitable society teas?"

Mary laughed. "Only my monthly musical evenings, and those by invitation. Should I scratch you from my invitation list?"

"Do you play?"

"Usually. I mostly prefer to introduce newly discovered talents, or well-known artists performing new works. But, yes, I generally cannot resist performing as well. It is a weakness of mine."

"Then by all means, include me on your list," Jack said. "Having heard you play briefly at Lady Halsted's, I am anxious to hear more. You play like an angel, my dear." He smiled so warmly that for once Mary believed his praise was genuine. She felt the uncharacteristic heat of a blush.

"And those other afternoons?" he prompted.

"Tuesdays are my only at-home afternoons. Most other days I'm out and about, visiting or shopping or just walking through the parks."

"Then I shall simply have to make an appointment," Jack said.

Mary laughed. "That would probably be best. But as long as

you're here now, let us make the best use of our time. I have my list just here," she said as she twisted around to reach into the hidden pocket of her overdress. The movement caused her thigh to brush against Jack's momentarily. She felt a tingle of awareness, and her eyes darted quickly at his. His smoldered, as usual, with false seduction. Such a look directed at her never failed to set her off, and she once again dissolved into giggles. The man was incorrigible. She shifted her position and resumed her search for the folded paper. She located it and produced it with a flourish.

"Let's see," she began. "Lady Daphne Hewitt?"

"A lovely young woman," Jack said, "but . . . well, perhaps a trifle bluestockingish for my taste. I fear she would make me feel the idiot more often than not."

"Strike Lady Daphne," Mary said as she crossed her name off the list with a tiny gold pencil. "Miss Langley-Howe?"

"Too beautiful," he said.

"I beg your pardon?"

"I am sorry, Mary. But she is simply too beautiful. Not that I object to such beauty on principle, you understand," he said, smiling. "It is just that I fear the competition for such a prize would set me at a disadvantage. Ever since Lawrence exhibited her portrait at Somerset House, Miss Langley-Howe has been surrounded by an army of young, handsome admirers. If truth be told, I would just as soon avoid that crowd."

"How unsporting of you, Jack," Mary said with a grin.

"Put it down to my advanced years, my dear," he said, "but I would simply rather not have to fight quite so hard for a moment of the lady's attention. Besides, I am not convinced the effort would be justified. My single brief encounter with the young lady showed little beyond her beauty to recommend her. Her conversation, if I may be so blunt, was insipid at best."

"That is one of the things I most admire about you, Jack," Mary said. "You are always thoroughly honest and forthright."

For a moment Mary thought she detected a shadow cross Jack's eyes before he quickly lowered them. But she decided it was nothing more than embarrassment at her compliment, and she liked him the more for it.

"And so we eliminate Miss Langley-Howe," she said as she

crossed that lady's name off the list. "Lady Camilla Redbourne?" she asked hesitantly, the pencil poised for another strike.

"Hmm, Lady Camilla," Jack said, bouncing an index finger against his chin in apparent contemplation. "Yes, I rather liked her."

Mary looked up in surprise. She distinctly remembered watching Lady Camilla, an otherwise pleasant young woman, tread repeatedly on Jack's toes during a country dance at the Seymour ball. Though comely enough and with a pleasing personality, she was often somewhat awkward, even clumsy. She had come very close to ruining a beautiful gray satin waistcoat Jack had been wearing when she tripped while holding a glass of punch. Mary had been sure Jack would not wish to endure further punishment in her company.

"Keep her on the list," he was saying. "I would like to get to know her better, I think. She seemed to have a very sweet nature."

Mary smiled in genuine pleasure. How surprising to find a gentleman willing to overlook the obvious disadvantages in favor of the truly important aspects of a young woman's character. Lord Pemerton was indeed a remarkable gentleman.

"Lady Camilla stays, then," Mary said. "Miss Radcliffe?"

Jack shook his head. "I think not."

Mary looked up sharply. He had surprised her once again, this time by his rejection of such a beauty. Marguerite Radcliffe was a bit older than most of the other candidates, but Mary had been certain that her striking looks and continental manners—inherited from her French mother—would have appealed to Jack.

"I am afraid I could not bear her somber temperament, my dear," he said. "You, of all people, should know how much I appreciate a sense of humor. Miss Radcliffe is altogether too serious. Once her stunning looks fade inevitably with age, I fear she would be intolerably dull. I would as soon not be buckled to such as her."

Mary was somewhat taken aback by this pronouncement, not being of the same opinion regarding the lady's temperament. But Jack returned a look that seemed to challenge any objection, so she shrugged her shoulders and crossed off Miss Radcliffe's name.

She sighed as she reached her personal favorite among the candidates. She was no longer prepared to predict Jack's reaction to any of these woman, so she had no idea what to expect.

"Miss Carstairs?" she asked.

"By all means, leave her on the list," Jack said with unexpected enthusiasm. His brows rose at Mary's looks of undisguised shock. "Surely you are not surprised, my dear? I very much enjoy Miss Carstairs's company. She has a quick wit and intelligent conversation. Besides, I know her to be a favorite of yours. How can I quarrel with my Mary's good judgment?" After a quick wink at Mary, he turned toward Olivia, bent over her embroidery. "Do you not agree, Mrs. Bannister?"

Olivia looked up and actually smiled, much to Mary's astonishment.

"I do indeed, my lord," she said. "If I may say so, I believe Miss Carstairs to be a delightful young woman. And so pretty."

Mary glared at Olivia, who had only nights before condemned Miss Carstairs for her plumpness. Why was she suddenly so enthusiastic? Even more surprising, what had happened to the ubiquitous scowl?

After her bold announcement Olivia calmly returned her attention to her embroidery. It was really quite remarkable. Olivia seldom spoke more than two words in Lord Pemerton's company, and generally made her disapproval of him plain, though unspoken. Mary and Jack looked at one another in question, grinned, and continued with the list. There was only one other candidate in whom Jack expressed an interest. Three candidates in all. So far. There were still many on the list yet to be presented to him.

Mary felt extraordinarily pleased with herself as she considered the three young women who had received Jack's approval. None were out-and-out beauties, though each was at least passably pretty. Each had been selected by Mary based on various other fine qualities, and she was happy to discover that those qualities had apparently not escaped Jack's notice. She had included a variety of ladies on her list, not knowing precisely what Jack would most admire. She could not be more pleased to have discovered that such a notorious womanizer was able to look beyond superficialities in his search for a wife. It was unfortunate that the marquess had developed such a questionable reputation over the years. There really was much more to the man than one had been led to believe.

She found herself staring at him in admiration—not of his handsome exterior, but of the man beneath, whom she was coming to know and appreciate. He was speaking of Lady Camilla when he caught her eye and stopped in midsentence. He placed his cup on the tea table and reached for her hand.

"Come, Mary," he said in that seductive tone that still had the power to unnerve her, despite its obvious insincerity, "let us dispense with lists and candidates. Run away with me. We could scandalize the world and elope to the Continent. There are some advantages to being a marquess. I can obtain a special license by tomorrow. Shall we do it, Mary?"

Out of the corner of her eye Mary briefly caught a look of disapproval on Olivia's face. The scowl was back. Surely Olivia understood that Jack was teasing. A man such as Jack could never be seriously interested in someone like Mary. Yet Olivia looked as though she feared he might be serious, though hardly a day went by when he did not joke about marrying her. Mary really found the whole thing excessively droll, and Olivia's wounded sensibilities only added to her own wicked amusement. She looked up to find twin devils dancing in Jack's blue eyes and dissolved into uncontrollable laughter.

Jack slowed his black stallion to a trot as he turned into the Hyde Park gates from Park Lane. He tipped his hat a few times in the direction of acquaintances as he made his way through the afternoon crowds toward the Serpentine. It was at the first bend that he had arranged to "accidentally" encounter Mary, who would be strolling with Miss Carstairs.

The very rich Miss Carstairs.

Jessop had been fortunate to find a former acquaintance who was now employed in the Carstairs home on Portman Square. After plying his friend with several pints, Jessop had unearthed a wealth of information—so to speak—on the expectations of the daughter of the house.

"Her papa's rich as Croesus and she's his only child," Jessop had announced with relish.

Apparently, the Honorable Mr. Carstairs, younger son of an earl, had wisely invested inheritances from an uncle and a grandmother, the results of which now amounted to a sizable fortune. Miss Lillian Carstairs, his sole heir, stood to inherit a lot. And her dowry was rumored to be a large amount of cash along with a small estate in Surrey. Another estate as well as the Portman Square house would be hers upon her father's death, along with the bulk of his fortune.

Lord knows Jack did not need yet another estate to worry about. But if the cash settlement were fat enough, it would not matter. Yes, he thought as he smiled to himself, he would even abide the plump Miss Carstairs in his bed if only her dowry were equally plump.

He thought of Mary's undisguised delight at his suggestion that they arrange a chance meeting in the Park. Her huge eyes had sparkled with excitement. Though she had not said so, he knew that she had been surprised at his interest in Miss Carstairs. She was obviously very fond of the young woman and positively gloated at her success in encouraging Jack's notice. When Mary's big hazel eyes had looked at him with so much warmth and gratitude, he had experienced such a powerful feeling of guilt that he had almost turned tail and fled. It truly pained him to betray that good lady's faith in him. But he could not allow such niggling doubts to interfere with his plans.

As he headed up the length of the Serpentine, Jack caught a glimpse of primrose muslin and knew immediately it was Mary. She was turned away from him, gesturing toward a family of ducks gliding on the water, her head tilted toward the lady at her side. But something in the way she moved, the way she stretched her neck upon her shoulders—always attempting to compensate for her short stature—gave her away. Jack smiled as he watched her, thinking how perfectly the bright yellow color of her dress suited her sunny personality.

Mary turned at that moment and caught his eye. A wide smile spread across her face as she recognized him. Their eyes locked momentarily as Jack's smile broadened in response to hers. When she finally turned away, took her companion's arm, and spoke to her, Jack realized he had almost forgotten about Miss Carstairs, so pleased was he to see Mary.

Miss Carstairs, in pink sprigged muslin, walked arm-in-arm with Mary as they approached Jack on the bridle trail. He pulled his stallion to the side of the path and dismounted. Keeping the reins in his left hand, he doffed his hat with his right.

"Good afternoon, Lady Mary, Miss Carstairs," he said as he bowed toward the two smiling ladies. "What an unexpected pleasure."

"Unexpected, Lord Pemerton?" Miss Carstairs said, smiling and raising her brows in mock astonishment. "Surely it is no great surprise to find Lady Mary and me about at this hour, along with all the world and his cousin." With a sweep of her free arm she indicated the crowd of people on foot, on horseback, and in carriages thronging every pathway in the Park.

"Indeed, ma'am," Jack replied, "it is no surprise to find two such fashionable ladies about at this fashionable hour. But it is my extraordinary fortune to have encountered you at all in this crush. May I walk with you awhile?"

"We would be pleased to have you join us, my lord," Mary said.

Unable to relinquish the reins—perhaps he should have brought a groom, but that would have looked too calculating—Jack was therefore unable to offer an arm to each lady, and so he merely walked beside them. He was amused to watch Mary's easy manipulation of Miss Carstairs to a position between them.

They strolled along in companionable conversation for some time. Jack found Miss Carstairs to be intelligent and quick-witted, and began to think seriously of her as his potential bride. She was most animated when discussing the collection of antiquities she had recently viewed at the home of Sir John Soane at Lincoln's Inn Fields. Mary had warned him of Miss Carstairs's fascination with the subject, but her apparent obsession didn't bother him all that much. Better that she should have interests of her own to keep her occupied, making it easier for him to pursue his own passions. He thought with longing of the house on Half Moon

Street. Miss Carstairs's dowry would be more than adequate to finance another lease.

Along with her pleasant conversation she had an engaging smile and pretty golden curls peeking from beneath her bonnet. She would be tolerable enough as a wife, Jack decided, until she became fat, which he had no doubt was her destiny. But by then perhaps she would have provided him with the necessary heir and a spare, and he could avoid sharing her bed.

After a few more minutes of polite conversation they encountered a group of gentlemen, some apparently known to Mary, who stopped to chat. Among them was Giles Hamilton, an acquaintance of Jack's from his days at Cambridge. As Hamilton was apparently unknown to either Mary or Miss Carstairs, Jack made the introductions. He stood back fascinated as he watched Mary probe the poor man for information about himself. Hamilton, normally reticent at best, was helpless against Mary's gregarious questioning. The odd thing was that she never came off as meddlesome, but rather as interested. And Jack knew instinctively that indeed she was. She really was a most remarkable woman.

In her indomitable way Mary had soon discovered not only Hamilton's acquaintance with Lord and Lady Bradleigh—to her obvious delight—but that while he and Lord Bradleigh had been at Cambridge together, both had been students of the classics.

"Does your interest in the classics extend to classical antiquities as well?" Mary asked.

"Indeed, it does," Hamilton replied. "In fact, I have a few small pieces of my own. A Hellenistic bronze figurine of Andromache is one of my most prized possessions. Do you have a special interest in antiquities, Lady Mary?"

"I regret that I have only a dilettante's understanding of the subject, Mr. Hamilton," she replied. "But Miss Carstairs," she said taking that young lady's elbow and skillfully maneuvering her into the conversation, "is quite a scholar, I believe. You may be interested in her account of a visit to view Sir John Soane's collection."

Jack watched with some anxiety as Hamilton, eyes wide with interest, spoke at some length with Miss Carstairs. Even more troubling was the way she gazed in open admiration at Hamilton.

It came as a bit of a jolt to Jack that he might actually have serious competition for the girl, particularly from such as Hamilton, whom he had always considered a very dull dog. He had been so cocksure that he could seduce her with his looks and charm and grand title, that she would willingly and eagerly accept an offer from him. He must not become so complacent about his abilities. He could ill afford to lose this game. But he recognized that there were other things to attract a woman besides the obvious. Look at Hamilton. An unlikely competitor, he was nevertheless successfully wooing Miss Carstairs through mutual intellectual interests. Jack was very much afraid that the man had the advantage of him.

Jack looked over at Mary, who was in conversation with one of the other gentlemen. She met his eyes and arched a brow as if to ask why he was apparently giving in so easily to defeat. He nodded in understanding and deftly insinuated himself into the conversation between Hamilton and Miss Carstairs.

Chapter 5

"Rumor has it that you have seriously entered the Marriage Mart," Lord Sedgewick said as he followed Jack into a somewhat private corner of the subscription room at White's, away from the hubbub of the faro tables. Lord Sedgewick lowered his lanky form into a wide leather-cushioned armchair, stretched his long legs out in front of him, and crossed his ankles. He swirled his glass of claret, took a swallow, then looked earnestly at Jack. "Tell me it ain't so," he said.

"Can't do that, Sedge," Jack said as he eased into a matching chair and reached for the wine decanter that had been placed on a small table between them. " 'Fraid it is so."

"Good God!" Sedgewick stared openmouthed at Jack, then shook his head in disbelief. "You could have knocked me over with a feather when Skeffington told me you were dancing attendance on the latest crop of debs. Said you were shopping for a bride. Told him he must have gotten it wrong. Not the marrying type, I said."

"Things have changed, Sedge."

"Ah. Right." Sedgewick looked distressed, obviously not wanting to bring up the tragedy that had made Jack head of his family. But Jack and Sedgewick had been friends for too long for there to be any awkwardness between them. Jack caught his eye and nodded, a signal that Sedgewick should not feel constrained to discuss the matter. Sedgewick took a deep breath and blew it out of puffed cheeks. "I suppose your poor mother is after you to secure the succession," he said.

"Yes," Jack said, "and rightly so. I recognize that my carefree days as an insignificant younger son are over. Strange. I suppose there are many who envy me my title. For me it has brought nothing but grief and loss of a freedom which I never fully appreciated."

"Never thought of it like that," Sedgewick said, "but I suppose you are right. Before . . . all this," he said with a flutter of long fingers, "you were quite the solitary man, were you not? No one to please but yourself. No responsibilities. Beholden to no one. Devil-may-care—"

"Just so," Jack said, interrupting before Sedgewick could further inventory his selfish ways. "But now—"

"Now you must marry and produce an heir." Sedgewick sighed loudly and sank further into the leather seat cushion. "Well, I suppose there are worse fates. Might work out all right, after all. Look at Bradleigh."

"Indeed," Jack said, grinning. "He is disgustingly happy. It is almost sickening."

"Oh, I don't know," Sedgewick said. "I think it's rather nice."

Jack raised his brows in question, but Sedgewick ignored him and took another swallow of claret. Jack had not been terribly surprised when their friend Bradleigh had chosen to marry a little over a year ago. After all, the man was an earl and had responsibilities. But to imagine Sedgewick considering the same step was too incredible to contemplate. But he had surely not imagined that wistful tone of voice.

"At least your mother ain't in Town arranging things for you," Sedgewick said. "You can make your own choice and present it to her a *fait accompli*."

"Yes. Thank God for that," Jack said.

"Gad, man, with your title and estates and fortune, you must have them lining up at your door. You can have your pick of the lot."

"Er . . . not exactly."

"What? Oh. You mean your reputation. Less than sterling, and all that. The gambling. The women. The—"

"There is that, of course," Jack said, quickly interrupting yet another list of iniquities. "But you would be amazed at how short memories can be when the title of marchioness is at stake."

"No doubt," Sedgewick said, smiling broadly. "So, then, what is the problem?"

Jack took another long swallow of claret before speaking. He had decided to confide in Sedgewick—in fact he *needed* to confide in Sedgewick, or someone. Only Jessop was aware of the nature of his problems, but even he was unaware of the extent of them. It was becoming an oppressive burden to carry alone. He needed to talk about it. He wanted to talk about it. Sedgewick was one of his closest friends; he could rely on his discretion.

"I am afraid the field is not as wide as it could be," he said in a strained voice. He found that he was more than reluctant, that it was almost physically impossible to say what he needed to say. He was ashamed. "I am able to consider only . . . an heiress." He almost choked on the word, then threw his head against the back of the chair and closed his eyes. He could not bear to look at his friend just yet.

"An heiress?" Sedgewick's voice reflected his surprise. Jack took a deep breath and slowly opened his eyes. Sedgewick's brow was knotted in confusion.

"I don't understand," Sedgewick continued when Jack did not respond. "I always thought you were well to grass before. And now that you have inherited your father's estates and fortune, not to mention whatever you picked up from James and Frederick, I assumed you to be as rich as old Midas."

"If only that were true!" said Jack with some vehemence. He leaned forward in his chair and rested his elbows on his knees. "The fact is," he said in a voice so quiet Sedgewick had to lean closer in order to hear, "what I inherited was a mountain of debts and six mortgaged and badly managed estates." He paused and took a deep breath. "I'm bled dry, Sedge."

"Good Lord! I had no idea."

"Neither did I," Jack said. "I have led a somewhat reckless life, as you know. But I always kept my financial affairs in order and assumed that my father and brothers did the same." He gave a ragged sigh. "I was badly mistaken." He dropped his head into his hands, and his voice shook with suppressed emotion. "This last year has been a nightmare."

Sedgewick reached out and briefly squeezed Jack's shoulder.

"Why have you not said anything before?" he asked in a tone of such concern that Jack was almost undone.

"I wanted to try to put things right," he said, trying to maintain his composure, but unable to completely disguise the anguish in his voice. He lifted his head and reached for the wine decanter. He poured another glassful, but did not immediately take a drink. He simply held it in both hands, moving it in gentle circles as he watched the swirling red liquid illumined by the adjacent fire to a ruby glow. He did not look at Sedgewick.

"It's beyond me, Sedge," he said. "I cannot manage it. I will have to sell off at least two of the estates now, perhaps others later. But they are in such poor condition they will probably not bring enough even to pay off their mortgages. I have had to pour funds from Broadhurst into Pemworth just to keep it going, and have been juggling rents between Goodwyck and Crutchley to finance repairs. The tenant farms and cottages on all the estates are disgraceful. I have had to put new men in place of the bailiffs, who, I am convinced, were lax at best, and in some cases may even have embezzled revenues."

"God, Jack," Sedgewick said, running his fingers through longish blond hair, "I am so sorry."

"Yes. Well, the point is I need cash and lots of it and I need it now. I have just about depleted my own resources." He brought the wineglass to his lips at last and drained it in a single swallow. Placing the empty glass on the table, he looked at Sedgewick and offered a rueful smile. "Hence, the need for an heiress," he said.

"I can see that," Sedgewick said.

"But I had as soon not have my financial situation made public. I don't believe I could bear for people to know that I was . . . that I was a . . . a . . ."

"Fortune hunter?" Sedgewick gave a shudder that shook his entire lanky frame. "Don't blame you, old man. Ugly label, that. Not a pretty situation."

"Indeed," Jack said. "And so although I have in fact publicly entered the Marriage Mart for the Season, I am only truly considering those young women who can help me out of this dreadful coil. But I hope I have been circumspect enough so as not to reveal my true situation. Not only would I feel thoroughly humiliated, but I suspect my choices would suddenly become severely limited if it were known that I have little more than a title to offer. And," he said looking Sedgewick in the eye, "I am counting on your discretion, my friend. You are the only one who knows the truth."

Sedgewick placed his hand on Jack's shoulder. "You know you can trust me, old fellow," he said in a gentle voice. "Anyway, things will work out in the end, you'll see." Suddenly, his eyes widened. "I have it!" he said with a huge grin that split his face in half and caused his eyes to crinkle into slits. "I shall play matchmaker for you and find just the right girl to help you out of your troubles."

"God help me!" Jack said, and both men dissolved into laughter, slapping one another on the back.

"What's this? Don't tell me that congratulations are already in order, Jack?"

Jack looked up at the familiar voice to find Lord Bradleigh standing over them. "Robert!" he said, smiling with genuine pleasure. "Well met. I did not know you were in Town. Do not tell me that connubial bliss has finally palled?"

"Not in the least, my friend," the earl said, grabbing a nearby armchair and flopping down casually into it. "You two should try it. Fact is, Emily is in an interesting condition, and we have come to Town to have a special wardrobe made up for her."

"Congratulations, old man," Sedgewick said as he grabbed Lord Bradleigh's hand and pumped it energetically.

Jack signaled to the waiter to bring an extra wineglass and turned to Lord Bradleigh. "That is wonderful news, Robert," he said. "Give my best wishes to your beautiful countess."

"Thank you," Robert said. "But what was all that backslapping I witnessed as I came in? I heard you were in the market for a bride, Jack. Shall I wish you happy?"

"Eventually, I hope," Jack said in a light tone. "But not quite yet. I was just telling Sedge how eligible I have suddenly become now that I have a marchioness title to offer. Mothers who once dragged their daughters away if I so much as entered the same room are now fawning all over me."

Robert laughed. "I know the feeling. I had to overcome my reputation, too, you may recall. Although mine was not quite so . . ."

"Sordid?" Sedgewick suggested. "Scandalous? Dissolute? Debauched?"

"Enough!" Jack exclaimed, holding up both hands in a defensive posture and laughing. "Sedgewick has done nothing this evening but catalog my sins," he said to Robert. "I really don't know why I abide the fellow."

"The man has no sensitivity," Robert said, grinning. "Never did have."

"Well!" Sedgewick said with mock outrage as he pulled himself out of his chair and stood. "I shall not remain here and be insulted. Besides, I have an engagement this evening and must be off." He turned to Robert and flashed his famous grin. "Good to see you, Robert. Give my regards to Emily."

"I will," Robert said. "Perhaps you will join us for dinner one evening?"

"I would be delighted," Sedgewick replied.

"Good. I will send a note round."

Sedgewick turned to Jack and smiled warmly. "Good luck, Jack," he said. "I hope you may be as fortunate in your choice of brides as our friend Robert has been."

"Thank you, Sedge," Jack said. "Thank you for . . . everything."

"Any time, old man." Sedgewick smiled and winked at Jack, then tugged at his waistcoat and straightened his cravat. "I'm off," he said and then wound his way through the many groups gathered in the subscription room, stopping to acknowledge acquaintances here and there, and was soon out the door.

Robert turned to Jack and raised his brows in question.

"I was commiserating with Sedge on the frustrations of having to seek a bride," Jack said, keeping his tone light. "The succession, you know." Though Robert had long been as close a friend as Sedgewick, Jack was unwilling just now to confide in him regarding his financial problems. It had been difficult enough to open up to Sedgewick. He wasn't up to a second round of painful disclosure just yet. Besides, he would as soon limit the number of people aware of his situation.

"I know how you feel," said Robert. "And I imagine you are

going about it in the same cold-blooded manner I once did. No expectations of a love match?"

"None."

"I thought not," Robert said. "Be careful, Jack. That's how I ended up betrothed to Augusta Windhurst." He shuddered and a spasm of distaste crossed his face. "What a lucky escape that was." He poured himself another glass of claret. "Have you singled out anyone yet?"

"There are a few I am considering."

"I wish you luck," Robert said with a rueful smile. "It is not an enviable task. At least you don't appear to have an army of female relations acting as matchmakers."

"No, thank heavens," Jack said. "Mother is persistent, but she is not tossing candidates my way." He slid down a little in his chair, feeling mellowed by the wine. "I have, though, received assistance from the most unexpected quarter," he said with a smile. "A most extraordinary woman has become my champion. Lady Mary Haviland."

"Lady Mary?" Robert said, his eyes widening in surprise. "I know her, Jack. She and Emily are good friends. You must have met her at our wedding."

"Indeed," Jack said, "she claims I did, but I regret that I have little recollection of the event."

Robert laughed, and Jack gave a weary shrug. He had been reminded of his sins more than enough times for one evening.

"You are correct in finding Lady Mary extraordinary," Robert continued. "Apart from Emily, she is one of the most delightful women of my acquaintance. She has a home in Bath, you know, which is where she and Emily met. Lady Mary was often at Grandmother's house in Laura Place. So she is in Town now? Emily will be pleased. Where is she staying?"

"She has taken a house in Upper Brook Street," Jack said.

"We must pay a call on her," Robert said. "I am glad to hear you have struck up a friendship with her. She is a delight, is she not?"

"Indeed," Jack said, smiling as he thought of Mary. "She is a most unusual woman. I don't believe I have ever met anyone so genuinely open and unaffected. She is the most thoroughly cheerful person I think I have ever known. And her laugh," he said, laughing himself, "is positively infectious."

"Yes," Robert said, smiling. "Amazing when you think about what she has been through. If anyone has a right to be less than cheerful, it is Lady Mary."

"What's that?"

"You know," Robert said. "Her father and all that." He took another sip of wine and turned toward an outburst at the other end of the room, where one of the groups crowded around a faro table had become suddenly animated.

Ignoring the noise, Jack stared at Robert. What was that about Mary and her father? He was unaware of any problems in her life. But then he suddenly realized he knew very little about Mary. He knew he liked her, was quite fond of her, in fact. But he knew nothing about her background other than her being the daughter of the late Earl of Assheton. She never spoke about herself, and Jack was forced to admit he had never asked. They spent most of their time talking about himself.

Robert turned his attention back to Jack. "I suppose all that money helps," he said. "I have often wondered, though, if Mary's current great wealth could ever really make up for the past."

Jack froze momentarily, the wineglass halfway to his lips. *All that money?* Her *great* wealth? Mary was wealthy? His little Mary was wealthy?

A smile spread across Jack's face as a new idea occurred to him.

Jack decided to walk home later that evening, after sharing a bird and a bottle with Robert. He needed time to himself to contemplate the plan that Robert's words had triggered.

He whistled as he headed along St. James's Street and across Piccadilly to Bond Street, feeling well pleased with himself. He was hailed by a few friends loitering in front of Gentleman Jackson's saloon.

"Why the big smile, Jack?" one of them asked, poking him in the ribs. "New ladybird on the mount?"

Jack joined in the general laughter that followed, shared a few ribald remarks, and then continued on his way. He received stares from several passersby as he headed up Bond Street with a spring in his step and a grin on his face. It was all too deliciously easy. He felt as though a goose had deposited a golden egg right into his lap.

Mary was rich!

He still could not believe it. Nor could he believe how stupid he had been not to have considered it as a possibility. But then he had never thought of Mary in that way. In fact, it was strangely disappointing to begin to think of her in that way now. He had found it unexpectedly pleasant, comfortable even, to have a purely companionable relationship with a woman. He thoroughly enjoyed the times he spent in Mary's company, despite—or perhaps because—there were none of the usual sexual undertones to which he was accustomed. He did, though, enjoy teasing her with suggestive comments for the simple pleasure of hearing her laugh.

Nevertheless, he was willing to forgo his comfortable friendship with Mary if her fortune recommended a more serious relationship.

As he dined with Robert, he had discreetly probed for information on Mary's situation, hopefully without giving away his having been unaware of it himself.

"She don't exactly flaunt her wealth," Jack had said when Robert had returned to the subject of Mary. He tried to keep his tone indifferent, affecting an attitude of fashionable ennui.

"No," Robert said, "she doesn't, does she? She lives well enough, but you certainly never see her dripping in diamonds or parading around in flashy carriages with showy horseflesh. Emily thinks that Mary sees her fortune only as a means to provide her the freedom to live exactly as she pleases. Beyond that, it is of little interest to her."

Jack cocked a brow in an attitude of casual disbelief, struggling to disguise his interest.

"Perhaps she doesn't fully appreciate the extent of it," Robert continued. "She only became aware of it very suddenly, after all."

Jack had been puzzled by this part of the conversation. He had not been able to get much additional information from Robert, who did no more than imply that the fortune had come to Mary upon her father's death. He had seemed more inclined to discuss some trouble with her father, but Jack had not paid much attention. He was more concerned with the subject of money, but he had felt uncomfortable probing any deeper. He had not wanted to arouse Robert's suspicions.

But surely, as the late earl's only child, Mary had always known of her expectations. Why should it come as such a surprise to her to inherit? He pondered this question as he turned onto Conduit Street and then George Street. He knew very little of the late earl, who had kept much to himself. Never, however, had he heard that the man was terribly wealthy. Perhaps he had been one of those eccentrics who had lived like a hermit but hoarded a fortune. That could explain why Mary may not have known of her expectations.

The fact was, he did not care how it had come about, he thought as he playfully kicked a pebble down the street. He could have Jessop look into it if it really mattered. The important thing was that Mary was as prime a candidate as any other woman on her list. Indeed, she was a far superior candidate because she had no father or brother or guardian controlling her fortune. Apparently, if Jack correctly interpreted Robert's implications, Mary had complete control. And that she was older and quite plain could be seen only as an added advantage. By God, but she would be easy pickings!

Fortunately, they were already on very friendly terms. He believed she was fond of him. However, he could not help but recall her deep, throaty laughter each time he had teasingly suggested a liaison between them. And on their very first meeting she had made clear her position on marriage.

I am quite happily and comfortably on the shelf, she had told him.

Nevertheless, Jack felt confident he could change her mind. After all, he thought with a wicked grin, he had had years of practice in wooing women of all types. Surely, a plain little thing like Mary could not help but be flattered by an offer from him. Jack was reasonably certain that she had no particular admirers. She was not, after all, the type of woman to generate that sort of interest. And it would likely be the only such offer she would ever receive, so why should she refuse him? She liked him well enough, didn't she? Well, if she did not, Jack was willing to seduce her if necessary. He thought briefly of how he might actually enjoy it. Though tiny, Mary appeared to be soft and round in all the right places. In fact, she was a perfect little Pocket Venus.

Yes, he thought, grinning to himself, he might just enjoy this after all.

As he passed by St. George's Chapel, the site of the most fashionable of *ton* weddings—a subject which, for the first time in fifteen years, did not have him quaking in his boots—he considered how best to make the move from friend to suitor. Though he was anxious to proceed, it was best that the change in their relationship seem gradual and natural. He did not fear that it would appear too unlikely, since they were often seen in one another's company. It was true that Mary was not his usual type; but the *ton* did not expect one to marry the same sort of woman with whom one might choose to dally. Anyway, he liked Mary. Everybody liked Mary. So much so, in fact, that a marriage to her would probably help to reestablish his credibility with the *ton* to a degree he could never have accomplished on his own. The more he thought about it, as he reached Hanover Square, the more perfect the whole thing began to sound.

He laughed aloud as he flung back the elaborate ironwork gate at the entrance to Number 26, elated at this surprising but delightful turn of events.

Chapter 6

"What do you think, Olivia? The green lutestring or the bronze silk?"

Mary alternately held up each dress in front of her as she surveyed her reflection in the full-length pier glass. She was partial to the shimmery effect of the bronze silk.

Olivia eyed her employer's reflection in the glass, then spun her around to look at her directly. Mary continued to hold up the bronze evening dress while her companion scrutinized it with a knotted brow. Finally, Olivia looked up and smiled as she reached for the dress.

"This is certainly beautiful, my dear," she said as she laid it carefully on the bed. "But I really do not believe the shade is quite right for you. Your pale coloring is, I think, better set off by this rich green," she said as she held up the other dress against Mary, turning her back around to face the mirror. "Besides, the subtle vertical pattern of the fabric . . ."

"Will increase the impression of height," Mary said, completing Olivia's thought. "I believe you are correct, Olivia," she said with a smile as she took one last look at it. "I shall wear the green." She handed the dress to her maid, who took it away for a last-minute pressing. She sat down at her dressing table and began to rummage through her jewel case, at last removing a simple pair of emerald earrings and a matching pendant suspended on a gold chain. Mary's collection of jewelry—all bought by herself within the last three years—was modest and unostentatious. Though she certainly had the means for much more, her tastes were simple. Besides, she always felt that, because of her small stature, any elaborate style of dress or accessory only made her look like a child's doll.

She laid the emeralds on the dressing table and began to unpin the braids coiled high in a crown on the top of her head. The long braids, being waist-length, toppled into her lap, and she began to carefully unbraid them.

"And what shall *you* wear this evening?" she asked, catching Olivia's eye in the glass as she seated herself on the end of a nearby chaise. "Oh, I know just the thing!" she exclaimed before Olivia could open her mouth. "That lovely pink satin with the darker rose underskirt."

"Oh, Mary. I do not think so . . ."

"Come now, Olivia. This is something of a special occasion. Jack is bringing his uncle tonight, you know."

"I know." Olivia gave a profound sigh.

"I am so excited to meet Mr. Maitland!" Mary said. "I have heard he has led a very adventurous life. He must have wonderful stories to tell."

"No doubt," Olivia mumbled.

"Mr. Maitland will act as your escort, my dear, while I take Jack's arm." Mary spoke with increased animation as she continued to unbraid her hair. "Is it not sweet of Jack to invite us to the opera tonight?"

"He is most generous," Olivia replied with something less than enthusiasm. "But, all things considered, Mary, I really wish he had invited a larger party. Only four of us! It seems so . . . so . . ."

"Intimate?" When Olivia shrugged in resignation, Mary threw back her head and laughed, one side of unbraided hair falling in brown waves over her shoulder. "You mustn't be so priggish, my dear," she said with a broad smile. "I believe Jack wishes only to express his gratitude for our help in his search for a bride. This singling out of us is merely his way of showing his appreciation. You know," she continued in an excited voice, "I truly believe he is close to the sticking point with Lillian Carstairs!"

"Do you?" Olivia said, arching a brow. "And yet lately he seems to spend more time in *your* company than in hers."

Mary looked up to catch Olivia's wary eye in the glass. It was true. Jack had almost become a permanent fixture in their drawing

room during the last week. But Mary was sure that was only because he felt especially at ease in her company, could lounge
comfortably in chair by the fire, and speak on any subject without
fear of offense. Her drawing room appeared to offer him some so-
lace from the rigors of *ton* propriety. She was pleased to be able
to offer him that respite.

"We enjoy one another's company," Mary said. "That is all.
We are friends." She watched as Olivia's brow furrowed and her
eyes narrowed. "Oh, please do not scowl!" she said. "Truly, we
are merely friends."

"But you cannot deny that he flirts outrageously with you."

Mary chewed on her lower lip in a valiant effort to suppress a
giggle. She loosened the last bit of braid and shook her hair free.

"And all you ever do is laugh," Olivia said, throwing her hands
up in exasperation. "I do not understand how you can have such a
cavalier attitude about that sort of behavior. It is most improper!
Why, I have often blushed at things he has said to you within my
hearing. I hesitate to think what he might be saying when he
whispers in your ear."

Mary could no longer control herself and dissolved into laughter. She covered her mouth with both hands and dropped her fore-
head onto the dressing table. Her entire body shook as she
shrieked with laughter, her eyes streaming with tears that fell onto
the fine white muslin table covering. She lifted her head slightly
and caught Olivia's reflection in the mirror—brows raised, trying
to look serious. But one corner of her mouth twitched upward, and
Mary was lost once again. She laughed until her sides hurt
and she could hardly breathe.

When she finally recovered her breath, she stood up, walked
over to a mahogany highboy, opened a drawer, and retrieved a
linen handkerchief. "My dear Olivia," she said with a hiccup as
she sat back down at the dressing table, dabbing her eyes, "how
you *do* make me laugh!"

Olivia smiled, but there was still a seriousness about her eyes
that Mary distrusted.

"I am glad I amuse you, Mary, I am sure. But I really fail to see
what is so funny about Lord Pemerton flirting with you. I, for
one, do not find it amusing."

"But don't you see?" Mary said as she reached for a silver hair-brush. "He is a handsome, titled gentleman and a rake of the first order. And yet he flirts with *me*. I laugh because it is so ludi-crous—that such a man should bother to flirt with someone like me." She began to run the brush through her hair. "But, he cannot help it, you see. It is second nature to him to flirt with women. All women. His behavior—flirtatious, flattering, suggestive, even se-ductive—is so ingrained that he cannot even stop himself from acting that way with someone as unattractive as myself. He does not mean a word he says, of course. And that is why I always laugh—that he should say much things to me as a sort of involun-tary reaction that he cannot control. It is too absurd!"

"No more absurd than your own pigheaded notion that you are unattractive," Olivia said with some vehemence.

"Now, Olivia." Mary turned around on her stool and fixed her companion with a stern look. "We have had this discussion be-fore."

As she watched the scowl on her friend's face melt into a look of concern, Mary began to experience an all too familiar frustra-tion, bordering on anger, that almost completely overwhelmed her former lighthearted mood. Why did people find it so difficult to believe that she was quite comfortable with her appearance? She had accepted from a very young age that she was not at all attrac-tive. But she had never become obsessed with the notion. There was nothing she could do about it, after all, so why repine?

The only claim to vanity Mary was willing to admit to was her desire to increase the impression of stature. She commonly wore shoes with higher heels than was fashionable, and she kept her hair long so that she could pile it ever higher upon her head. And she was very conscious of posture, always keeping her back straight and her head high. But none of this was done in any pre-tense of beauty. She was simply tired of sometimes feeling like a child in a room full of adults.

Mary almost never gave into any feelings of regret for her lack of beauty. She was extremely happy with her life and her many friendships; she really had nothing to complain about. But, if she were perfectly honest with herself, she had to admit that there were times—not often, but there were times—when she wished she were not ugly. When she wished that Jack's false flattery were true. But those were rare, fleeting moments, and she dismissed them immediately. She knew better than to dwell on what could never be.

For a moment the image of her father's face—wild-eyed and furious—appeared in her mind's eye.

How glad I am that your mother never lived to see what an ugly creature she spawned.

Yes, she had learned the truth about herself at a very young age, from the one person in the world who should have loved her.

But she had overcome her father's cruelty in the end. She was a free and independent woman now. What matter that she was not beautiful?

She turned back toward the dressing table and continued brushing her hair. "Well, Olivia," she said in a cheerful voice, "how shall I have Sally dress my hair this evening? I must be sure to dazzle Mr. Maitland."

Olivia took one last look in the mirror and sighed loudly. She was not at all sure about the appropriateness of the pink satin dress that Mary had insisted she wear. For one thing, the bodice was much too low-cut, she thought as she tugged at it one more time. Perhaps she should ask Mary if she might borrow a piece of lace or a fichu to cover up the expanse of bosom revealed by the daring cut of the neckline. But, no, Mary would only laugh at her prudishness. Besides, she had generously provided Olivia with a lovely cream silk shawl embroidered with pink roses. She would simply keep it tightly wrapped about her, claiming she felt a chill.

It was a shame, though, to cover up such a lovely dress, she thought as she fingered the softness of the fabric. Mary had ordered it for her at the beginning of the Season, and she had yet to wear it.

"You look positively beautiful!" Mary had exclaimed when Olivia had first tried on the gown at the modiste's salon.

As she studied her reflection once more, Olivia was forced, not without some pleasure, to agree. The color gave a soft, pink glow to her complexion, and even her brown hair—with only a few noticeable strands of silver—seemed to show new auburn highlights. The cut of the skirt was less full than she was used to, displaying her still slender figure. She had put on almost no weight in all these years since Martin's death, though she seemed to have become slightly more buxom in her middle age. Or perhaps it was just the dress.

Martin would have loved it, she thought wistfully.

But her late husband would not have loved the company she would be keeping this evening—to be escorted by Edward Maitland! Poor Martin would be turning over in his grave—if only he had one. She supposed he could still be outraged in his watery resting place at the bottom of the Cape of Trafalgar. In any case, Olivia was outraged enough for both of them.

She turned deliberately away from the mirror and walked toward the bed where she had earlier laid out the silk shawl, a pair of evening gloves, a reticule, and a fan. The latter, kept for special occasions, was a memento from the days of her marriage. Her eyes strayed briefly to the table next to the bed where she kept a miniature of Martin on a tiny stand.

Dearest Martin, give me strength.

It was a petition often made before an evening out with Mary. She had grown more or less used to her employer's odd starts, taking up with one after another of Society's most outrageous rogues. But an evening practically alone with two of them! It was almost too much to bear. Well, she was paid to act as Mary's companion, and she would do her job, difficult though it sometimes was. For when all was said and done, she adored Mary.

She had been with Mary for three years, ever since Mary had established herself in Bath after her father's death. Mary had not particularly wanted a full-time companion, and had been very open about her displeasure with those strictures of Society that refused to allow a spinster to live alone.

"I take leave to tell you," Mary had said during their first meeting, "that I resent having to hire a companion at all. I will not have you trailing after me except when absolutely necessary. In fact," she had said with some indignation, "I suspect we will actually see very little of one another."

Despite their shaky beginnings, the two women had developed a fast friendship, once Mary had overcome her general misgivings about servants and employees, born of the grim years of closely guarded isolation in her father's castle. She had been especially vulnerable in those early days, so soon after leaving Castle Assheton. But Mary had quickly grown stronger and soon became fiercely independent and very private. As far as Olivia was aware, Mary never again spoke of those unhappy years in her father's castle. Though she had a passion—no, more like a hunger—for the company of people, and had friends and acquaintances by the score, Olivia doubted she opened up to any of them about her past. She kept that part of herself locked deep inside, behind a thick shell of self-protection that seemed impenetrable.

Though Olivia accepted that after years of isolation Mary craved human companionship, she could never quite comprehend that proclivity for unsuitable friendships that caused her to seek out every rascal in the land—Lord Pemerton, for example, she thought as she pulled on elbow-length gloves.

This project of Mary's to help find him a bride was very worrisome. There was something about this particular rake that made Olivia most uneasy. Perhaps, though, it was Mary and not the marquess who was the real cause for concern. She had not failed to catch the special sparkle in Mary's eye whenever she was near the marquess. Despite her apparent worldliness, Mary was really quite naive and innocent, and could easily be hurt. In fact, it was only Mary's ridiculous belief in her own unattractiveness that most likely kept her safe from harm, causing her not to develop false hopes or illusions. But at the same time, it also most likely prevented her from ever finding true love and happiness—which, to Olivia's way of thinking, meant finding a husband.

It was past time to give up all this foolishness with rakes and such, and get serious about the future. Olivia determined in that moment, as she tied the reticule to her left wrist, that she would help her friend to find the happiness she deserved by searching out a husband for her. Oh, she knew there were certain difficulties, but she did not believe they would be insurmountable with the right man. But how on earth was she to find the right man if Mary persisted in associating with that horrid Lord Pemerton?

Olivia had draped the creamy silk shawl tightly around her shoulders when a peremptory knock on her bedchamber door drew her attention. Before she should respond, the door was flung open and Mary stood there, hands on hips, slippered toe tapping furiously.

"What on earth are you doing in here, Olivia? Jack and Mr. Maitland have arrived. Are you *quite* ready?"

"Goodness, Mary, I am so sorry. I suppose I must have lost track of the time." With one last look in the mirror she pulled the shawl more tightly about her shoulders and turned toward the door. "I am ready."

Mary stopped her with a hand to her shoulder. "Oh, no you are not." She turned Olivia around and pushed her back into the room. "Give me that shawl," she said as she grabbed for the silky garment.

Olivia clasped the shawl to her breast. "No!"

Mary tugged harder, and Olivia pulled it tighter; but finally it fell away, leaving Olivia feeling half naked. Her hands instinctively flew to her exposed bosom. Mary shook out the shawl—now slightly wrinkled from the brief tug-of-war—and folded it neatly over her arm. "Now, let me look at you," she said as she gently took Olivia's hands, pulled them away from her bosom, and held them out in front of her while she studied the dress from top to toe. "Outstanding!" she said at last, dropping Olivia's hands.

"But—"

"No buts, Olivia. And no shawl, until you agree to wear it properly. My dear, you look wonderful—why in the world would you want to cover up your assets? Good heavens, if I looked like you I would walk tall and proud."

Olivia laughed. "Mary, you *do* walk tall and proud."

"Well, there you have it, then. If a plain old thing like me can face the world with confidence, how much more so should one such as you? You are a beautiful woman, Olivia. Condescend to let the world gaze upon you with admiration." She reached over and kissed Olivia on the cheek. "Or, if not the world, then at least our two escorts this evening. Now," she said forcefully, "shoulders back. Chin up. Bosom thrust majestically forward."

Olivia dissolved into laughter upon this last instruction. "Oh, Mary," she said, impulsively hugging her friend, "I do love you."

Mary hugged her back, then released her. "Ready?"

"Yes, I suppose so."

"Then here is your shawl," Mary said. Olivia took it and began to drape it once again across her shoulders. "But do *not* wrap it about you like a shroud. Here," she said, pulling it away from Olivia's shoulders until it hung loosely down her back. "It should fall gracefully from your arms, just so. Do not wear it as if you were freezing to death." She took Olivia's arm, and both women headed out the door and downstairs toward the drawing room where their guests awaited.

"Suppose I *do* become chilled?" Olivia asked with a smile. "What then?"

"I am sure Mr. Maitland will think of something."

"Mary!"

"And so, dear lady," Edward Maitland said as he turned toward Mrs. Bannister, "you must tell me your impressions, thus far, of Catalini?"

Jack smiled as he watched his uncle continue in his attempt to defrost Mary's companion, leaning close in order to be heard over the din of voices, but never quite touching her. He would know not to take too many liberties with such a woman, but instead would use all his skill to make her feel comfortable, to make her feel as if she were the only other person in the room. Noting the wobbly smile on Mrs. Bannister's face, Jack was certain his uncle was making progress.

Uncle Edward—the younger brother of Jack's mother—was one of his favorite people in all the world. Though now in his late fifties, he was still a handsome devil, with a thick mane of silver hair and sparkling blue eyes. Still a bachelor, he had led a more or less rakehell existence for over thirty years, and had therefore been a source of inspiration to Jack. As a boy, Jack had been drawn to his uncle's enthusiastic approach to life and intrigued by overheard whispers hinting at a scandalous reputation.

In his youth Jack had never himself aspired to such a reputation. It was only after his disastrous betrothal to the beautiful Suzanne had soured him on all so-called respectable women that he had taken his uncle as mentor in hedonism. Their attachment had caused some concern with Jack's family; but as a younger son less attention was paid to him than to his brothers, and so after a while, no one much cared.

If they cared now—now that he was the marquess—it was of no concern to Jack. Uncle Edward would always be welcome in Jack's home—more welcome than many other relatives, in fact.

He had invited Uncle Edward this evening with the intention that he should distract—in his inimitable way—the formidable Mrs. Bannister, while Jack began his seduction of Mary in earnest. When he had first called on his uncle at his town house last week, that gentleman had been most enthusiastic in his agreement to go along with Jack's scheme.

"It has been some time since I have faced such a challenge," Uncle Edward had said upon hearing of his own role in the evening's plans. His interest had been piqued at once by Jack's description of the unflappable and dour Mrs. Bannister. His face had broken into a mischievous grin. "I trust my skills are up to the task."

"I have no doubts on that score, Uncle."

"You flatter me, boy. And so, tell me of this young woman—Mary, is it?—who has so captured your attention. A beauty, is she?"

"Not exactly," Jack said with a sheepish grin. "She is not at all my usual type, in fact."

"Respectable, you mean?"

Jack laughed. "Yes, she is that. But different in other ways as well. Perhaps I should explain."

Jack had then related to his uncle all the ugly details of his financial situation and his need for a rich bride.

"I beg your pardon for having to say this, my boy," his uncle had said, shaking his head in disbelief, "but your esteemed father was a prize idiot. How could he have let things go so far? Does my sister know? Is that what has caused her decline this past year? Good Lord, if the man were not already dead, I believe I would kill him."

"Mother has not been herself since the accident," Jack said in a tight voice. "I have not been able to speak with her about these matters. Her heart has been broken, Uncle. It is grief that continues to afflict her, not financial difficulties. You know how devoted she was to Father. Losing him was enough of a blow. But to lose James and Frederick, too. And little Jason, her only grandson. I do not think she will ever be the same. I would be a cad to even consider adding to her suffering."

Uncle Edward had paced the length of his study several times, running his hands through his thick hair in an agitated manner. "I wish I could help you, my boy," he said at last, "but my own resources are—"

"Thank you, Uncle," Jack interrupted, "but I think my plan with Mary is my best—nay, my only—alternative."

And so Uncle Edward had agreed to help out by distracting Mrs. Bannister, which he seemed to be doing very well at the moment, judging from that lady's flushed countenance. As he watched, Jack was suddenly struck by how attractive Mrs. Bannister looked this evening. He had never really paid her much attention. Of course, he had sized her up at their first meeting as a woman still handsome for her age—he guessed she was in her mid-forties—with good bones, clear skin, and bright green eyes. But her perpetual scowl had detracted from any real beauty, and her obvious disapproval had caused Jack to dismiss her entirely. But she was not scowling this evening. Under his uncle's spell her expression had softened, and she was actually smiling. She looked quite lovely, in fact.

Jack smiled, thinking what a joy it was to watch Uncle Edward in action. The old roué could still out-charm the best of them. Jack doubted even his own formidable skills could have defrosted Mrs. Bannister quite so easily.

Assured that his uncle had matters well in hand, Jack was able to turn his full attention to Mary. He tucked her tiny hand in the crook of his arm as he led her out to the lobby area during the interval. Upon their return he guided her into her chair without relinquishing her hand. As the music began once again, he gently forced open a pearl button at the base of her glove and drew tiny circles on the exposed skin of her wrist—a tactic that never failed to titillate other women.

Mary seemed not to notice.

Twice during the next act, when Mary turned to him with a

smile of appreciation for the music, he had brought her hand to his lips.

She had giggled.

Several times he leaned close and whispered suggestive comments in her ear, once even allowing his lips to brush her neck.

She had burst out laughing.

In fact, Mary laughed so much during the last act that many eyes were drawn to their box. Jack was puzzled. Although Mary had, from the beginning, laughed away his attempts at flirtation, he was much more assiduous in his attentions this evening and had expected a different response. He had certainly never experienced such difficulties with other women.

She was obviously not taking him seriously.

He watched her profile while she stared spellbound at the stage as the opera reached its finale. She was practically oblivious of his presence. *Well, my dear,* he thought with a resigned sigh, *it seems I shall have to take a more direct approach.*

Chapter 7

Mary sat at her beloved pianoforte and absently picked out a tune while listening to her companion discuss the rout they had attended the previous evening. For reasons that escaped Mary, Olivia had apparently found the evening highly entertaining. Mary had been bored.

"Did Sir Henry tell you about his recent travels to the West Indies?" Olivia asked, comfortably ensconced on the brocade-covered sofa near one of the two large windows overlooking the street below. Her workbag was carelessly tossed at her side. She did not look up from her embroidery. "He is considering purchasing a sugar plantation in Jamaica," she continued. "Would it not be lovely to travel to such exotic locations?"

Mary gave a deep sigh. Sir Henry Lambton had clearly piqued Olivia's interest, for she had mentioned him no less than a dozen times this morning. A middle-aged widower with two young daughters, the man was obviously on the lookout for a new wife. Mary sincerely hoped Olivia was not getting any ideas.

She stopped playing and looked across at her friend, who was bent over her embroidery hoop. "Olivia," she said, "you are not setting your cap for Sir Henry are you?"

Olivia looked up with a startled expression. "Me?"

"For if you are, I take leave to tell you that you could do much better for yourself, my dear. Sir Henry is a dead bore."

Olivia gave a sniff and returned her attention to her work. "He seemed a nice enough gentleman. But I assure you, I am *not* setting my cap for him. I only thought that perhaps you—"

"I am glad to hear it," Mary interrupted. "If I thought you were seriously considering marrying again, I could recommend several other gentlemen who would be much more interesting than Sir Henry." She paused as a wicked thought crossed her mind. "Only look at how attentive Mr. Maitland has been." She grinned at the furious look her companion directed at her embroidery. "Now, *there's* an interesting man for you, Olivia."

"Mary, *please*."

"Olivia!" Mary studied her friend closely as she stabbed viciously at the stretched silk. "You are blushing!"

"Hush, Mary. You are being ridiculous."

"Am I?"

Her head still bent over the embroidery hoop, Olivia continued to ply her needle, but raised her eyes toward Mary with an imploring look. Suddenly, she gave a startled squeak and brought a finger quickly to her mouth. "Blast!" she muttered as she studied the pricked finger.

Mary had only been teasing, but had she in fact struck a sensitive chord? They had only met Mr. Maitland on two occasions: at the opera two nights ago, and yesterday when he had come by to take her and Olivia for a drive in the Park. Mary had liked him at once. He reminded her so much of Jack. During both occasions, though, he had been particularly solicitous of Olivia. Mary had dismissed his behavior as no more sincere than that of his nephew. The two of them had enough charm between them to coax all the birds from all the trees in all the parks of London. Surely Olivia had not taken him seriously?

But perhaps Mary had misread his attentions. Olivia was a very attractive woman, after all. She had no idea what sort of conversation the two of them had shared at the opera. Jack had kept her too busy with his own silly flirtation. The few times she had glanced over at them, however, she had noticed Olivia smiling and apparently enjoying herself. Good heavens, she thought as a smile spread across her face, could it be that . . . could they have . . .

"Olivia," she blurted before completing her thought, "is there something you have not told me?"

"I beg your pardon?" Olivia asked with a puzzled look as she wiped her finger on a linen handkerchief.

"About you and Mr. Maitland, I mean. You seemed very cozy

together at the opera, and he could scarce keep his eyes off you yesterday in the Park. Have you two formed an attachment?"

"Good heavens!" Olivia exclaimed.

Her outraged tone was somewhat offset by the blush that crept up her neck all the way to her hairline.

"What a foolish notion," Olivia continued in an exasperated voice. She did not look at Mary, but instead busied herself with adjusting the fabric in the embroidery hoop. "The very idea! For one thing, I hardly know the man. For another, he is a rake, and, like your friend Lord Pemerton, a consummate flirt. He flirts with me. That is all. There is nothing more to it than that."

As Jack flirts with me, Mary thought wistfully.

Apparently satisfied with the new position of the painted silk, Olivia began rummaging through her workbag and finally pulled out a skein of green silk thread. She moistened the end of the silk and, turning around slightly toward the sunlight streaming in through the window behind, rethreaded her needle. She then looked up at Mary with a determined tilt to her chin. "Unlike you, my dear," she said, "a gazetted rake holds no appeal for me." She then bent back over her embroidery, plying tiny green stitches with intense deliberation. Her face, however, Mary was quick to notice, was still colored with a rosy blush.

Mary was not by nature a matchmaker. Her project to find Jack a bride was entered into on a whim, as a source of diversion. And though it looked as if she might be making progress in that quarter—Jack seemed to have shown a marked partiality for Miss Carstairs—she would not willingly attempt such a project again. It had all been too confusing, with Jack showing a preference for the least likely candidates while cavalierly dismissing the most obvious.

But the very idea of Olivia and Edward Maitland was almost enough to change her mind about matchmaking. There had been a spark of something between them, she was sure of it. There needed only a bit of kindling to ignite it.

It was almost irresistible.

"It is true," she said, turning back to the pianoforte and picking out a tune in an attempt at nonchalance, "that Mr. Maitland has a reputation as a rake. But he is older and more mature now. The wild days of his youth are surely long past."

Olivia continued to ply her needle with silent intensity.

"Nevertheless," Mary continued, "he is still quite attractive, is he not?"

"I suppose so," was the muttered reply.

"And so very charming and witty. Do you not agree, my dear?"

"If you say so," Olivia said in a voice so soft Mary had stopped playing in order to hear.

Mary was prevented from pursuing this very interesting discussion by the sound of voices in the hall. She was not normally at home to callers on Wednesdays, so she was extremely curious to know who it might be. Her eyes were trained on the double doors when they were swung open by the butler. When she spied a familiar figure behind him, she was filled with an unexpected thrill of excitement. Her face broke into a huge smile.

"His Lordship, the Marquess of Pemerton," the butler announced. "And Mr. Edward Maitland."

Mary was only vaguely aware of the sound of embroidery hoops clattering to the floor as she rose to meet her guests.

Jack smiled as his eyes caught Mary's. She had risen from the bench at the pianoforte and was moving across the small drawing room toward him with an outstretched hand.

"Jack!" she exclaimed with flattering enthusiasm. "And Mr. Maitland. How lovely."

Jack took her proffered hand and brought it to his lips, then turned it over and placed a quick kiss on her palm. Her eyes flashed with amusement. After she had turned to greet his uncle, Jack took her arm and led her back toward the pianoforte. He noticed, out of the corner of his eye, that Uncle Edward was helping Mrs. Bannister to retrieve something—sewing articles or some such thing—from the floor where they had apparently fallen and scattered.

"I hope you do not mind our dropping by like this, unannounced," he said. "But we were in the vicinity and, since it is not Tuesday, I thought it safe to call."

Mary gave a throaty chuckle. "You are quite safe," she said.

"No other callers are expected. And you must know, Jack, that you are always welcome. Olivia and I had just about exhausted our store of amusing conversation, so your timing is quite perfect."

"You were playing?" he asked, nodding toward the pianoforte, noting for the first time what a particularly beautiful instrument it was, with a satinwood case inlaid with rosewood in a rambling floral pattern. It must have been a very expensive piece. Jack chastised himself for not noticing it before; it was almost the only outward sign of Mary's wealth.

"Just dabbling," she replied with a dismissive wave of her hand. "Nothing serious."

Jack had not considered Mary's music when developing his plan for the morning. But now that he thought on it, it might be just the thing to encourage the proper mood. Yes, just the thing. "Will you play for us now?" he asked, indicating that she should be seated on the pianoforte bench.

"Now?"

"Jack has told me of your skill, Lady Mary," said his quick-thinking Uncle Edward, now sharing the sofa with a blushing—blushing?—Mrs. Bannister. "It would be an honor to have you play for us."

Mary turned back to Jack with a questioning look.

"Please, Mary. Nothing would give me greater pleasure than to listen to your sweet music." He took her hand to his lips once again.

"All right," she said, laughing. "It is my greatest pleasure as well. What would you like to hear?"

Jack bent over the stack of sheet music piled on the edge of the instrument and searched through the top few selections. His eyes were drawn to a score handwritten in a fine, spidery scrawl. "What is this?" he asked.

"Oh," Mary said as she took the score and fondly thumbed through it, "it is a Scarlatti sonata transcribed for the pianoforte."

"Your own transcription?"

"Yes."

Jack was genuinely impressed. "Then you must certainly play it for us," he said. "Shall I turn the pages for you?"

"You read music?" she asked with a teasing grin.

"I am not totally without accomplishments, my dear."

"Very well, then," she said and settled in to play.

Jack had heard Mary play on two previous occasions and had been struck both by her technique and her passion. She seemed almost to lose herself in the music, which played nicely into his plans for the morning. He would need to catch her off guard if everything was to go according to plan.

Once again, he was impressed by Mary's performance. She was truly gifted, he thought, watching her small hands fly across the keyboard in a skillful interpretation of the complex baroque patterns. He lifted his eyes to her face, expecting fierce concentration, and found instead an almost peaceful contentment. It had been no jest, then, that this was her greatest pleasure. Though he turned the pages for her, she seldom actually looked at the score, often closing her eyes, her body swaying gently to the melody.

When her fingers at last stilled on the final chord, she sat quietly for a moment, breathing deeply, her eyes half closed—clearly she had forgotten the presence of her audience.

Jack bent slightly over her. "Beautiful," he whispered.

She suddenly came alert, looking up at Jack and smiling. The sound of gentle applause came from the other side of the room.

"Wonderful!" Uncle Edward said with enthusiasm. "Wonderful." He turned to look at Mary's companion, who was smiling fondly at her employer. "Do you not agree, Mrs. Bannister?"

"I have lived with Lady Mary for three years," she said, "and have never ceased to be impressed by her talent. I am most fortunate to be so often an audience."

While they spoke, Jack had seated himself at Mary's side on the bench. She had grinned and moved over to allow him room. When Uncle Edward turned to make some remark to Mrs. Bannister, Jack tilted his head down toward Mary's and placed his lips close to her ear.

"I must speak with you in private," he said in a soft whisper. "It is very important."

Her eyes widened, sparkling in expectation, and a huge smile split her face. "Is it—"

He interrupted her with a finger to his lips. "In private," he repeated. Her smile grew even broader, if that was possible. In a flash of insight he knew what she was thinking. She expected him to announce his formal intentions, or even a betrothal, to Miss Carstairs or one of the other candidates. He could almost feel her excitement, her giddiness, as she seemed almost to bounce right off the bench. He gave her a stern look. She nodded and turned, with the greatest equanimity, toward the sofa across the room.

"Thank you for your kind words, Mr. Maitland," she said. "I am glad you enjoyed it. Music is my greatest passion, you know. But I have others as well. For example, I share an interest with Olivia in exotic plants. We have quite a collection, do we not, Olivia?"

"Yes, we do," Mrs. Bannister said with a somewhat puzzled look.

"Our small conservatory boasts several rare specimens," Mary said, favoring Uncle Edward with her most engaging smile. "Perhaps you would be interested in seeing them, sir?"

Jack tossed his uncle a pleading look. He knew of Jack's plans and had in fact been invited along for the express purpose of somehow removing the ubiquitous companion from the scene. Uncle Edward had accepted his task with unexpected enthusiasm. Mary's suggestion simply made the job easier. Uncle Edward was quick to take advantage.

"Indeed," he said rising, "I would be pleased to view your collection. Can you spare Mrs. Bannister for a few moments, if she will agree to accompany me?"

"Of course," Mary said. "Jack and I will await you here. Perhaps I will play another piece for him." She smiled at Jack and he nodded.

Uncle Edward offered his arm to Mrs. Bannister who looked as if she were being asked to dance naked down St. James's Street. A deep scarlet blush colored her entire face. Eyes cast down, fingers barely touching Uncle Edward's sleeve, she directed him, with obvious reluctance, out of the drawing room and toward the conservatory.

Once alone, Mary was again bursting with excitement. "Tell me!" she demanded, grasping his arm.

Jack studied the situation for a moment and decided he needed to recapture the languorous calm that had followed her playing.

"In due time," he said. "First, I would like you to play for me once more."

"Jack!" she shrieked with impatience.

He definitely needed to soften the mood. "Mary, my sweet," he said in his most seductive tone, "indulge me. I do not often have the pleasure of hearing you play. You must know your talent is extraordinary. One more piece. Please, Mary."

She furrowed her brow and wrinkled her nose in frustration, then heaved a profound sigh. "All right, if you insist. What shall it be, then?"

"You choose, my dear."

She sifted through the sheet music, discarding several before pulling one out and setting it on the music stand. "This is a new sonata by Herr Beethoven," she said. "I think it is quite lovely. Shall I play the adagio for you?"

"Yes, my dear, if you please."

As before, she was soon lost to the music. The slow, haunting melody seemed to engulf her with its passion. Her mobile face evoked all the sadness, the wretchedness, the longing, and finally the rapture of the music. Jack could not say for certain whether the emotional power of the piece came solely from the notes laid down by the composer, or from Mary's own intensity of expression. He was moved in a way he had not thought possible.

But throughout, he never lost sight of his ultimate goal. The particular ardor of the piece—how fortunate that Mary had selected one by the passionate Herr Beethoven—set the mood perfectly for what he hoped would follow.

When she played the final notes and slowly slid her hands from the keyboard, it was obvious she was still absorbed by the emotion of the music: head thrown back, eyes half closed, lips slightly parted. She was breathing heavily. Before she could overcome her rapt state, Jack made his move.

He quickly pulled her onto his lap and clasped her tightly to his chest. "Mary, Mary," he said softly, gazing down into her eyes, suddenly wide with confusion, "you are so vibrant, so full of passion. Even since we first met, I have tried to resist you, my dear. I can do so no longer."

He lowered his lips to hers and kissed her.

Chapter 8

Mary returned Jack's kiss almost without thinking. She molded her body to his and wrapped her arms tightly about his shoulders. It had been so long!

She forced her thoughts into somewhat better focus when his lips left hers and began to trace a path down her throat and up her neck. What on earth was going on? One moment she was lost to Herr Beethoven, and the next she was lost to Jack.

Jack!

She couldn't believe this was happening, that she was actually being kissed by Jack. Oh, he had always flirted with her, to be sure, but it meant nothing. It had, though, become more and more difficult of late to steel herself against his often very physical flirtations. She had almost gone mad the other night at the opera when he had toyed with her hand throughout the last act, and had even brushed his lips against her neck at one point. She knew, though, that it was merely his way with women and signified nothing. She often had to remind herself that it was naught more than meaningless flirtation, just a game he played.

And yet this was no game, she thought, moaning slightly as his lips and tongue tantalized her neck, his silky black hair tickling her cheek. But perhaps this *was* just a game. He was a consummate rake, after all. Was it possible they had simply entered a different level of play—a level of which she had no experience and no understanding of the rules?

"Mary, sweet Mary," he muttered as his lips found her jaw, her brow, her eyes. Finally, they returned to her lips, moving over them gently.

Ah well, she had wondered, after all, what it would be like to be kissed by Jack, a rake of the first order. Now she knew. It was quite wonderful. She had enjoyed his flirting. Now she would enjoy his kisses. Later, she would worry about what it all meant. When his tongue teased the seam of her lips and forced its way inside, she was lost once again to all rational thought and gave herself up to the wonder of pure sensation.

After a few minutes Jack raised his head slightly. "Marry me," he whispered against her lips.

What?

Mary's feet came back to earth with a thud. What had he said? She could not have heard him properly. He had simply spoken her name. Her foolish mind was playing tricks. She had heard *marry* when he had simply said *Mary*. Idiot! She pulled away from Jack's embrace and looked up at him.

"Marry me."

There. He had said it again. There was no question about it this time. *Oh, my God.* She searched his face for some hint of the teasing amusement she had come to expect from Jack, but found nothing to indicate that he was joking. Could he possibly be serious? She sat in dumbfounded silence, her thoughts a blur, as she listened to him speak.

"You can bring on an endless parade of candidates," he was saying, his deep blue eyes gazing longingly into hers, "but there is only one woman I want." He pulled her closer. "I want *you,* Mary. I want to marry you. Will you have me, my dear? Will you marry me?"

Her mind was reeling. She couldn't seem to grasp what was happening. "You want to marry me?" she asked, her voice rising in an unnatural squeak.

"More than anything."

"Truly?"

"Truly."

Something was very wrong here. This couldn't be happening— not to her. She must be dreaming. That's it—she was dreaming. This was too close to what she had desired in the deepest, most private recesses of her heart to be real. She was dreaming. Foolish dreams.

All at once the dream was invaded by an image of her father—

eyes flashing, a malevolent grin on his face as he sat opposite her in the carriage on their return from her aborted elopement to Scotland.

"Foolish girl," he had chided. "You must know that no man will every marry you. Did you seriously think you had actually attracted a man? A pitiful-looking, puny little creature like you? How could you have imagined any man would want you?" He had snorted with derisive laughter. "That Morrison chap was willing enough to disappear once I paid him off. He did not care this much for you," he said, snapping his fingers in front of her face. "And no other young men will come sniffing around now, you may be sure. You shall not even have my fortune to bribe them, for I will not give it to you. You shall have nothing from me, girl." He had thrown back his head and laughed and laughed.

But he had not known—or had forgotten in his increasing madness—about the trust fund set up by her mother. He had not known, and neither had she at the time, that she indeed had a fortune to offer in compensation for her ugliness. Her father had not known.

But then, neither does Jack, she thought, pulling her attention back to the present and dismissing the unpleasant memory of her father. Jack could not possibly know about her fortune. And even if he did, what would it matter to him? He was a marquess, the head of an important family. He owned property all over England. He would have no need for her money. If this was not a dream and if he truly wanted to marry her, then it must be for herself. The thought was comforting, almost as much as his thumbs, gently stroking her jaw while he looked down at her in question, awaiting her response. *He wants me for myself,* she thought as a bubble of hope lodged itself in her heart.

All these years she had accepted the truth of her father's words, accepted the fact of her unattractiveness, her ineligibility. Even when she had discovered that she had access to a fortune, she had resolved never to use it to buy her way into a marriage. She would rather be alone than face that ignominy. And so she was resigned to her single state. But here was Jack—handsome, witty, charming, worldly, wonderful—apparently wanting to marry her.

But of course, he did not really know her. He did not know the truth about her. And when he did, he would not want her.

Thoroughly confused and befuddled by his closeness, she extricated herself from his embrace, stood, and walked across the room. She stood behind a small upholstered armchair, her hands gripping its back tightly in an attempt to stop their shaking. If Jack was not joking—and apparently he was not—then she was just about to toss away an opportunity she had never dreamed could be hers.

It was the second worst moment of her life.

"Thank you," she said in a quiet, trembling voice. "I am sensible of the honor you have shown me by your offer. But I cannot marry you, Jack."

"Why not?" Jack asked, walking toward her. He halted before he was close enough to touch her, stopped by the pain and confusion in her eyes.

He did not understand her rejection. There was no question that she had enjoyed their kiss. Indeed, he was certain she had. But then, he had never yet failed in a seduction. He knew exactly how to entice a woman, how to lead her without fail toward the ultimate surrender. Every sensual move was precisely choreographed. He had had no doubts about his ability to seduce Mary. Women like Mary were generally more difficult to entice initially, but were ultimately more susceptible to seduction. He had expected a spinster of her years to be stiff and unyielding at first, requiring special care and patience so as not to frighten her. In fact, her response—her lips matching the pressure and movements of his own, opening at last to allow his tongue entrance, her arms wrapping around his shoulders and pulling him into a more intimate embrace—had been so unexpected that he had almost lost control. Oh god, but she was a passionate little thing!

And so now she was apparently going to play hard-to-get. He found himself feeling a twinge of disappointment that his Mary would stoop to such hackneyed tactics. He would not have expected it of her. But he must remember that after all, she was a woman, and when it came right down to it, they were all the same. She was no better than Suzanne, who had convinced him of her affection then jilted him for a grand title. His young and naive heart had been further outraged when Suzanne had made it clear that, though married to another man, she was willing to bestow her favors upon Jack if he was interested. This, from the woman with whom he had shared what he thought to be the purest love. What a young fool he had been.

He had vowed fifteen years ago that he would never again allow a woman to claim his heart. Suzanne had taught him a valuable lesson. All women were faithless, inconstant, scheming manipulators. Even Mary. All right, then, he would play along with her little game. He could be as manipulative as any woman.

She was breathing heavily. Jack watched the rise and fall of her bosom with some admiration. If he could just get beyond this obligatory scene, he began to believe that marriage to Mary—with her sweetly rounded little body and her passionate nature—would not be so very unpleasant after all.

When his eyes strayed from her splendid bosom, he saw she was gripping the back of a chair so tightly that her knuckles were white with the strain. There was nothing coy in her attitude. Her eyes were downcast. She had not spoken.

"Mary?" he prompted in a soft, coaxing tone. "Tell me why you cannot marry me."

She looked up at him finally, a haunted look in her eyes that stunned him with its intensity and pain. There was a crease of anxiety across her brow. Was there something after all, some insurmountable obstacle to a marriage between them? His stomach knotted suddenly in fear that his plan might actually fail.

She took a few more steadying breaths. "I know that you need to marry, Jack." Her voice was not the usual deep, husky purr he had grown so fond of, but instead was a fraction higher in pitch, as if her throat were tight. "And I know you have said you do not much care who you marry. But you must not allow that indifference to extend to me, Jack." Her voice had become higher and more plaintive. "I am not the right woman for you. You know I am not. You would be better suited to Miss Carstairs . . . or Lady Camilla Redbourne."

She let go of the chair back and began to pace the short distance in front of the fireplace, the skirts of her striped sarcenet dress swirling about her as she walked. Her hands were clasped tightly in front of her. Finally, she looked up at him, her brow still creased.

"Jack," she said, "you are handsome and titled and important. Surely you owe it to your family—your mother, at least—to choose someone more appropriate. Someone," her voice cracked after a brief pause, "someone young and beautiful and innocent."

This may not after all be the typical cat and mouse game he had expected. Her distress seemed genuine. He did not believe the anguish in her eyes could have been feigned. Poor Mary. Was she really so convinced of her own worthlessness? Jack suddenly realized that his concern for her feelings was very real. He wanted more than anything to persuade her that he wanted her, if only for her own self-esteem. He hated to see her so downcast and vulnerable. He wanted his sunny, cheerful Mary back.

He reached out and gently unclasped her hands—dear God, they were trembling!—and took one in his own. "Mary, my dear," he said softly, looking down into those huge hazel eyes, "youth and beauty are extremely tenuous ideals, open to a vast array of individual interpretations. Let me make my own judgments. How old are you, Mary?"

She looked at him for a long time before answering. "Twenty-nine," she said at last, her eyes dropping to watch their entwined fingers.

"A full eight years my junior," he said, gently squeezing her hand. "Compared to an old ruin like me, my dear, you must certainly be considered youthful." He flashed her a grin, hoping to tease her into a smile. But when she raised her eyes to his, her brow was still furrowed—whether in confusion, disapproval, or disbelief, he could not be certain. He smiled and brought her hand briefly to his lips. "And so we can eliminate age as an obstacle," he continued. "And now," he said taking her chin in his other hand, "let us address the issue of beauty."

Her head snapped downward, but he gently forced her chin back up so that she had to look at him. He must tackle this subject with some caution.

"It is true, my dear, that neither of us can claim the sort of classical beauty that Society and Art have idolized as the latest fash-

ion. But just because we are not perfect does not mean we are unattractive."

"Of course not!" Mary said with some vehemence. "You are
very attractive, Jack, very handsome."

"As are you, Mary."

"No!" She tried to twist her face away from his, but he kept her
chin firmly tilted up to look at him.

"Yes, you are handsome, Mary," he said gently.

Her eyes darkened momentarily in what seemed like anger, but
she blinked and it was gone, replaced by a look of weary resignation. "You don't have to lie to me, Jack," she said in a whisper so
soft he was barely able to hear.

"Mary, Mary," he said, stroking her jaw. "I am not lying. It is
true that you don't have the beauty of, for example, Lady
Bradleigh—or Miss Langley-Howe. Not many are so fortunate.
But there is so much more to you, Mary. Don't you realize that a
man could drown in your eyes, my dear? They are the most beautiful eyes I have ever seen. And your skin," he said, running the
back of his fingers along her jaw and down her throat, "is positively translucent, like the purest alabaster. And your smile"—he
ran his thumb along her lower lip—"can light up an entire room."

She looked up at him in confusion. Had no one every before
told her these things, ever complimented her? The words he had
spoken were not false flattery, but were absolutely true. Had no
one ever told her she was attractive? Ah, Mary. He pulled her
close and held her against him, gently running his hands along her
back. Had this sweet, talented woman been overlooked for so
long that she could not recognize her own worth? How he wanted
to smooth that furrowed brow.

"And I absolutely adore your crooked nose," he said, planting a
quick kiss upon it.

"Really, Jack!"

"But I do," he said, kissing it again. "It gives you character."

"Character!"

"Yes," he said, pulling her closer, "a far more valuable com-
modity than surface beauty, my dear. It will serve you well in
later years. When Miss Langley-Howe has faded to a bland mid-

dle age, you will still be a handsome woman with a face of great character."

He bent down to nuzzle her neck and felt her suck in her breath. She might not trust him yet, but at least she was not indifferent to him physically.

"You are sweet to say such things to me," she said at last in a raspy voice. "In fact, you cannot imagine how much it means to me. But, Jack, this is madness. We both know I am not the sort of woman you desire."

"Mary," Jack said roughly, his lips hovering just above hers, "if you do not believe I find you desirable, then you have not been paying attention."

He kissed her, pulling her body close against his. She responded by curling her arms tightly around his waist and returning his kiss. And then almost immediately he felt her pull back. He continued kissing her nonetheless, until her hands moved to his chest and pushed. He let go, and she moved away at once. Her hands flew to her mouth, and her eyes were wide and unnaturally bright. She turned her back to him.

"Mary?" He placed a hand gently on her shoulder, but she shrugged him off, taking a step farther away from him. "What is it, my dear? Are you upset that I kissed you? Well, I will not apologize. I have told you that I find you desirable. I am afraid I also find you quite irresistible." He took a step closer, but did not touch her. "Come, Mary. Admit that you enjoyed it as much as I did. You see how compatible we are? That is important in a marriage."

Although she was still turned away from him, he could see her swallow almost convulsively and thought she might be crying. Oh, Lord. This was turning out to be more difficult than he could ever have imagined.

"Marriage is out of the question," she said at last in a trembly voice. "I have told you that I am not the right woman for you Jack. I have told you that you need someone young and beautiful and innocent."

"And I have told you, Mary," he said as he stepped closer and placed both hands lightly on her upper arms, "that I find you both young and beautiful. I thought we had effectively eliminated all your misconceptions of unsuitability."

"Except one," she said in a husky whisper.

He felt her stiffen beneath his hands, though she did not shrug him off. She stood very still and said nothing.

"Mary?"

After what seemed an interminable silence, she turned around once again to face him. Her stricken look was almost enough to break Jack's heart. He moved his hands slowly down her bare arms and took her hands. She clasped them tightly in return, digging a fingernail painfully into his palm. He ignored the discomfort as he studied the anguish in her face. What could possible be causing her such distress? He was fairly certain it had nothing to do with him. Suddenly, he experienced another moment of fear that this scheme of his wasn't going to work after all. She was going to tell him something—something that would make it impossible for him to marry her. He held his breath as he waited for Mary to continue, for all his plans to crumble into so much dust.

"Young and beautiful and innocent," she repeated. He watched her swallow with difficulty and take a deep breath. "I cannot marry you, Jack. Nor anyone else. I am not . . . innocent."

Chapter 9

"Mary? I do not understand," Jack said

He looked thunderstruck. Mary was mortified. How she wished Jack had never kissed her, and never filled her head with all those sweet lies, had never forced her to tell him what she knew she had to tell him. She pulled her hands from his, stepped back slightly, and dropped her eyes to the floor. She could not look at him. She could not bear to see the scorn, the disappointment, the disgust she knew would be in his eyes when she told him.

She opened her mouth to speak, but no words would come. It was as though her throat had swollen shut, allowing no sound to pass. She swallowed with difficulty and tried again. But once more, no words came. She could not seem to catch her breath. Her mouth was open, but she could not seem to breathe. She began to feel disoriented and dizzy.

Oh, my God.

"Mary!" Suddenly Jack swept her into his arms and carried her to the sofa where Olivia and Mr. Maitland had sat earlier. He roughly knocked aside Olivia's workbag, sending an embroidery hoop clattering across the floor, and gently laid Mary onto the sofa. All at once his hands were roughly moving over her thighs, and Mary felt as if she ought to panic, but did not seem to be able to focus her thoughts enough to do so. She felt him rummaging through her skirts and finally locating a hidden pocket. He reached inside and pulled out a tiny silver vinaigrette that Mary always kept with her, though she had seldom needed it. He flipped open the lid and thrust it under her nose. Though she kept the tiny sponge soaked in lavender water rather than vinegar, the fragrance was nevertheless soothing.

"Take slow, deep breaths," Jack was saying. "That's it. Breathe deeply. You will be all right in a moment."

She listened to his words and obeyed. And he was right. In a few moments she was breathing easily and very conscious of Jack leaning over her in a disturbingly intimate manner. Good heavens, had she almost fainted? How mortifying! This was indeed turning into the second most humiliating experience of her life.

Embarrassed for Jack to see her in such a state, she attempted to sit upright, but a firm hand on her shoulder kept her down.

"A few more minutes, Mary," he said. "You will only make yourself dizzy if you sit up too soon." He gently massaged her hand, which Mary suddenly realized he had been holding the whole time. "Are you feeling better?" he asked after a few moments.

"Yes," she muttered.

"Good girl. Now, let's very slowly raise you up." He took both her shoulders and slowly brought her upright. She swung her feet to the ground. "All right?" he asked.

"Yes. Jack, I'm so sorry—"

"Is there a sherry decanter nearby, or shall I ring for one?"

"No, please, don't ring. There is a decanter on the table over there, just on the other side of the pianoforte."

Jack rose and walked across the room. Mary watched, still embarrassed, as he poured her a glass of pale sherry. She grabbed the vinaigrette, which Jack had placed on a nearby side table, and stuffed it back into her pocket, not wishing to be reminded by the sight of it of her missish behavior. He returned to the sofa, sat down next to her, and placed the glass at her lips.

"Drink this," he ordered.

She took the glass from his hand and sipped the sherry. When Jack gave her a stern look, she took a long swallow. The smooth, nutty-flavored liquid traced a warm path down her throat. She felt its calming effects almost immediately. Jack took the glass from her and placed it on the side table. He then reached for one of her hands and held it between both of his own.

"Mary? Are you—"

"I am fine now, Jack," she said quickly, interrupting him. "Thank you. I . . . I am so sorry. I do not usually . . . it is just that I . . . Oh, God. I am so embarrassed." She turned her face away from him.

"Don't be," he said, placing a hand softly on her cheek and gently turning her face toward his. "You were upset, distraught." He stroked her cheek and jaw briefly before dropping his hand. Her face felt warm where he had touched her. "If you are feeling better now," he said, "I would like to try to continue our conversation. It is very important to me. Do you think you can, Mary?"

"Oh, Jack. This is so hard for me."

"I know, my dear."

"No," she said forcefully, "you do *not* know. No one knows. Well, except for Olivia. But I have never spoken of this to anyone else. I wish . . . I wish I did not have to speak of it to you. But your marriage proposal gives me no choice."

She looked up into his eyes and saw nothing but concern. He did not speak. She closed her eyes and forged ahead before she could lose what little nerve she had left.

"When I was seventeen," she began, "something happened to me—something that makes it impossible for me to consider marriage to you or anyone else. There was this young man, you see—"

"Mary!" he interrupted. She opened her eyes and found Jack looking down at her with something like relief. "My dear, is all this about some youthful indiscretion? Is that all it is?" He was smiling broadly, practically laughing. "Oh, Mary!" All at once he took her in his arms and held her close, whispering in her ear. "Do you think it matters to me? Do you think it makes any difference to me?"

"But—"

"Mary!" He bent and kissed the top of her head. "I thought you were going to admit to secretly being among the fashionably impure, that you had had a string of protectors. But my dear, a moment of passion some dozen years ago? How can you think—"

"It was not precisely a moment of passion," she muttered against his shoulder.

He pulled away slightly and gazed down at her with a stricken look. "Oh, God, Mary. Was it . . . did someone . . . force you?"

"I was not ravished, if that is what you are thinking," Mary said, pushing herself away from Jack, feeling unexpectedly angry. She had never fully understood—though she had accepted it—how the loss of a young woman's virtue was such a heinous offense. But it angered her even more to think that if she had been forced, if she had been raped, then the loss of an insignificant little membrane would have been more easily overlooked.

"I was a very willing participant," she announced boldly. She immediately wanted to take back her words. She felt the heat of a blush creep up her neck and face.

"I am glad to hear it," Jack said with a smile. "Tell me about it." He had taken her hand once again.

She dropped her eyes to watch the movement of his fingers over her own. "I was seventeen," she said. "I was . . . unhappy at home. I wanted to get away. So I eloped with a young man who was visiting the neighborhood. Peter Morrison was his name. We were headed for Scotland, but my father caught up with us at Cheltenham." Mary smiled ruefully as she recalled how she had always secretly referred to those events as her own private Cheltenham tragedy. "But it was too late," she continued, her smile fading. "We had spent one night together. I was already . . . ruined."

Jack squeezed her hand when she did not immediately go on. "What happened next?" he prompted.

"My father took me back home."

It seemed a ridiculously inadequate description of what had really happened. She recalled, once again, that carriage ride from Cheltenham with her father. Mary had sat silently, staring out the carriage window, her nose bandaged, one eye swollen shut. It had been the worst day of her life. And Peter's behavior had only forced her to face the truth of her father's cruel taunts. She had thought Peter loved her, but he hadn't even said good-bye. It was true, then, what her father had said—that he had only been interested in her fortune, that without it she was worthless as a human being, as a woman.

Somehow during the horrible trip home she had developed a kind of desperate resolve, a fierce determination to survive. She would no longer allow herself to be hurt by her father's gibes about her ugliness and worthlessness. It had been difficult. Once home again at Castle Assheton, her father had not ceased chiding her. Indeed, she knew that he derived perverse pleasure from it. She had been finally convinced, then, that he was in fact mad, somehow mentally deranged; but that knowledge had not made her life any easier. She accepted the truth of his words with resigned indifference; but she had never accepted or forgiven their deliberate cruelty, despite his madness. She had never forgiven him. She had hated him as much as he hated her.

My father took me back home.

It was all she could say, though it had been so much more than that.

"What became of the young man?" Jack asked. "Peter Morrison?"

"My father paid him off. I never saw him again. I heard later that he had joined the army and was killed at Talavera."

"Ah, Mary," he said, bringing her hand to his lips. "I am truly sorry you had to suffer such an ordeal. Were you very much in love with him?"

"Not really," she said after some thought. "In retrospect I can see that I did not really love him."

"And what makes you think, my dear, that this unfortunate episode of a dozen years ago makes you unsuitable to be my wife?"

"Because I am not . . ." She paused and looked up at him in confusion. What was he saying? Of course she was unsuitable. "A . . . a gentleman," she continued, "especially one as important as a marquess, cannot possibly marry a woman who . . . who is not . . ."

"Yes, he can," Jack said. "Mary, no one can tell me whom I can or cannot marry. No one. Besides, I cannot imagine anyone objecting to my marrying you—except perhaps to say that I am not good enough for you." He took her other hand and then brought both hands to his lips, kissing each one in turn.

Oh, but he is a devil, thought Mary, *seducing me with words and kisses*. How she wanted to believe him!

"My sweet Mary," he was saying, between kissing her fingers one by one, "you believe that a single youthful indiscretion—one that apparently only you and Mrs. Bannister even know about—makes you unsuitable. And yet my own wicked, miserable past is an open book that all of Society has read. If anyone is unsuitable, it must surely be me. Ah, Mary, it is I who should be begging you to forgive my disreputable past, not the other way around. Will you forgive me, Mary? Will you have me, despite my wretched, soiled life?"

Mary was unable to answer because Jack had once again claimed her lips. Her mind was reeling again, unable to believe he was serious. Did he really want her, knowing that she could not come to him untouched? Did it really not matter to him? Oh, how she wanted to believe him—this fascinating man who set her senses on fire. Should she say yes? Should she agree to marry him? Should she grab at this unexpected opportunity for happiness?

Happiness. Would she truly find happiness with Jack? A foolish question, she thought as his lips tantalized her ear and throat. If she was honest with herself, then she must admit she was already halfway in love with him. And that, of course, was the real problem. It would be so easy to fall in love with him. And it would be so easy for him to break her heart. She must not forget that he was a rake, a libertine, a habitual womanizer who would no doubt be unfaithful to her from the start. How could she bear it?

And what exactly did he expect from her? She understood it was important that he marry, now that he was head of his family. He was obviously not seeking a love match, just a wife. Was he proposing a marriage of convenience between two friends? And would that be such a bad thing, after all? She pulled away from his lips and looked him in the eye. He smiled at her seductively.

"I need to understand something, Jack."

"Yes, my dear?"

"What exactly do you expect from me if we marry? What sort of marriage are you proposing?"

He gave her a huge smile, his eyes bright as if he knew she was going to accept him, as if that would make him happy. "Mary, Mary," he said, running a knuckle along her cheek, "you are the most delightful woman I know. You are in fact the only woman I

have ever called a friend. You know, better than anyone, that I
must marry. I am simply proposing that we take our already close
friendship one step further. We enjoy one another's company. We
laugh together. Good lord, Mary, we have more in our favor already than most married couples. We like each other. And"—he
brushed his lips lightly against hers—"we are certainly compatible physically."

"But do you think," Mary said in a soft whisper, "that you
could ever love me?"

Oh, Lord. He was unprepared for such a question, though he
should have expected it. He had hoped to avoid any mention of
love. *Love!* Why did women always need declarations of love!
Fifteen years ago, he had been coerced by the beautiful Suzanne
into such a declaration. But the truth was he had meant it—young,
naive fool that he had been. He had loved her totally and he had
believed her own words of love to him. He had discovered too
late that she had only wanted his connections and money—it was
believed that even the younger son of a marquess was sure to
have a comfortable fortune. When a wealthy earl some twenty
years her senior had made her an offer, she had jilted Jack without
a thought. Two years later—bored and restless—she had offered
herself to Jack. He had been disgusted and turned her down.
Words of love, indeed. Women were incapable of such feelings.

And so was he.

But now Mary wanted a declaration of love, did she? Well, he
was prepared to give her anything she wanted at the moment. He
desperately needed her to accept his proposal. He had thought this
would be so easy, that she would fall into his arms in gratitude.
He had been totally unprepared for the torrent of emotions he had
unleashed. Poor Mary. She was so thoroughly convinced she was
unworthy. Mary, unworthy! She was probably the most worthy
person he had ever known. It had torn at Jack's heart to listen to
her admission of having been "ruined" so many years ago. Her
apparent shame had touched him deeply and caused him to suddenly consider in a new light the inequities in the ways Society,
himself included, had always treated women in this regard. How
unjust that a sweet woman like Mary should be made to feel dis-

graced for all her life by a single moment of physical surrender, whereas a man such as himself could, and did, publicly flaunt dozens of indiscretions without the least fear of censure.

Jack felt sure that he had successfully eliminated Mary's past as an obstacle to marriage. He could feel her capitulation when he kissed her. And yet there was apparently one more complication to face: a declaration of love. Should he give her what she wanted? Is that what was required? Could he carry his deceit that far?

He looked down into Mary's big hazel eyes and knew he could not go that far. His seduction and proposal were deceitful enough. He owed this sweet little woman at least some measure of honesty.

He took Mary's face in both his hands and looked deeply into his eyes, willing her to trust him. "I am very fond of you, Mary. I can promise to keep you close and protect you for all the rest of my days. I can offer you security, friendship, affection . . . and, yes, passion, too. And, God willing, children. But I cannot promise more, Mary. I am not capable of offering more to any woman. But I offer you all that I can. Will you be my wife, Mary?"

"Jack, I—"

Mary's response was cut off by a great rattling of the drawing room doors. *Damnation!* He needed more time. At least Uncle Edward was doing his best to announce their return. Mary lost no time in removing herself from his embrace. Quickly straightening her skirts, she strode casually to the pianoforte and begin sorting through the stack of sheet music.

"Ah, here they are, Jack," she said with such an air of calm nonchalance that he could hardly credit that she had only a few minutes before been so overcome with emotion she had practically swooned. "We had almost given up on you two. Did you enjoy the conservatory, Mr. Maitland?"

"Indeed we did, Lady Mary," Uncle Edward said, casting a swift questioning glance at Jack. "And we were having such a fascinating conversation that I am afraid we lost track of time."

Uncle Edward smiled at Mrs. Bannister, who, Jack noted, was blushing once again. Perhaps his uncle had fared better with his lady than had Jack. Blast it all! How was he to finish his business with Mary?

Neither Mrs. Bannister nor Mary took a seat, so it was obvious the visit was at an end. While his uncle chatted briefly with the ladies, Jack turned to Mary and raised his brows in question. She nodded, but he had no idea what it meant. He felt oddly nervous.

As good-byes were said and hands were shaken all around, Mary turned to Jack as he headed toward the drawing room doors. "About that business we discussed, Jack," she said.

"Yes?"

"I shall inform you tomorrow when I have made a decision. Will that be all right?"

He let out the breath he had not realized he had been holding. "Of course, my dear," he said, taking her fingers to his lips one last time. "I look forward to hearing from you."

The drawing room doors closed behind them, and he and his uncle followed the butler down the stairs to the front hall.

"How did it go, my boy?" Uncle Edward whispered through the side of his mouth.

"I am not certain," Jack said, watching the back of the butler, hesitant to say anything in front of Mary's servants.

Uncle Edward's brows shot up in surprise. "Difficult?" he asked.

"You might say that," Jack said uneasily.

"Good lord! What—"

"Later, Uncle," Jack said, casting a significant glance at the butler.

"Of course," his uncle murmured, nodding his head in understanding. "Have you seen the conservatory?" he asked, raising his voice slightly. "No? Well, you must ask to see it, my boy. It is full of wonders, I assure you. In fact, I cannot tell you when I have encountered such a delightful, rare specimen as I was privileged to behold this morning."

"Indeed?" Jack said, smiling as he took his hat and walking stick from the butler. "You must tell me all, Uncle."

Chapter 10

When Mary turned away from the drawing room doors as they closed behind Jack and his uncle, it was to find Olivia in an uncharacteristically unladylike pose—on her hands and knees, bottom thrust in the air, as she reached for something underneath the sofa. Mary was unable to suppress a gurgle of laughter at the sight.

"Olivia!" she said. "What—"

"Now, how on earth did this get under here?" Olivia asked as she retrieved her workbag, leaning back on her heels and holding it up in front of her. She quickly rummaged through the bag. "But where is my other hoop?" she asked in a distracted voice as she looked around the room.

"I believe it rolled over here somewhere," Mary said as she walked toward the fireplace. "Ah, yes. Here it is," she said, bending to retrieve the missing embroidery hoop from behind the pole-screen. She handed the hoop to her companion, who had risen from her kneeling position and was now brushing off her skirts.

Olivia seated herself once again on the sofa and began to rearrange the disordered contents of her bag, and then carefully smoothed on her lap the half-worked painted silk picture that she had been stitching for several weeks. It was a representation of Summer from a set of the Four Seasons copied on silk from paintings by Sir Francis Wheatley. Mary had given the kit to Olivia as a present, having often admired the quality of her companion's needlework. Her fine stitches were set off beautifully by the delicately painted faces and hands of the figures.

Mary watched dispassionately as her friend gently smoothed the silk and examined her work. She found an odd source of tranquillity in the mundane activity, which allowed her to begin the slow process of subduing the still overwhelming emotions resulting from Jack's visit. She affected an attitude of studied calm as she strolled toward one of the windows and gazed out at the street below. She caught a glimpse of Jack and his uncle, perched side by side in Jack's glossy black curricle as it rounded the corner into South Audley Street. They appeared to be laughing.

"Mary?"

"Hm?"

"How did my workbag happen to find its way beneath the sofa?" Olivia asked in a suspicious tone. "I am certain I had stuffed it behind a cushion after Lord Pemerton and Mr. Maitland arrived."

"Oh," Mary said with a casual shrug, "I suppose Jack must have knocked it aside when he laid me down."

"When he what?" Olivia's voice was an astonished shriek.

"Well, I had become somewhat faint, I am ashamed to say. Jack was most solicitous, I assure you."

"Mary!" Olivia was suddenly at her side, an arm placed gently around her shoulder. "What happened, my dear? Are you all right?"

"I am fine," Mary said, although she felt nothing of the kind. Jack's proposal had her brain in such a whirl she thought her head might spin right off her neck and fly around the room. The image that notion conjured up caused Mary to giggle nervously.

"Mary?" Olivia's arm tightened.

The concern in her voice was Mary's undoing. She curled her face into her friend's shoulder. "Oh, Olivia," she said, her voice cracking, "I am so confused. I do not know what to do!"

Olivia's arms came around her and held her tightly. She said nothing, but rocked Mary gently in her arms like a child. And suddenly, Mary felt like a child. She wanted someone older and wiser to tell her what to do, to make her feel better, to encourage her to take a chance on Jack, to tell her everything would be all right. Olivia was the closest thing to a mother she had ever had. Perhaps she could help Mary to sort out her confused feelings. She clung to the older woman as though she were her last hope.

"What happened, Mary?" Olivia asked at last, still holding

Mary in her arms. "What did that wretched man say to upset you so?"

"He asked me to marry him," Mary muttered into Olivia's shoulder. She stifled an involuntary giggle. It was all so absurd— and so wonderful.

Olivia pulled back and looked down at Mary with a stern glint in her eye. After a moment her eyes softened and she placed an arm around Mary's shoulders, moving her gently toward the sofa. Mary seated herself next to her friend and looked at her in question.

"You do not seem surprised," she said. "I wish I could say the same for myself."

"Mr. Maitland hinted to me what the marquess was about," Olivia said. "He was forced to say something when I was bound and determined not to allow you to remain alone with the man for more than a few moments. It was his role, it seems, to ensure you and Lord Pemerton had time for a private conversation."

"Are you not interested in what happened?" Mary asked.

"I would not dream of prying into your private affairs," Olivia said as she reached for her workbag. "But if you wish to talk about it," she continued, looking up at Mary with a fond smile, "I am here to listen."

Mary did indeed wish to talk about it. She was anxious for Olivia's advice. The problem was, where to begin?

"He kissed me," she blurted without thinking.

"Well, then," Olivia said, "it is no wonder you fainted." She pulled her tambour out of her workbag and began to carefully stretch the silk picture between the hoops. "So he has proposed marriage. What did you tell him?"

"I promised him a decision tomorrow." Mary rose from the sofa and began to pace across the room. "What am I going to do, Olivia?"

"What do you want to do?"

"I do not know." It was not an entirely truthful statement. There was really no question about what she *wanted* to do.

"Do you wish to be married?" Olivia's head was bowed over her needlework, her tone inscrutable.

"I have never considered it, as you must know," Mary said.

"You alone know the truth of my circumstances. Well . . . you and Jack. I had to tell him, of course."

"And what was his reaction?"

"He claimed it did not signify."

"Well, then," Olivia said, her head cocked to one side, eyes still on her work, "I must say that Lord Pemerton has more character than I had imagined. And so with that perceived obstacle neatly overcome, how do you *now* feel about the prospect of marriage?"

"It is such a new idea," Mary said, still pacing, "that I have not yet grown accustomed to it." She stopped, looked at Olivia, and grinned. "It is tempting, to be sure."

"I have always prayed that you would find the right gentleman and settle down to marry," Olivia said. "You cannot expect to continue forever with your vagabond existence—moving from Bath to London to Brighton to country house parties season after season. You need a more settled life, my dear—a home and a husband."

Mary stopped pacing and turned to look at her friend. "You believe I should accept him, then?"

Olivia looked up. "I believe you need a husband. It is not for me to say who that husband should be."

"You have never liked Jack."

"I do not dislike Lord Pemerton," said Olivia, returning her attention to her needlework. "It is just that I have not always approved of his behavior. He has such a wild reputation, you know. I have simply been concerned about what associating with him might do to your own reputation. You cannot deny that it is most unusual for an unmarried woman to cultivate a friendship with a rake."

"Yes, I know," Mary said with a smile. She could not completely explain the perverse pleasure she had always found in pursuing acquaintances with some of Society's most notorious gentlemen. Perhaps it was just to prove her father wrong, to prove that she could indeed capture, however innocently, a gentleman's interest. Somehow, though, it was different with Jack.

Mary walked once again toward the window and propped an arm against the wide embrasure. She gazed absently at the street below as a milkmaid, a heavy wooden yoke laden with milk pails balanced on her shoulders, made her way toward a neighbor's service entry with a quick-stepped grace that belied her heavy burden. Farther down the street a drayman carefully maneuvered his cart load of vegetables into the narrow mews alley. How commonplace it all seemed, Mary thought, when for her the morning had been nothing less than extraordinary.

"Mary?" Olivia said, interrupting Mary's momentary reverie. "Are you in love with Lord Pemerton?"

Mary continued to observe the normal late-morning routine played out on the street below as she considered the question. She wasn't entirely certain she believed in love. She had never personally experienced love, to be sure, nor had she much exposure to love between others. Perhaps if her mother had lived, she would have had an example to which she could aspire, for it was certain her father had loved her mother to distraction. Even after her death he had been so obsessed with her memory he had had no affection left for his only child.

She had thought Peter was in love with her. His words and actions certainly had implied as much. But he could not have loved her, for he had not even fought for her. He had not really cared for anything beyond her father's money.

As for her last three years in Society, it was difficult to cite examples of couples in love. To be sure, she had seen many a starry-eyed debutante, agog over her first suitor. But that was not love. There were betrothed couples and married couples who were obviously fond of one another. But because so many marriages were arranged between virtual strangers, and propriety forbade excessive displays of ardor or tenderness, one could never really be certain of any mutual affection. Of course, her friend Emily had married Lord Bradleigh for love, as all the world knew—a year later there was still occasional gossip about the precipitate ending of Lord Bradleigh's first betrothal at his own engagement ball— and so Mary had to admit that loving relationships did exist for some.

But not for her.

"No," she said, finally, "I do not believe I am in love with Jack. I am quite fond of him, though. And he is certainly handsome and charming." Not to mention that the thought of his kisses made her weak in the knees.

"Is he in love with you?" Olivia asked.

Mary recalled with no little embarrassment her similar question to Jack. What on earth had prompted such a bold query? "No," she replied, "he stated quite clearly that he is not. And I am glad he did, for if he had admitted to a grand passion for me, I would not have trusted a word he said. He was, in fact, quite honest with me, I think. He is fond of me and he needs a wife."

"But you have known all along that he was looking for a wife," Olivia said, gazing at Mary with some concern. "You have been trying to find him one, for heaven's sake. Why has he suddenly turned his eye toward you? Oh, my dear," she said, dropping her embroidery and bringing both hands to her cheeks, "I did not mean to suggest that you are not worthy of his interest. It is just that—"

"That I am not the sort of woman one would expect Jack to marry."

"No!" Olivia said in a frustrated tone. "That is *not* what I meant at all. I only wonder why he did not speak sooner, before allowing you to present him to all those other young women."

"I believe," Mary said after some consideration, "that he is more comfortable with me than with any of the other young women I have brought to his attention. Perhaps he just decided he would rather marry a friend than a stranger. And I think he . . . he k-kissed me so . . . well, so he could determine if we would be . . . compatible . . . in that way."

"And were you?" Olivia's brows raised in question.

Mary paused for a moment as she recalled the fire Jack's kisses had ignited. Her experience at seventeen had certainly not prepared her for such passion, nor for her own response. These things certainly were different, she thought wickedly, when the participants were more mature. "We were extremely compatible," she responded at last.

"So. You are fond of him," Olivia said in clipped tones. "He is handsome and witty, and you enjoy his kisses. It sounds to me as if you have made your decision."

"No, I have not. But if I had," she snapped, tossing an accusing look at her friend, "I can see that you would disapprove. Why do you dislike him so?"

"Mary," Olivia said in a softer tone, "I do not—"

"You have always disliked him!" Mary's voice had become almost a shout. "You have scowled and scoffed and chided since the moment you met him. You have never once acknowledged a single positive quality—not his good looks, or charm, or wit, or—"

"Mary!" Olivia dropped her needlework and sat up straight, her eyes round with astonishment. "I never meant—"

"You would think he was some kind of ogre, the way you have behaved toward him. How will you treat him when we—" Mary stopped as her hand flew to her mouth. What was she saying? She was railing at her closest friend, and for what? She suddenly realized she had been pleading Jack's case as though she had already agreed to marry him. But that could not be. She had not yet made up her mind. She had not.

She turned to Olivia and grimaced at her friend's almost frightened look. "Olivia," she said in a contrite voice, "please forgive me. I had no cause to shout at you like that. It is just . . . I am just . . . rather agitated by this morning's events. I am sorry."

Olivia's eyes softened and she smiled. "It sounds to me as though you have decided to accept Lord Pemerton."

"No." She had not decided. There was much to consider. She was not sure she entirely trusted Jack. She had *not* decided.

Olivia's smile broadened. "And yet you defend him so eloquently." She paused and her brow furrowed slightly with concern. "What is it, then, Mary? You seem to be arguing with yourself, not with me. What is troubling you, my dear?"

Mary sighed deeply, walked across the room, and plopped down rather ungracefully on the other end of the sofa. "I do not know. I suppose I am just confused by it all," she said. "It is so sudden, after all. I have always enjoyed Jack's lighthearted flirting. But I never expected *this*," she said, spreading her hands, palms up, in front of her. "I am afraid, I suppose, of acting too hastily and making an irrevocable mistake."

"You believe marrying Lord Pemerton might be a mistake, then?" Olivia asked in a bland voice as she returned her attention to her needlework.

Mary looked at her friend, smiled, and shook her head. "You would make a shrewd diplomat, Olivia, the way you fling one's words back in one's face, giving them an altogether different meaning. You have never approved of Jack and are very deftly attempting to get me to decide against him."

Olivia finished her stitch, then looked up and laid a hand over Mary's. "You must not think that, my dear," she said, gently patting Mary's hand. "As I told you, I have always wished for you to have the opportunity for marriage, a home, and family. The happiest days of my life were those spent with my dear Martin. Knowing how fond I am of you, how could you suppose I would wish anything less for you? If you believe Lord Pemerton can offer you that sort of happiness and security, then you certainly have my blessing." She squeezed Mary's hand briefly. "I only want you to be sure."

"But how can I be sure?" Mary asked in a plaintive voice.

"Only you can answer that, my dear," Olivia said, releasing Mary's hand, but adjusting her position so that she was turned toward Mary. "If you have doubts, then you must face them, weigh them, analyze them. If, in the end, you believe you cannot marry Lord Pemerton, then you must have the courage to tell him. On the other hand, if you are able to eliminate your doubts, then you must follow your heart."

Mary reached over and kissed Olivia's cheek. "You are right, my wise friend," she said. "I have some serious thinking to do." She rose from the sofa and shook out her skirts. "Would you be terribly disappointed if we did not attend Lady Sewell's card party tonight after all? I should prefer, I think, a quiet evening at home in order to consider my decision."

"Of course I do not mind," Olivia said. "I think it would be best. Besides, I could use an early night for once!"

"Poor dear. I do keep you busy, do I not?"

Olivia smiled and returned her attention to her needlework.

"I shall just go and pen a note to Lady Sewell, then," Mary said. She left the drawing room and headed down the stairs to the small study on the first floor. She pulled a chair up to the front of a mahogany secretaire. The open flap was already littered with books, letters, and lists, as well as writing paper, two quills, and a silver wax jack. She quickly penned a note of apology to Lady Sewell.

After melting the sealing wax and carefully applying it to the folded paper, she fell back in her chair and heaved a great sigh. She glanced around the room, searching for any other trivial activity that would allow her to put off thinking about her decision for another few moments. But thoughts of Jack kept intruding.

She would probably be a fool to reject his offer. It was certainly the only opportunity she would ever have for a husband and family—something she had never before allowed herself to consider, so remote were the chances of it ever happening. Any other woman in her situation would jump at such a rare opportunity. She wanted to jump at this opportunity. So why, then, did she hesitate?

She could not have admitted it to Olivia, but her real concern, her most fundamental fear, was that she would lose her heart to Jack and that he would never be able to return her affection. If she screwed up her courage and decided to marry him, she must take care to protect her heart. She had spent most of her life steeling herself against her father's hatred. Over the years she had developed so many layers of armor around her heart that it was surely almost completely safe from harm. A simple tightening of that armor would, she hoped, act as a safeguard against any assault—however unintentional—from Jack.

If she married him, she would accept his offer for what it was and nothing more: a promise of security and companionship and perhaps even physical passion. It would have to be enough.

If she married him, she would accept him for what he was and not expect any miraculous change of character. She would always remember that he was a habitual womanizer and would probably be unfaithful from the start.

If she married him, she would learn to ignore his infidelities and remember that those other women had nothing to do with her. She would never question him about his private activities.

If she married him, she would learn to take what happiness she could and be grateful for it.

It should not be that difficult, after all. If nothing else, twenty-six years under her father's roof had taught her one thing: no expectations meant no disappointments. She would never expect from Jack what he could not give.

If she married him.

Chapter 11

"Jack?" Edward Maitland asked as his nephew was shown into the breakfast room of his town house the next morning. "No, no, Jayston, this cannot be my nephew. Black Jack has never been known to show his face at such an ungodly hour. This must be some impostor. Show the blackguard out."

Jack smiled as he sauntered into the room, passing an amused glance over the brightly colored silk banyan and matching tasseled cap his uncle wore. "It is no less wonderful to see my dissolute uncle up and about so early. And," he said, flicking the gold tassel hanging over his uncle's ear, "in such charming dishabille."

"You like this?" Edward asked, holding his arms out in display. "I had it off a Turkish sultan I met years ago on my travels. Embroidered by one of his more accommodating wives."

"Lovely," said Jack.

"At least I can claim not to be properly dressed at such an hour," said Edward, motioning for Jack to take a chair across the table from him. "What brings you here this early, looking so disgustedly bright and fresh?"

"I was hungry," Jack said, taking a seat. "I have come to be fed."

Edward laughed. "Jayston?" he said to the hovering butler.

The butler nodded and without a word turned to the sideboard. He soon presented Jack with a steaming cup of coffee and a plate piled high with scrambled eggs, bread, and jam. "I will have Cook prepare another beefsteak, my lord," he said as he left the room.

Edward glared at Jack and raised his brows in question. "So?" he asked.

Jack grinned and flung his arms wide. "I feel like a new man, Uncle," he exclaimed. "I can actually begin to see an end to my troubles. I am rejuvenated. Exhilarated. Invincible!"

Edward eyed him warily. "You are certain she will accept your offer, then?"

"Of course she will."

"How can you be so sure?" Edward asked, rising to refill his own cup of coffee. "I thought you had some difficulty yesterday."

"I had just about convinced her when you—with deplorable timing, I must say—returned with Mrs. Bannister. She was ready to surrender, I tell you." He slathered a slice of bread with jam and took a large bite. "I expect her formal acceptance today," he said through a full mouth.

"Well," said Edward, returning to his chair. He stared hard for a long moment at Jack. "I suppose I am to wish you happy, then," he said at last in a flat voice.

Jack held a forkful of eggs halfway to his mouth. "I would appreciate a little more enthusiasm, Uncle. It is a wonderful thing, after all."

"Is it?"

"Indeed it is," Jack said as he replaced the fork on his plate. "I cannot imagine why you are less than sanguine about the thing. You know my situation. I thought you agreed that this was the only solution."

Edward leaned back in his chair and sighed. "Yes, yes, yes," he said, fluttering a hand dismissively. "I understand your dilemma. And I agree that marriage is your best recourse. But . . ."

"I have no idea what your objections are, Uncle," Jack said after another mouthful of egg. "But I promise you my good spirits will not be dashed. I feel like shouting from the rooftops. But please, feel free to rail on about the evils of marriage and my unsuitability to be anyone's husband. Lecture all you want. I shall listen politely, but I assure you, the thing will be done. And today."

"I was not about to prose on against the noble state of matrimony," Edward said in an impatient tone. "I realize it is too late for that. And useless, considering your circumstances. It is simply . . ." He paused, shaking his head.

"Go on," Jack prompted. "It is simply what?"

Edward continued shaking his head. "I am not sure, my boy. But I cannot help wondering if Lady Mary is the right choice."

"Because she is no beauty? Uncle! She is very, very rich. That makes her the *perfect* choice."

"But are *you* the right choice for her?"

"Ha!" Jack gave a crack of laughter as he slammed a palm on the table with a force that sent dishes bouncing and rattling. "Of course I am not good enough for her," he said with a grin. "How could I be? If I have been a dissolute libertine, who taught me to be so? Who took me to my first whore? Who introduced me to every gaming hell in Town? Who taught me to scoff at Society's rules. Who—"

"Enough!" Edward interrupted, holding up a hand and laughing. "I admit to having done all those things and more, and would do so again. Jack, my boy . . . I have always seen you as a reflection of my younger self. You were the only member of our stiff-rumped family who understood and appreciated my particular approach to life. I have always loved you, Jack, probably because we are so much alike. That is why I know you would be wrong for Lady Mary."

Jack sobered instantly. He had not expected such circumspection from Uncle Edward, of all people. "I know that I am not even remotely suited to be a good husband," he said. "I had expected to finish out my life in blissful bachelorhood, following in your footsteps. But that is no longer an option for me. And if—when—Mary accepts me, you can be sure I will not forget what I owe to her. I would not willfully harm her in any way. But tell me, Uncle, why the sudden concern for Mary?"

"I know I have no right to interfere." Edward removed the cap from his head, tossed it on the table, and ran his fingers nervously through his silver hair. "Blame it on Mrs. Bannister," he said with a sheepish grin.

"Mrs. Bannister?" Jack smiled and cocked a brow in question.

"While we were in the conservatory yesterday," Edward said, "she was quite talkative."

"What a shame," Jack said in a sarcastic tone. "I thought you were seducing her."

"I would have liked nothing more, but she never stopped talking long enough to allow me to do so. She was afraid, you see, of leaving Lady Mary alone with you. It seems Mrs. Bannister does not trust you."

Jack snorted.

The door opened and Jayston returned at that moment and placed before Jack a huge, steaming beefsteak swimming in its own juices. Jack eyed it ravenously—the eggs, it seemed, had only whetted his appetite—and lost no time slicing off a large, juicy chunk.

"Anyway," Edward continued when the butler had departed once again, "to keep Mrs. Bannister out of the drawing room for more than a few minutes I had to hint—rather broadly, I confess—about your intentions. She was shocked, to put it mildly. I expected a flurry of outraged objections, but to my surprise she spoke only of Lady Mary and how devoted to her she was, how concerned she was for her happiness. She went on at length, though with very few details, about the suffering that poor lady had endured in her life. She was worried that you might be the cause of additional heartache."

Suffering? What sort of suffering? Jack wondered as he speared another piece of beefsteak. He vaguely recalled Lord Bradleigh's having mentioned something about Mary's painful past, but he couldn't remember precisely what he had said. Anyway, it was unimaginable that anyone as perpetually cheerful and full of life as Mary could have done much suffering. Perhaps they were merely hinting of her failed elopement—a painful experience, to be sure. But, good Lord, that was a dozen years ago.

"I know something of Mary's past," he said. "She knows I don't hold it against her. Besides, if you and Mrs. Bannister are so concerned about my breaking Mary's heart, then you may rest easy. I was very honest with her. She knows I am not offering her my heart, and I do not believe she is offering hers to me. It is to be an amicable arrangement, nothing more. She understands that."

"I hope you are right," said Edward. "Mrs. Bannister made me very uneasy about the whole thing. She was very forceful in her opinion that Lady Mary is more vulnerable than she lets on, that she would never be free of the ghost of her father."

"Her father?"

"Assheton," said Edward. His brow furrowed and his voice turned somber. "I remember him slightly. A very odd fish. There were rumors at one time that he was not quite sane." Edward's gaze drifted off into the distance, eyes narrowing as if he were trying to drag up an elusive memory. "What must life with him have been like for that poor girl?" he said almost to himself. "You know," he continued, returning his attention to Jack, "I cannot recall ever hearing that the man had a daughter. You would have thought if she had been out in Society these ten years or more we would have known of her. Did you have any knowledge of her before these last few weeks?"

"I am said to have been introduced to her at Bradleigh's wedding last year," Jack said. "But I have no recollection of it. I remind you, Uncle, that she is not the sort of woman either of us would have given a second glance, and therefore it is not so unusual that we might have overlooked her all those years."

"You could be right, I suppose," Edward said in a less than convincing tone. "But I wonder . . ."

"Look, Uncle, if Mary has been unfortunately overlooked and lonely all these years, she will be so no longer. She will be my marchioness and therefore in great demand. Besides, it will not be as cold an arrangement as it sounds. I am really quite fond of her, you know. And," he added with a grin, "she is surprisingly passionate."

"Indeed?" said Edward.

"Yes," Edward said, "and that is all you shall have out of me on the subject. I may be a rogue and a scoundrel, but beneath it all I am a gentleman born and bred. Suffice it to say that the idea of marriage to Mary is not a completely unpleasant one," he said as he finished the last of the beefsteak.

Olivia sat at her dressing table and pondered her future as she pinned her chignon into place. She had expected to be with Mary for years to come, but Lord Pemerton's offer changed everything. Although she had always hoped Mary would someday find a nice gentleman to settle down with, she had never actually expected it. In the three years she had been with her, Mary had shown a complete lack of interest in courtship or marriage; and so Olivia had more or less determined, reluctantly, that marriage for her employer was unlikely.

It just went to show how unpredictable life can be.

She had left Mary alone the previous evening to ponder her decision. It was clear to Olivia—though perhaps not to Mary—that Mary had already made up her mind. And so she must consider what to do when Mary no longer needed a paid companion.

Prior to her employment with Mary, she had been companion to an elderly woman, and then chaperone to a young girl in her first Season. It should not be difficult to secure another post, although the idea of beginning a new life in a strange household was not one she relished. Not for the first time that morning, she wished that Martin was still alive. How she would love to have a home of her own once again, and her dear Martin to curl up against at night. Though she adored her present employer, how much more preferable to have a life she could call her own. It was not impossible. Perhaps she would marry again.

Marry again? Where had that notion sprung from? She blushed for the benefit of the room as the image of Edward Maitland came to mind. Her hands flew to her cheeks as she stared at her reflection in the dressing table mirror. What was wrong with her? A respectable middle-aged woman had no business harboring thoughts of such a man. She should be ashamed of herself.

And yet, he had been so charming yesterday. No, it was more than charm. She had been the object of his considerable charm on other occasions. Yesterday, his comfortable presence had reminded her somehow of Martin, open and friendly and compassionate. How odd to liken him to Martin. Two more different men she could not imagine. Nevertheless, for a short time yesterday she had felt a closeness with Mr. Maitland that she would have found unthinkable had she not experienced it.

She had been nervous and awkward in Mr. Maitland's company and had chattered like a magpie at first. When he made it clear that Lord Pemerton intended to make Mary an offer of marriage, she had been stunned. Her first instinct had been to protest, believing the man to be a heartless scoundrel. But it was not her place to object, and besides, it would have been rude to denounce

Lord Pemerton's character in front of his uncle. Instead, nervous and confused, she had rattled on about Mary.

"She is such a sweet woman. She deserves so much happiness."

Edward had laughed. "Your knotted brow tells me you are worried she may not find that happiness with my nephew."

Olivia had felt herself blush. "I only want Mary to be happy," she said.

"I have met Lady Mary only these few times," he said, "but I liked her at once. I can understand your fondness for her. She has such a vivacity about her—one cannot help but to be drawn to her. And as for Jack, you mustn't be deceived about his character, dear lady," he said, laying a hand momentarily on her arm. "He may be a rascal in public—which, correct me if I am wrong, seems to intrigue Lady Mary—but in fact, he is a good boy at heart. He has certainly been a dutiful and loving son to my sister."

"You are correct about Mary's strange affinity for scoundrels," she said, darting a glance at Mr. Maitland, who laughed. "I have never completely understood it. But I am relieved by your assurance of Lord Pemerton's true nature. Mary has not had much experience with men of good character."

Before she knew what she was doing, Olivia had begun to speak altogether too freely about Mary's past. Mr. Maitland had not apparently made the connection with the late Earl of Assheton and had been amazed to learn that Mary was his daughter.

"I am not surprised to hear that Lady Mary led a somewhat less than happy life in her father's castle," he had said. "I met him only a few times, but it was enough to know that I never cared to meet him again." His nose had wrinkled and a visible shudder had passed through his upper body. "I was thoroughly uncomfortable in his presence," he had continued. "It was his eyes—a slightly vacant look, but with an odd sort of wicked amusement behind it, as if he was secretly laughing at everyone. He had a way of looking at you—a piercing, steady glare down his long nose—that made you squirm to get away."

Olivia had been fascinated to add Mr. Maitland's impressions of the late Earl of Assheton to the information she already had from Mary. She began to put together a more complete picture of the man whose probable madness had made life miserable for his only daughter. It had touched her somehow that Mr. Maitland seemed to understand.

Olivia reached for her best lace-trimmed morning cap and forced thoughts of Mr. Maitland from her mind. She tucked her chignon snugly under the cap's full crown and tied its ribbon beneath her right ear as she turned her thoughts once again to her most immediate concern. She really must begin to make plans to find another post; although she supposed there was still a remote possibility that Mary would reject Lord Pemerton's offer. Olivia sincerely hoped that she would—and not because she would lose her position. She honestly believed Lord Pemerton would ultimately cause Mary a great deal of unhappiness.

Mary was not being quite honest with herself, Olivia thought as she gave one last fluff to the lace framing her face and rose from the dressing table. She had observed Mary's many acquaintances and even friendships with rakes, rogues, and libertines. Olivia had always disapproved on principle, but had seldom actually had cause for concern. It was somehow different this time. Mary's friendship with Lord Pemerton had stirred her apprehension from the start. Olivia had even attempted to encourage the marquess's interest in Miss Carstairs and others, in hopes of putting an end to his association with her employer.

Mary was never more vibrant than when in his company. She never spoke of any other gentleman with such admiration. Olivia believed Mary was in love with Lord Pemerton, though she probably would never admit it, even to herself. More to the point, she was convinced the marquess would probably never have more than the most casual affection for Mary. Such a situation was bound to end in heartbreak for poor Mary. The pain of her father's physical abuse would be nothing compared to the emotional pain she would endure with such a man—a man who could probably not be faithful if his life depended on it. Did Mary honestly believe she could accept his womanizing? Did she really believe she could ignore the possibility of sharing him with countless other women? Olivia certainly could not have accepted it.

She wondered if Martin had had mistresses. He was away at

sea so much of the time, she supposed it was possible. But it was not an idea she cared to explore.

The point was, though, that the marquess—most likely in all innocence—was playing to Mary's deep-rooted feelings of insecurity and inferiority, which she took such pains to disguise. Mary had made great progress in her three years of independence, but it was too short a time in which to completely rebuild the confidence that had been stripped away by her father. She was still very fragile. She needed a patient, compassionate man whose love would lead to a final healing. She would need a strong pair of arms to hold her when the inevitable nightmares came. They were less frequent of late, but nevertheless a concern.

Olivia knew she spoke out of turn, but she had done her best yesterday to hint at Mary's vulnerabilities when speaking with Mr. Maitland. Since she knew it was not her place to speak to the marquess directly, she hoped that his uncle would repeat to him some of what she had said.

Of course, she thought as she gave her collar and sleeves one last adjustment before heading downstairs, she might be worrying over nothing. Mary might not accept him after all.

Olivia made her way down to the breakfast room and opened the door. Mary was there before her and looked up with a brilliant smile that lit up her face like a candle.

"Is it not a glorious morning?" she said, her eyes flashing.

Olivia nodded and forced a smile, knowing in that instant that Mary had made her decision.

Chapter 12

Jack felt extraordinarily pleased with himself and with the world at large as he twirled his newly affianced bride around the dance floor at the Duchess of Portland's ball. *What a clever fellow I am*, he thought, *to have effected such a coup.*

He had known, of course, that Mary would not refuse him. How could she? Nevertheless, he had been surprisingly nervous when, in response to her note, he had arrived at Upper Brook Street last Thursday. When he had been greeted by a smiling Mary, who announced her intention of accepting his proposal, he had grasped her by the waist and swung her through the air. She had laughed with him—that rich, throaty laugher he had always thought delightful, but which he now found to be unexpectedly provocative—and he had kissed her again with genuine pleasure.

"When, Mary?" he asked when they had both come back to earth. "When will you make me happy? Very soon, I hope?" He had crooned into her ear in his most persuasive tone, hoping she would agree to a quick marriage. He was anxious to get on with it.

"It was a monumental enough decision to accept your proposal, Jack," she had said. "Let me get used to the idea. Please, don't rush me."

Slightly disappointed, he had agreed to wait until the late summer when he would take her to Pemworth for the wedding. She had, though, given him permission to announce their betrothal immediately. That alone would be enough to hold the creditors at bay until his marriage.

Ah, sweet Mary, he thought as he looked down into her big hazel eyes. She was going to provide him the means to dig himself at last out of the quagmire of debts he had inherited. He was sincerely grateful to her and would attempt—he really would attempt—to be an accommodating husband. He was fond of her, after all, regardless of the fact that she in no way represented the sort of woman he preferred. At least, he thought as pulled the diminutive bundle in his arms closer, she was not completely unattractive to him. And he was relieved that she was not the naive virgin he had expected. He would not, after all, have to worry about an awkward, apprehensive wedding night. In fact, he found that he quite looked forward to bedding Mary, whose responsiveness so far had pleasantly surprised him.

Jack glanced around the ballroom, noting many smiles and nods of approval as he spun Mary around to the strains of an unfamiliar waltz. He had not been wrong in predicting an engagement to her would go far toward re-establishing for himself—or rather, establishing, since it had never actually existed—a measure of respectability. After the initial astonished reaction to his announcement in the *Gazette*, he had heard nothing but warm and sincere congratulations. It seemed that by choosing a woman liked and respected by everyone from the most stiff-necked dowager to the most notorious rake, he had done immense credit to himself. He met with continued congratulations and praise at every turn.

"Well done, Jack."

"A wise choice, my lord."

"She will make you the perfect hostess."

"Never would have guessed you had so much sense, Jack."

"Lady Mary is a great favorite of ours, my lord. We are so pleased to see her settled."

"How astute of you, my boy, to recognize the lady's superior nature."

"A sensible woman, my lord. She will make a fine marchioness."

He chuckled to himself, marveling once again at the extraordinary cleverness he had shown by betrothing himself to a woman who could solve his financial woes, warm his bed, and repair his reputation all at once. It was almost too perfect. He grinned with uncontrollable self-satisfaction and gave Mary's waist a gentle squeeze.

But most satisfying of all, the thing so wonderful that all other considerations paled in comparison, was the information he had had from Mary's man of business. Mr. Fleming had journeyed from Bath especially to meet with Jack and discuss settlements. Mary had chosen not to attend their meeting yesterday afternoon, claiming complete confidence in Fleming and, Jack was intrigued to note, an apparent lack of interest in the whole business.

He had approached the meeting with some trepidation, anticipating endless awkward questions on his own financial status. He had come prepared to utilize his best Superior Marquess tone to deflect the worst of the probing. But such had not been necessary, as Fleming had been thoroughly professional, not even raising a brow when presented with Jack's circumstances. In fact, it had been Jack and not Fleming who had almost lost his composure, for what he learned from Fleming was so stunning, so incredible that he had been almost knocked off his pins.

Mary's fortune amounted to something close to a quarter million pounds!

Jack had done his best not to look flabbergasted, to maintain a casual calm in discussing such a sum. Once able to think clearly, he began to appreciate Fleming's conscientious management of Mary's affairs. It was due to Fleming's insistence, and not any particular request from Mary, that trust funds were established to protect the fortune for any children they might have, as well as arrangements for the bulk of the estate to revert to Mary in the case of divorce, annulment, or childless widowhood. This provision did not overly concern Jack as he would certainly never willingly consent to end the marriage, and intended to set about producing an heir as soon as possible. All in all, his future was settled and he was well pleased.

What a sly little thing she is, he thought as he looked down at Mary once again. Who would have guessed she sat on such a fortune? He believed most of the *ton* would be as astonished as he was to discover she was worth a quarter million pounds. It followed, therefore, that no one would think him a fortune hunter.

How perfectly everything had fallen into place. He could not have planned things better if he had tried.

The waltz ended, and Jack tucked Mary's hand into the crook of his arm as he led her into supper. Although his cheeks ached from constant smiling, he was so proud of himself he could not seem to stop grinning like a fool. Mary looked up and returned such a brilliant smile that he knew she must be as happy as he was. He suffered a momentary pang of guilt that she was happy for very different reasons. Good Lord, he hoped she was not in love with him. No, Mary was too sensible for such foolishness. She was no doubt happy to be marrying at all, to have her future settled at last, to have a man to look after her, to stoke her long dormant passions. She was getting precisely what she needed, he thought as they entered the crowded supper room; and so was he. It was ridiculous to harbor needless guilt over such an excellent arrangement.

"Everything seems to be happening so fast," Mary said to her friend Lady Bradleigh. They sat side by side in Mary's carriage as it made its way down the Strand back toward Mayfair. The two ladies had spent the morning selecting fabrics at Layton & Shears on Henrietta Street, and were now on their way to Mrs. Gill's on Cork Street to have them made up into new dresses—Mary for her wedding clothes and the countess to accommodate her rapidly expanding waistline. "I feel as though I am moving along at a normal pace," Mary continued, "while the rest of the world speeds past—I have no time to react or consider or focus my concentration for even a moment." She reached over to squeeze her friend's hand. "I am sorry, Emily. I must sound terribly foolish."

"Nonsense," Emily replied with a smile. "I understand completely. I remember feeling as though I was being swept along by a swift tide once Robert and I announced our betrothal. I had wanted to wait, to allow the gossip to die down. But Robert was very . . . impatient." She smiled shyly at Mary, who grinned as she noted the faint blush that colored her friend's cheeks.

"I suppose we are alike in that respect, at least," Mary said. "Neither of us ever expected to marry and . . . well, here we are, both tied to very handsome, eminently eligible, titled gentlemen.

Who would have dreamed two years ago that such a thing was possible?"

"Certainly not I," Emily said. "For myself, at least. I always had a niggling suspicion that some gentleman would win your heart, though, Mary. From the first, you always seemed to be surrounded by gentlemen. I used to marvel at how comfortable you were with them."

"Yes, I have always found it easy to make friends with gentlemen," Mary said. "It was more difficult with ladies. You and Olivia are my only close female friends, you know."

It was odd, but until she had spoken the words just now, Mary had never realized how few women she called friends. Olivia, through proximity alone, was an obvious confidante. More than that, they shared a bond from the early days of Mary's independence, through which Olivia had helped her adjust, and for which Mary would be forever grateful. She had been friends with Emily since they had first been introduced in Bath just over two years ago. Emily's golden beauty had impressed Mary almost as much as her total indifference to it. But most of all, Mary had recognized in her a kindred spirit—an intelligent, educated woman who was, for all intents and purposes, alone in the world. Since Emily's marriage to Lord Bradleigh, Mary had missed that shared, though unspoken, understanding. Now, with her own impending marriage to Lord Bradleigh's friend, a renewed level of camaraderie had sprung up quite naturally between the two women.

"I suspect many ladies were jealous of your unaffected and easy manner with the gentlemen," Emily said, drawing Mary's attention back to their conversation.

"Perhaps," Mary said, gazing out the carriage window as they turned from the Hay Market into the heavy traffic of Piccadilly. "They certainly behave differently toward me now. It is almost disconcerting the way people even look at me since our engagement was announced. You would think I was suddenly a different person, though of course I am as plain and insignificant as I ever was."

"Never plain, Mary," Emily said in a gentle voice. "And hardly insignificant. You are to be a marchioness, after all."

"It is silly, is it not," Mary said, "how a title, or even the anticipation of a title, can make all the difference to Society? All this toad-eating will take some getting used to, I assure you."

"I know what you mean," Emily said, her green eyes flashing with amusement. "It took me quite some time to become accustomed to being 'my lady'. At first, whenever someone addressed me as Lady Bradleigh I kept looking over my shoulder expecting to find Robert's grandmother." Emily laughed at the remembrance, and Mary's laughter soon joined in.

The carriage had by now made its way to Old Bond Street where it stopped and a footman handed the ladies down. Arm in arm, they ignored the jostling of strutting beaux and preening dandies as they walked the short distance to the narrow Vigo Lane and then onto Cork Street, where they arrived at the small but elegant salon of Mrs. Gill, lately experiencing a new popularity due to numerous plates in *Ackermann's Repository*. As the proprietress and her assistants fell all over themselves to serve a countess and future marchioness, Mary caught Emily's eye and had to stifle a giggle at this further example of the obsequiousness to which she was more frequently subjected of late.

After almost two hours of reviewing fashion plates, selecting designs, and being measured, poked, and pinned, the two friends returned to the awaiting carriage on Bond Street and journeyed the short distance to Grosvenor Square to partake of a restorative tea at Bradleigh House.

The countess's condition caused her to tire easily, and so Mary planned to enjoy a quick cup and perhaps a biscuit, and then to be on her way. But Emily refused to let her depart so quickly. She, too, had few close friends and appeared to relish the idea of a long and comfortable coze with Mary. She shamelessly probed her friend on the subject of her betrothal.

"I have always been fond of Jack," Emily said as she eyed the tea tray with a look of longing, as though she fought the desire for another biscuit. She wrenched her eyes away and turned her body toward Mary on the other end of the sofa. "He has a shocking reputation, I know," she continued. "But then, so did Robert, so I do not give such talk any consideration. I suspect that, like Robert, Jack is quite ready to settle down and give up his rackety ways.

He appears to be most solicitous of you. I find you on his arm at almost every affair we attend."

"Yes," Mary said, "he has been all that is considerate and attentive. In fact, I have found it surprisingly pleasant to have a constant escort rather than merely a companion. Oh, I still bring Olivia along, for propriety's sake. But everyone knows that I am with Jack, which, I am ashamed to admit, gives me no little satisfaction. Of course, Mr. Maitland, Jack's uncle, is also a constant presence of late. He and Jack are quite close, you know." She smiled conspiratorially at her friend. "But I have begun to suspect the man is more interested in Olivia's company than Jack's."

Emily's eyes widened in surprise. She reached for a biscuit as she raised her brows in question.

Mary laughed. She had known her friend would ultimately surrender, as she always did, to Mrs. Dawson's excellent biscuits. "I must say, it gives me wicked pleasure to imagine my prim and proper Olivia falling victim to such a rakehell. Of course," she said as she reached for a biscuit herself, "the *ton* must feel the same about Jack and me. I know we make a rather unconventional couple."

"I think you make a wonderful couple," Emily said. "I cannot tell you how pleased I am that Jack chose you for his bride. But then, how could he help falling in love with you."

Mary almost choked on her biscuit. Is that what people believed? That Jack was in love with her? Surely not.

"Jack is not in love with me, Emily."

"Never say so! Of course he is."

"No, he is not," Mary said. "He admitted as much to me. He said . . . he said he was not capable of loving any woman."

"Oh, dear," Emily said in a troubled voice echoed by her furrowed brow. She reached over and squeezed Mary's hand. "Did he really say that? The poor man," she said when Mary nodded. "It must have something to do with his first engagement."

"His what?"

"Oh, heavens! Have I spoken out of turn? I thought you would have known." When Mary looked puzzled, Emily gave a sigh and continued. "I suppose there is no point in keeping it from you." She eyed Mary warily. "Robert told me about it. It was a long time ago—it must be a dozen or more years ago, in fact. Jack was, according to Robert, a very naive and idealistic young man. A dreamer if you can believe it. Even fancied himself a poet while at Cambridge. He is said to have fallen violently in love with the daughter of a neighbor and soon became engaged to her. I recall that her name was Suzanne. But at the last minute, within days of their wedding, she threw him over for someone else. I don't know the details, only that he was heartbroken."

"Good Lord," Mary said. "I had no idea."

"Robert says he was never quite the same after Suzanne's desertion. He became cynical and reckless and wild. But until now, he has never shown the least interest in any other woman . . . except for . . . well . . . you know. But he is certainly fond of *you,* even if he cannot admit to being in love with you. It is a good start."

A good start. Yes, Mary had believed that herself, being fairly certain he was fond of her. But with her new knowledge of his past, she was also fairly certain he would never be any more than that.

"Mary," Emily said in an anxious tone, "you must give him time. His heart is hardened by that unfortunate episode. But it was a long, long time ago, and I am convinced he will eventually open his heart to you. How could he fail to do so?" She smiled warmly at Mary. "In the meantime, I wonder if it might not be a good idea for you to encourage him to speak of Suzanne? It might bring you closer together and could help him to put the past finally behind him."

"I doubt he will want to speak of it," Mary said, feeling suddenly very uncomfortable. "After all, he has never mentioned it before." She took a long sip of tea and sighed. "But perhaps you are right. Perhaps one day I will broach the subject and see how he reacts."

It was, however, the last thing she intended to do. Dragging up old wounds from Jack's past could potentially lead to questions about her own past, about her father—questions she had no desire to answer. If Jack was fond of her now, what would he think of her if he knew what she had allowed herself to endure in her father's castle all those years? What sort of pathetic coward would he think her if he knew how she had come by the crooked nose he claimed to find so adorable? Or the pale alabaster skin he so often praised?

She did not want Jack to know these things. She did not want anyone to know these things. Though she had a new life now, she would forever be ashamed of her past. She could not bear the thought of Jack's contempt if he were ever to learn what a poor, weak creature she really was.

If he was at least fond of her now, there was no possibility he could ever love her if he knew the truth of her nature. And she must be doubly cautious to guard her own heart as well. If there was to be any hope for a comfortable arrangement between them, they must each put their pasts behind them. Resurrecting old wounds could only lead to renewed pain.

She would not tell him about her father.

And she would never ask him about Suzanne.

Chapter 13

"I have not seen this in an age," Olivia said as she held up a coral-colored Norwich shawl retrieved from the depths of the mahogany clothespress. "You ought to take it along, I think."

Mary reached for her shawl and ran her fingers over its fine texture. "Yes, I shall probably need every wrap I own for those cool Devon evenings." She placed the shawl among the pile of garments and accessories heaped upon a chaise in her dressing room, where she and Olivia were deciding which items of her wardrobe to take to Pemworth Hall. Every so often her maid, Sally, came to remove the pile of clothes for airing or cleaning prior to being carefully packed in trunks for the journey to Devon.

Mary had experienced an uncharacteristic bout of nerves over the trip to Jack's primary estate, where she would meet her future mother-in-law and other members of Jack's family. It was one thing to be accepted among London Society where she was well known; but to face Jack's family, who must surely have been expecting someone quite different for his bride, caused Mary a good deal of consternation.

Jack had been very reassuring when he had sensed her uneasiness. "Mama will adore you, my dear," he had said. "You must forgive her, though, if she seems a bit reserved at first. You must understand that she has been overcome with grief this last year. I am certain, however," he said with a roguish grin, "that a wedding will greatly improve her spirits."

And so she and Olivia were preparing for the trip to Pemworth Hall, where in three weeks' time she and Jack would be married in the family chapel.

"What about these, Mary? Shall you be needing them as well?"

Olivia smiled as she held out a sturdy pair of brown leather half boots that had certainly seen better days. Olivia often teased Mary about this particular pair of boots, telling her that a woman of her wealth could surely afford to replace things when they became worn.

"Oh, by all means," Mary replied, retrieving the faded, scuffed boots from Olivia and clasping them fondly. "They are my most comfortable boots, you know. Jack tells me there are some rugged walks along the shorelines and I am sure they will be just the thing."

"Has he told you much of Pemworth?"

"Oh, indeed," Mary said. "He has spoken at length about what to expect in terms of the house, the grounds, the servants, the tenants—everything. It is obvious he loves the place. He grew up there, you know. Whenever he speaks of Pemworth, it always leads to some tale of his youth or childhood." She chuckled as she recalled some of Jack's more amusing tales. "I have learned much about him these past few weeks."

It was true. Though she had set out to avoid discussions of the past, such stories always seemed to crop up. He loved to speak of his childhood at Pemworth. Occasionally he would ask some general question about her own childhood. She had become adept at short, noncommittal responses, followed by the ruthless steering of the conversation toward other topics. Nevertheless, she had relished Jack's fond reminiscences. She found she had an almost insatiable desire to learn more about her future husband.

Of course, the more she learned the closer she came to falling in love with him.

"I am pleased you are spending so much time together, getting to know one another," Olivia said as she shook out a linen chemisette and added it to the pile. "It will make it easier for you in the early days of your marriage—fewer surprises."

"The only thing I have found surprising thus far," Mary said as she rummaged through a drawer of laces and ribbons, "is how fondly he speaks of his home and family. I am sure you will agree there has always been a cynical edge to Jack's charm. But I believe I have uncovered his soft spot. He has spoken warmly, and at length, about his happy childhood with loving parents and lively siblings." Mary looked up, winding a length of pink ribbon around her fingers. "I wonder," she mused, "what it must have been like—growing up with a family who loved and cared for each other."

Her gaze accidentally encountered Olivia's concerned frown, and she quickly turned back to the ribbons. She was sorry she had spoken that thought aloud, but it was one that crossed her mind often lately. She was truly fascinated by Jack's stories of home and family. He might as well have told her he had been raised by a band of gypsies—it could not have been more foreign to her. She certainly had no personal experience of the sort of unconditional love implied in Jack's stories of his parents and brothers. She had always believed her mother would have loved her, had she lived. Her portrait at Assheton Castle had suggested a sweetness of character and gentle nature. Mary herself had loved the mother she had never known—or, more precisely, the idea of her mother—but had never truly experienced the sort of love she imagined Jack had received as a child. She had not even felt such love with Peter, the brash young suitor to whom she had given her heart and body. He had not offered her love, merely an opportunity to escape her father—which was a good enough reason at the time to feel love for him.

"Mary?" Olivia's stern voice broke into Mary's reverie. "I trust you are not giving into envy that the marquess is more fortunate in his family than you have been."

"If I were to do that," Mary said with a chuckle, "I would no doubt be consumed with envy for every person I meet. No, no, my dear. I am not repining my own difficulties, only trying to imagine how different life must have been growing up as part of a family such as Jack's. Besides," she said, her voice sobering, "my own misfortunes can be nothing compared to his. After all, he lost most of that loving family—very tragically."

"Poor man," Olivia said. "Has he spoken much of the accident?"

"Not directly," Mary replied. "I have, though, often noted a flicker of sadness in his eyes when he speaks of his father or brothers. But then he speaks cheerfully of building a family of our own to romp the shores of South Devon. At such times I am almost overwhelmed with longing to bring him that happiness."

When Jack spoke of Devon or his childhood, Mary was reminded of Emily's description of the dreamy, idealistic, happy young man Jack had once been. She could almost believe it when he embarked on a remarkably poetic description of the beauties of Devon. More and more she was convinced he had turned his back completely on that naive young romantic—driven, she supposed, by the rejection of his fiancée—and had deliberately embarked upon a life of reckless libertinism that had since become second nature to him. She found herself longing to bring him back to a more peaceful contentment, to resurrect that happy dreamer. She felt sure that, given time, she could make him love her.

"Is that what you want, to make him love you?" Olivia asked.

Mary was mortified to realize she had spoken her thoughts aloud. "No," she said quickly, "I did not mean it. That is not what I want or expect. I will take whatever Jack has to give, and I will do my best to make him happy."

Silently, though, she thought with some surprise that she indeed wanted him to love her.

Just once in her life she wanted to understand what it meant to be loved.

After two days on the road they had at last reached the grounds of Pemworth. Jack rode his stallion alongside the carriage that held Mary and Mrs. Bannister as they wound their way through the lush green park. He realized suddenly how anxious he was for Mary to see his principal home, how important it was for her to love it as much as he did. He may have had less than admirable motives for wanting to marry her, but he intended to do his best to make her comfortable. It was the least he could do, considering all that she was providing him.

They were soon at the gatehouse, where they were heartily met by Old Crook and his wife, who had kept the gates at Pemworth for most of Jack's life. They were obviously expected, and the Crooks were very anxious to meet his future marchioness. After introductions and congratulations, they resumed their way along the winding avenue of lime trees. Jack cantered alongside the carriage, chattering with Mary through the open carriage window, pointing out the red deer which stocked the park as well as some of the more interesting plantings arranged by Capability Brown in the last century.

Some considerable distance later, the rolling woodland parted to reveal the splendor of Pemworth Hall. Jack was gratified by Mary's gasp of surprise at her first sight of the magnificent Elizabethan structure.

"Oh, Jack!" she exclaimed. "How beautiful!"

Indeed, the old place looked quite lovely from this distance, its pink tufa stone glistening in the sunlight, its triple row of mullioned windows reflecting the shimmer of the ornamental pond, its array of fanciful chimney stacks animating the skyline. The sight never failed to fill his heart with longing. He watched as Mary's face lit up with pleasure as they approached the Hall. He only hoped she would still be as pleased when she noticed the shabbiness and signs of neglect that would become obvious as they drew closer.

Thanks to Mary's fortune, he had no doubt that before too much longer some of that shabbiness would be eliminated. Pemworth would be restored to its original glory.

Bless you, Mary.

When they came to a stop at the center of the curved driveway, Jack dismounted and assisted the ladies out of the carriage. They were met at once by Grimes, the elderly butler, and Mrs. Taggert, the housekeeper. There was obviously an air of suppressed excitement among the staff over the impending nuptials. As Mrs. Taggert led them into the Great Hall, Grimes supervised a pitifully small number of footmen and grooms—the staff had been greatly reduced over the past year—as they unloaded the carriages.

The Great Hall was one of the few rooms at Pemworth that remained intact in its original Elizabethan grandeur. The massive hammer-beamed ceiling soared two floors above them, and huge tapestries lined the walls above the carved oak paneling. The tapestries were faded, the paneling dull and cracked, and the black-and-white marble floor showed cracks and chips. It was nevertheless a grand room, and Mary squeezed his arm and began to express her appreciation of its beauty when the double oak doors at the opposite end of the hall were flung open with a crash. Two small girls and several dogs of various breeds came barreling into the Hall, followed closely by three women.

"Uncle Jack! Uncle Jack!" exclaimed the smallest of the girls as she dashed forward holding her skirts up above her chubby knees.

Jack quickly relinquished Mary's arm and knelt down to scoop up his youngest niece. "Hullo, Lizzy," he said, giving the child a kiss on her upraised cheek.

"I have a new pet frog," she said. "Would you like to see it?"

"Perhaps later, Lizzy," he said, grinning at Mary. "First, allow me to introduce you. Lady Mary Haviland, Mrs. Bannister, this is my niece, Lady Elizabeth Raeburn."

More introductions followed in the confused and clamorous atmosphere of children, dogs, and servants. Jack gave his mother a long embrace and was pleased to watch her expression of surprise and approval as she was introduced to Mary. Alicia, James's widow, was as haughty and cold as ever, offering two limp fingers to Mary and a nod to Mrs. Bannister. Sophie, her ten-year-old daughter, was, he was sorry to note, looking as wan and solemn as when he had last seen her. The poor little thing had never quite made sense of the loss of her father and brother. Charlotte, Frederick's widow and four-year-old Lizzy's mother, was more effusive in her welcome to Mary, but then he had always liked Charlotte.

"We shall let you get settled, my dears," his mother said, "and hope you will join us all for tea in the yellow drawing room."

His nieces had been ushered out along with the dogs by their governess and nanny, and his sisters-in-law headed toward the drawing room. His mother took Mary's arm as she led her up the carved oak staircase toward the living quarters on the second floor. The two women chattered together easily while Jack trailed behind.

"I trust your journey was reasonably comfortable, my dear," his mother said. "The roads here in Devon can be rather beastly at times."

Mary laughed. "I have a very solicitous coachman, my lady. Even so, I believe your son must have given strict orders not to jostle us unnecessarily, as we fairly crawled over certain patches of rutted lane."

"As well he should," his mother said, tossing a glance over her shoulder and smiling at him. "He was acting on my instructions, after all, to convey you to your new home in a leisurely, comfortable fashion."

"I am at your service, *mesdames*," Jack said as they navigated the long corridor of the west wing.

"I am glad to hear you say so, my dear," his mother said. "I shall expect you to acquaint Mary with all the grounds and tenant farms and such, while I introduce her to the special requirements of running this old place. I am so pleased you were able to come a few weeks early, my dear," she said, patting Mary's arm. "It will give us time to get to know one another."

"I am looking forward to it, my lady," Mary said, flashing one of her brilliant smiles. "Though Jack has spoken so much of Pemworth and his family that I feel I already know you all."

"Then we must concentrate on those things he would *not* tell you," his mother whispered, leaning her head close to Mary, who laughed.

Jack was pleased to note Mary's apparent ease with his mother. He knew she had been a bit nervous about this meeting, but Jack had been certain it would go well. He had never known Mary to be awkward or shy in anyone's presence. He was especially relieved, however, at how well his mother had taken to Mary, though he had never really worried about that, either. Everyone liked Mary.

He was also pleased to see that Mary was given one of the more beautiful suites, with a view over the back gardens to the sea beyond. The two women shooed him away to his own suite, but he returned sometime later to escort Mary and Mrs. Bannister to the yellow drawing room.

"Oh, Jack," Mary said as he led her through the house, "Pemworth is absolutely beautiful. No wonder you love it so."

He found himself extraordinarily gratified by her praise and pleased to think that she would probably become as fond of the place as he was. When they reached the yellow drawing room— an astute choice on his mother's part, as it was the one room in the old house that showed few signs of shabbiness or wear—he saw that they were to be joined by the vicar and his wife. It was a lively and talkative group for tea—everyone obviously anxious to know all about Mary.

His future bride handled herself very well. Even the dour vicar was apparently charmed by her cheerful vivacity, he thought as he watched the man smile flirtatiously at Mary. But then, how could anyone fail to smile in her presence? She brought a little sunshine into every room she entered. As he watched Mary's face light up with a broad smile, he marveled that he had ever thought her plain. She was positively glowing at the moment in her bright aquamarine dress. His eyes were drawn to her mouth, stretched across her face in her usual smile. He had once thought that mouth too wide and the lips too full. Now, suddenly, all he could think of was how velvety soft those lips had felt beneath his. He chuckled to himself as he realized with some surprise that he actually found his future bride attractive after all.

Jack watched as Mary chatted with his mother, her big eyes dancing with some amusement, her distinctive laugh filling the air. He was astonished to see his mother pat Mary's hand and laugh with her. The poor thing had been so sad and frail since her bereavement, he had often feared for her health. But as he watched, she showed the first signs of joy he had seen in over a year. He was moved more than he could say by that smile on his mother's face.

Bless you, Mary.

After a short time his two nieces were allowed to join the adults. Both girls dove hungrily into the platter of strawberry tarts topped with the distinctive yellow clotted cream for which Devon was famous. Lizzy launched herself onto her mother's lap, but the solemn-faced Sophie planted herself on the needlepoint settee next to Jack.

"I am happy to see you again, Uncle Jack," she said around a mouthful of tart.

"And I you, Sophie," Jack said as he tousled her dark curls.

"You are to be married?" she asked. "To that lady over there?"

"Yes, Sophie. Lady Mary will soon be your aunt."

"That's nice," Sophie said. "I like her. She has a nice face."

"She does, doesn't she?" Jack said with a grin as he glanced again in Mary's direction. "I am glad you like her."

"Mama says I will never find a good husband now that I will not be the daughter of a marquess," Sophie said. Her high, clear voice had echoed through the room just at a moment when conversation had lulled. Jack cringed at the sudden quiet and turned a fulminating gaze on his sister-in-law.

"She says it's not as good to have a marquess for an uncle," Sophie continued, oblivious to the strained silence in the room as she reached for another tart. "Mama says there won't be any dollerie—whatever that is—for me and Lizzy, and so we will never find husbands. But that's all right," she said as she licked at the clotted cream. "I don't want a husband, anyway."

Jack reached out a hand and brushed a crumb from Sophie's cheek, then tilted her chin up to look at him. "Your mama is wrong, Sophie," he said, slanting a glance at Alicia, who sat looking down at the hands twisting in her lap. "Your old uncle Jack will make certain you and Lizzy have *dowries,* and your Aunt Mary and I will search high and low for the perfect husbands for you. Not just anyone will do, you know, for the *niece* of a marquess."

Sophie seemed satisfied with that explanation and went on to discuss the new ponies on a neighboring estate.

Some time later, after the vicar and his wife had departed and the children had been collected by their governess and nanny, Jack seated himself next to his mother. She smiled warmly at him and squeezed his hand.

"I am so pleased with your fiancée, my dear," she said, glancing over at Mary who was in animated conversation with Charlotte. "She is positively delightful. I must admit, I had expected some fragile, aloof beauty who would have no more than two thoughts to rub together." She smiled and shook her head, then lowered her voice when she continued. "I should have known better, Jack. I should have expected you to show more sense than James did when he chose Alicia." She bit her lower lip, then broke into laughter along with Jack.

Jack was filled with gratitude and relief to hear his mother laugh once again and to see her smiling and happy as she chattered on about the wedding. Everything was going to be all right now.

Bless you, Mary.

Chapter 14

Mary had fallen in love with Pemworth. As she strolled along its shoreline with Jack, she was more happy than she could say that it was to be her home. Over the last week or more she had ridden and walked over most of the estate with Jack, discovering, through his eyes, all the unique beauties of the South Devon coast. She found the setting of Pemworth fascinating in its diversity—its northern approach lush with laurel, beech, and lime, and its southern gardens dropping off suddenly to the sea below. Gentle coves alternated with rugged cliffs and caves along the shoreline, where one could still find remains of prehistoric creatures embedded in the rock. Jack had once led Mary along a narrow hawthorn-lined path to an isolated hill where a stone circle stood mysteriously silhouetted against the sun. She had loved it all and would be happy to spend the rest of her days exploring the area.

Mary had also spent a great deal of time with the marchioness, of whom she had grown extremely fond, learning about the workings of the house as well as its history. She had been particularly pleased to discover a large music room tucked away in a seldom used portion of the east wing. It was obvious that the room and its contents—including pianoforte, harpsichord, clavichord, harp, and other assorted instruments from the previous century—had also seen little use, most pieces either covered in Holland cloths or layers of dust. It seemed the more recent generations of Raeburns had had little interest in music. The marchioness, a dabbler by her own admission, was excited to learn that Mary would be able to bring the joy of music back to the old Hall. Mary was no less excited by the prospect of making use of such fine old instruments, but thought to add a new Broadmore to the collection as well.

During her time spent with the marchioness, Mary also learned a great deal more about Jack through her eyes. He—along with her two granddaughters—was all the poor woman had left, and she doted on him. It was just as clear that he doted on her as well—he was so gentle and solicitous with her, as he was with his two nieces. The entire family had suffered so, and they all looked to Jack for reassurance, for security, for comfort. Mary looked over at Jack as he guided her down a narrow path to a secluded cove, and wondered that he didn't crumble beneath all that responsibility.

Even with so many family and estate matters on his mind, he still found time to be attentive to herself. She had begun to believe that he truly desired her to be happy and comfortable at Pemworth, that perhaps he did have some affection for her after all. It was her fondest hope, for she no longer denied her own feelings. If she had fallen in love with Pemworth, so had she fallen in love with its master—completely, irrevocably, hopelessly in love.

It was only a few hours earlier when this realization had come upon her quite unexpectedly. After a tour with his mother and Mrs. Taggert of the larders, kitchen gardens, and greenhouses, Jack had agreed to meet her near one of the fish ponds secluded among the rear gardens—a favorite spot of his. As she approached through a narrow opening in the yew hedge, she stopped as she saw Jack kneeling at the side of the pond next to young Sophie. They appeared to be involved in an intense conversation, judging from the serious look on the little girl's face, and Mary had been reluctant to intrude. As she watched, Jack smiled broadly and reached for a sketchbook lying next to Sophie. He removed a blank sheet and began to fold it, turn it, fold it again, and yet again, and within minutes he had created a miniature sailboat. Sophie laughed and clapped her hands together, fairly bouncing with glee. It was the first time Mary had seen the little girl so much as smile.

"Your papa taught me to make these," he said to Sophie as he handed her the tiny paper boat. He looked warily at the little girl as she turned the boat over and over, examining its clever construction. "He loved boats, you know. All kinds of boats." His gaze softened as Sophie smiled up at him, and Mary realized what he was doing. He did not want his niece to have a fear of boats as a result of what had happened to her father and brother.

"He and your Uncle Freddie and I used to sneak away from our tutor to go sailing." He grinned at Sophie's look of patent disbelief that her father would have done anything so naughty. "Sometimes, when there wasn't time to hike down to the shore and launch a skiff, or when we were afraid of being caught, we would escape here and have paper boat races on the pond." Sophie's blue eyes widened, and a small hand flew to her mouth as she giggled. "Shall we see how seaworthy this one is?"

Sophie nodded her head, and Jack guided her hand to gently position the tiny boat on the pond. It bobbed precariously for a moment, then righted itself and floated calmly before them. Sophie giggled with delight.

"Shall we give her a skipper?" he asked. When Sophie looked puzzled, Jack plucked a nearby dandelion and tucked it into one of the folds of the boat.

"Captain Dandelion!" Sophie exclaimed, and both niece and uncle laughed boisterously.

When Jack let go, a sudden breeze swept the tiny boat toward the center of the pond. "Oh, famous!" Sophie exclaimed, bouncing on her knees with childish enthusiasm as the paper boat bent with the breeze and skittered across the surface of the pond. She and Jack laughed and cheered it on for a few more moments until the little boat became lodged against a clump of reeds and came to a halt. Sophie was momentarily disappointed, but generally pleased with the whole operation.

Mary, delighted and touched by Jack's thoughtful attention to the wan-faced, solemn little girl, was at that point about to emerge from the yew hedge and make her presence known, when Sophie stopped laughing and turned toward Jack with her more usual grave expression.

"Will you teach me how to make a paper boat?" she asked in a tentative voice.

"Indeed, I will," Jack replied, smiling at his niece before kissing her on the cheek. "Your papa would insist on adding such an important skill to your list of accomplishments. Perhaps we can meet here again tomorrow. Just now I am promised to Mary. We are to take a skiff into the cove—"

"You're going sailing?" Sophie asked, her eyes huge with alarm.

"Yes, we—"

"But you can't!" Sophie wailed.

Suddenly, she was sobbing uncontrollably and Jack pulled her small body onto his lap and wrapped his arms around her. Mary had almost rushed forward then, moved by the little girl's distress, but checked herself. Sophie would probably not appreciate a virtual stranger witnessing her private anguish. She stayed where she was, hidden by the yew hedge, feeling intrusive and helpless.

"What is it, sweetheart?" Jack asked at last in a soothing voice. "What has upset you so?"

Sophie turned her red, tear-stained face up to his. "If you go sailing, you'll die," she said in a tremulous voice.

Jack hugged her close, and Mary caught the suspicious glint of moisture in his eyes. "No, no, sweetheart," he said, rocking Sophie in his arms. "I promise you, I won't die. What happened to your papa and Jason was an accident." He pulled away and tilted Sophie's quivering chin up to look at him. "Do you understand, Sophie? It was an accident."

"No, it wasn't," Sophie said in a petulant voice. "I overheard Old Crook tell Tommy Hopkins that the sea had a hunger for Raeburn men."

Jack visibly flinched, a glint of anger darkening his eyes momentarily, but he said nothing while Sophie continued.

"The sea swallowed up Papa and Grandpapa and Uncle Freddie and Jason because it particularly likes Raeburn men. It will swallow you up, too, Uncle Jack, and then there will be no Raeburn men left at all." She began to sob again and buried her face in Jack's shoulder.

Jack held her head against him and gently stroked her dark curls. "Sweetheart," he said softly, "Old Crook did not mean it literally. It was just a figure of speech. Do you understand what that means?"

When Sophie shook her head without looking up, Jack explained about figures of speech, and also about why Old Crook had made such a remark. He told her about two colorful Raeburn ancestors who had been lost at sea centuries before, but also recounted lively tales of a string of Raeburn men who had lived their lives out to natural ends. A few of the stories had even elicited a tentative smile from Sophie. After a few more minutes, she had quieted and seemed to accept Jack's explanation that last year's tragedy had in fact been a freak accident, and not something preordained by the Fates. After further discussion he had promised Sophie that, just to be on the safe side, he would not take Mary out on the cove just yet. Sophie seemed satisfied with that capitulation. She threw her thin arms around Jack's neck.

"I love you, Uncle Jack," she said, and then pulled away and looked at him again with that serious expression of hers. "And so did Papa. I know, 'cause whenever Mama used to say mean things about you, he got real mad. Sometimes Mama would call you a 'shameless liverteen'—I never knew what that meant, but I knew it was mean 'cause Papa always yelled at her for saying it. He would say, 'Jack's the best of us, Alicia, and don't you forget it.' You *are* the best, Uncle Jack. I love you."

Jack hugged the little girl tightly and whispered something in her ear. *I love you, too, Jack,* Mary thought as she brushed away a tear. There would be no more equivocating with herself. She could no longer deny the truth of her feelings. She loved him. This moment of profound realization had crept upon her quietly, not like the thunderbolt she would have expected. It was akin to the dawning of understanding when one resolved the answer to a riddle or mathematical problem: simple, clear, and right—a truth that had existed all along but had to be discovered. She loved him.

When Jack rose to take his leave, Mary blinked furiously and then walked slowly toward the pond. She offered a bright and affectionate greeting to Sophie, and the little girl shyly smiled in acknowledgment, then stood, picked up her sketchpad and excused herself as she returned to the Hall. Mary smiled and took Jack's arm, and they strolled together in companionable silence over the headlands before descending carefully along the crumbling sandstone to the gentle cove below. Jack seemed pensive after his encounter with Sophie, and Mary left him to his own thoughts while hers were filled with new respect and admiration for this remarkable man she was coming to know and love so well.

Jack took her hand as they walked along the hard sandy beach. "See that small opening in the bluff just over there?" he asked, pointing with his other hand toward the red sandstone cliffside up ahead. "You would never guess, but it actually disguises a very large and impressive cave."

"Really?" Mary squinted, trying to make out the entrance, but saw little more than a dark fold in the cliff. "How fascinating. Did you play there as a child?" she asked.

"No, we were never allowed near it. You see"—he leaned toward her and lowered his voice conspiratorially—"it has always been used by smugglers to temporarily store their contraband."

"Smugglers? Oh, how wonderful!" Mary said with genuine excitement, being intrigued by such a romantical notion. "Tell me more! Were the Raeburns involved? But, of course, they must have been, this being Raeburn property and all. Oh, do tell me, Jack—were your ancestors gentlemen smugglers?"

Jack looked at her and flashed a sheepish grin. "My grandfather, I am told, was very much involved with the free traders. There are additional caverns, you see, running from the cellars at the Hall, and it is said they were often used as a means of escape whenever the prevention men showed up." He helped Mary over a large, jutting rock, and turned to look back at the cave entrance. "And do you recall the little pavilion along the headlands path— with the great lantern suspended from its roof?" Mary nodded. "Well, it is said Grandfather built it for the sole purpose of providing a signal point for the free traders' vessels, to alert them when it was safe to enter the cove."

"That pretty little pavilion?" Mary laughed. "And I thought it a mere garden folly."

"As you were meant to think."

"Is it still used?" Mary asked. "For signaling, I mean?"

Jack did not immediately respond, and Mary began to wonder if she had not intruded on some very private business.

"Not that I know of," Jack said, obviously choosing his words carefully. "I suspect my father may have been involved with the local gentlemen in some way, though I have never known for certain. As a younger son, I was less in his confidence about such things than James might have been."

"And you are going to tell me that *you* were never involved?" Mary asked with amused disbelief.

"Well . . ." Jack hesitated and kicked at the sand. "Freddie and I once—on a dare, you understand—acted as lookouts during one particular shipment." When Mary chuckled with delight, he smiled and continued. "We were very young, you know, and it was only just that once."

Mary threw back her head and laughed. When Jack glared at her with mock outrage, she laughed harder. "To think," she said, still chuckling, "that a notorious rogue such as yourself should be embarrassed by a little smuggling!"

Suddenly, he grabbed her around the waist and pulled her close against his chest.

"You mock me, woman," he said in a seductive whisper. "You must pay the price for such insolence."

He did not move for a long moment, his black hair falling rakishly over one brow, his eyes boring into Mary's with an intensity that had her almost dizzy with anticipation before he finally lowered his lips to hers.

Instantly, a kind of fire ignited between them. Jack did not offer the slow, gentle exploration of lips she had come to expect, but instead plundered her mouth in a wildly sensuous assault that caused Mary's knees almost to buckle. She sensed a hunger in him she had never felt before, and the implications of that hunger sent her heart soaring. She wrapped herself more tightly around him, delirious with love and desire.

Finally, after some minutes, he pulled away, leaving Mary breathless and bereft with longing. He looked down at her, his blue eyes dark with passion, the backs of his fingers stroking her cheek with a tenderness that caused her heart to flutter violently in her chest.

"Do you know how eager I am for our marriage, my love?" he whispered against her lips. "Do you know how happy you have made me?"

He found her lips again, and Mary thought she might have discovered at last what it meant to be loved.

As Olivia strolled through the parterred rear garden, she was convinced she had made a mistake. She had closely observed Lord Pemerton since their arrival at Pemworth Hall, and now felt that she must have misjudged him. She had never understood what perverse reasoning had led him to betroth himself to Mary, but she had not trusted whatever reasoning that might have been. It had never seemed right, somehow, though she could not have explained why. She did not believe he truly cared for Mary, and therefore Olivia had been less than sanguine about their marriage.

But since their arrival in Devon, she had begun to question her earlier misgivings. The marquess lately appeared to have a sincere affection for Mary. When Mary chatted with the marchioness or played with the children, Olivia had often observed Lord Pemerton watching her with a look in his eyes that spoke of more than fondness. Perhaps he was in love with her after all. She certainly hoped so. Mary deserved as much, and more.

Olivia paused at an opening in the tall clipped box hedge that surrounded the garden as she gazed at a new vista through aligned openings in a series of hedge walls that ended at an obelisk some distance away. She wandered through the opening and found herself in a very different, less formal, decidedly overgrown rose garden. Its air of decay was actually very appealing, and Olivia's admiring gaze swept the length of it.

"Do you like roses, Mrs. Bannister?"

The gentle voice nevertheless startled Olivia, who turned to find the marchioness seated on a stone bench in one of the garden's corners, a book open on her lap. Not for the first time, she was struck by the resemblance of Lady Pemerton to Mr. Maitland, mostly around the eyes, though where he was fit and hearty she was thin and frail. She seemed a sweet woman, though, and had shown a generous hospitality. Olivia smiled and joined Lady Pemerton on the bench. "I do love roses," she said, "but I confess to a weakness for gardens of all sorts. I have enjoyed strolling through the Pemerton gardens. You must be very proud of them."

"I am proud of what they *could* be," the marchioness said, her gaze traveling from one end of the garden to the other. "I am afraid they have become rather overrun of late. I do not understand how Hopkins, our head gardener, has allowed such a thing to happen. I shall have to speak to Jack about it. Perhaps Lady Mary would like to undertake a project to improve the gardens once she and Jack are married."

"She would enjoy that, my lady, I am sure."

"You have known Lady Mary long?" the marchioness asked, closing the book on her lap after first marking her place.

"I have been in her employ for three years, my lady."

"Then you know her well. I find myself excessively pleased with Jack's choice for a bride." She cocked a brow and her blue eyes twinkled. "What do *you* think?"

"I believe Lady Mary is very happy with the match," Olivia said cautiously. "She would make any man a wonderful wife."

The marchioness laughed. "You are very circumspect, Mrs. Bannister. I suppose you question whether or not Jack would make any woman a wonderful husband. No, no," she said, smiling and waving a dismissive hand, "you need say nothing more on the matter. I am fully aware of Jack's reputation. But do not forget, I have known him all his life and am aware more than anyone of the true man who lurks beneath that rackety notoriety. I believe Mary is just the sort of woman he needs to bring him back to himself, to take him away from the dissolute sort of life he has led for so long."

Olivia was surprised at the plainspoken manner of Lady Pemerton and hoped she was right about her son, but she said nothing. The marchioness chattered on.

"He suffered so over that wretched business with Suzanne, you know."

Olivia, wondering who Suzanne was, gave a puzzled look.

"Oh, I suppose he does not speak of her, does he?" the marchioness said.

Olivia shook her head, still puzzled, and the marchioness sighed. "They were betrothed years ago, but the silly chit threw him over at the very last minute. He was devastated, you see. But, good heavens," her voice rose with frustration, "that was ages ago, and it is high time he found some happiness for himself."

"I know what you mean," Olivia said without thinking. "I have harbored similar hopes for Mary, after all the pain and suffering she went through."

"Good Lord, Mrs. Bannister," the marchioness said, sitting bolt upright and laying a hand on Olivia's arm, "what are you saying? In what way has Mary been made to suffer?"

Olivia felt an embarrassed blush warm her cheeks. There must be something singular about the Maitland family that encouraged her to such intemperate speech. She had said more than she ought to Mr. Maitland, and was now repeating her folly with his sister. She clamped her lips shut, afraid to utter a word lest she blurt out some further confidence.

"Mrs. Bannister?"

Olivia took a deep breath and considered her words carefully. "I am sorry. It is not my place to speak of my employer's private concerns. I will only say that Mary did not have a particularly happy upbringing. If you wish to know more, you will have to ask Mary."

"I will do that, Mrs. Bannister," the marchioness said. "And you must not fear that I will hint of any indiscretion on your part. You have not told me anything specific, after all."

"Thank you, my lady," Olivia said with a relieved sigh. Before she could embarrass herself any further, she changed the subject. "How are the wedding plans coming?" she asked.

"Splendidly," the marchioness replied. "Mrs. Taggert has things well in hand. It is to be a simple affair, you know. A brief ceremony in the family chapel followed by a wedding breakfast in the state dining room. Both Jack and Mary have requested a small party, and only a few friends and family members have been invited. I had asked Alicia and Charlotte and their girls to spend a few additional weeks here, to help Mary adjust to the family. Other guests should begin arriving as early as tomorrow."

"Is Mr. Edward Maitland expected?" Olivia could have bitten her tongue straight off. She could not imagine what perverse notion had caused her to ask such a question. She squirmed uncomfortably on the bench and cast her eyes down to the hands in her lap.

Lady Pemerton's eyes narrowed briefly as she gave Olivia a significant look. "My brother is expected tomorrow," she said.

Olivia made no sign of acknowledgment, continuing to stare at the hands in her lap as they twisted the muslin of her walking dress. She wished she could think of something innocuous to say, to change the subject again, but in fact she was too embarrassed to open her mouth.

Suddenly, the marchioness smiled brilliantly and patted Olivia's hand. "Good heavens, my dear, this is wonderful! I had given up all hope for poor Edward."

Olivia blushed.

Chapter 15

Mary strolled arm in arm with her future mother-in-law through the Long Gallery, listening, fascinated, to stories of each of the Raeburn ancestors depicted in the collection of portraits from Elizabethan times forward. The marchioness paused before a more recent painting of three dark-haired young boys shown outdoors in a beech grove: the tallest boy leaning negligently against a tree, another seated on an overturned log, and the third on his haunches with his arms around the neck of a large hound. Mary watched the Marchioness chew on her lower lip as she stared at the painting.

"You will be especially interested in this one," she said after a few moments, composing herself and turning toward Mary with a smile. "It was painted by Reynolds about thirty years ago. The impish-looking one with the dog is Jack."

Mary looked more closely and indeed recognized the intense blue eyes of a younger version of Jack. She smiled broadly. "He looks deceptively sweet, though his eyes do reveal a rather mischievous scamp."

"He was that," the marchioness said, "but sweet-natured as well. That's Frederick next to him and James behind."

"They were all handsome boys," Mary said as she studied the painting. "You must have been very proud."

"I was and am," the marchioness said. She gave a ragged sigh. "It is a horrible thing to outlive one's children. But," she said, brightening somewhat, "I still have Jack. And I am counting on more grandchildren, you know."

Mary blushed, but returned an embarrassed smile.

The marchioness squeezed Mary's hand, which was resting on

her arm. "I am so pleased about this marriage," she said. "And I am so very proud of Jack. He has shown remarkable good sense in betrothing himself to you. I believe that you will make him very happy, my dear."

"I hope so," Mary said with conviction. "I will certainly try my best to do so, my lady."

The marchioness smiled radiantly. "It is gratifying to see one's children happily settled and loved." When Mary blushed again, she continued. "You *are* in love with Jack, are you not? Yes, I can see that you are. How clever of you to see beyond the rather reckless, rakehell reputation he has done so much to foster. He is very deserving of your love, my dear. Ha! Listen to me. You will think me a silly, doting mama."

"Nonsense," Mary said. "I am pleased Jack has such a loving family, my lady."

"You must consider us your family as well, my dear. You are to be a Raeburn, after all. You must feel free to call me Mama if it pleases you."

"Thank you," Mary said, her voice catching slightly. "I would be very pleased to do so. My own mother died when I was born, so I have never had the privilege of calling anyone Mama."

The marchioness patted Mary's hand, and they moved on to the next picture.

"Oh, but this one is you!" Mary exclaimed as she stood before an enormous full-length portrait. A beautiful young woman with long, full powdered hair stood in the foreground of an ethereal, indistinct landscape, a rose in one hand while the other lifted her overdress slightly as she appeared to step toward the viewer. Mary recognized the unmistakable brushwork of Thomas Gainsborough. "How lovely," she said as she relinquished Lady Pemerton's arm and stepped back to better appreciate the painting.

"Yes," the marchioness said, "I believe this is the best—that is to say, the most flattering—of all my portraits. My husband insisted it be hung here in the gallery along with all the previous marchionesses. Oh!" she exclaimed suddenly, turning to take both Mary's hands in her own and holding them out before her, "we must commission a bridal portrait of you! You will be required to hang in this gallery along with the rest of us, you know." She chuckled and squeezed Mary's hands. "Have you sat for a portrait recently, my dear?"

"No," Mary said, "I am afraid I have never had my portrait painted."

The marchioness's jaw dropped in astonishment. "Never?"

"Never." Mary smiled at the woman's incredulous look.

"But, your father was an earl. And I gather you were his only child. He never thought to have you painted? Even as a young girl?"

"No, my lady." Mary was becoming decidedly uncomfortable as she always did when the subject of her father came up in conversation. Her instinctive reaction had always been to abruptly change the subject. But she did not wish to appear rude to the marchioness.

"Good heavens, child," the older woman continued, "what *can* he have been thinking?"

"Is it not obvious?" Mary replied softly.

"No, it is not. Forgive me, my dear, but I do not understand."

Mary took a deep breath. "One only has to look at me to understand," she said. "I am not beautiful, or even passably pretty. My plainness was a source of great disappointment for my father. I cannot imagine he would have ever considered committing my likeness to canvas."

"Oh, my dear," the marchioness said, "you cannot mean that. For one thing, you are not the least bit plain. For another, *all* parents find their own offspring attractive. It is a result of loving them so completely, and also, I suppose, in seeing them as a reflection of oneself. It is a vanity of all parents, I am afraid, myself included."

"But, you see," Mary said in a low, husky voice, "my father did not love me. In fact, he hated me in part because I *was* a reflection of himself, for in appearance I resembled him and not my beautiful mother." Mary had never before said such a thing to anyone, and could not for the life of her imagine why she did so now. But there was something in the sympathetic blue eyes of the marchioness along with a general warmth and kindness about her that quite disarmed Mary.

"Never say so, my dear!" the marchioness said, an expression of shock and concern on her face. Still holding Mary's hands, she squeezed them tightly. "Surely he did not hate you."

"Oh, but he did. He told me so often. He could barely stand the sight of me."

"Oh, Mary!" The marchioness looked stricken, one hand flying to her mouth. After a moment, when Mary could not seem to move, the marchioness placed a gentle arm around her shoulder and led her to a large, comfortable sofa near the center of the Long Gallery. She seated herself at Mary's side and clasped her hand. "You did not have a . . . happy life with your father, then?"

Mary gave a disgusted snort. "Hardly," she said in a sarcastic tone that she instantly regretted. She took a deep breath and went on. "My father was not . . . completely sane, you see. My mother's death sent him into an emotional decline from which he never recovered. He blamed me for her death."

"You?"

"It was giving birth to me, after all, that killed her. He never forgave me for that. Or for being ugly. He considered her death a waste when all it produced was me. I have often wondered," she said in a wistful tone, "if he would have loved me if I had at least resembled my mother instead of him."

Mary looked back at the marchioness and saw such pain and shock in the woman's eyes that she felt her own control slipping. "I am sorry," she said in a shaky whisper. "I should not . . ." And suddenly she could no longer speak. No more words would come. Then, without warning, she was overcome by sobs that wracked her entire body. She was vaguely aware that Lady Pemerton's arms came around her and held her tightly. But she could not seem to stop sobbing as a riot of emotions overwhelmed her: sadness, regret, anger, shame.

Mary hated herself for displaying such weakness, most especially in front of her future mother-in-law. She had worked so hard to overcome her particular vulnerabilities, to keep all those old demons at bay, but once her composure had cracked, she found it difficult to rein them back in. And the shame of her outburst only caused her to sob harder. She concentrated on her breathing, taking deep gulps of air between sobs, hoping she could at least regain physical, if not emotional, control of herself.

The marchioness continued to hold her, rocking her gently against her thin breast.

"There, there," she said, as if speaking to a child. "There, there."

Finally, Mary's sobs subsided to quiet tears. She seemed to have no control over the tears, which streamed unchecked down her face. She gently pulled away from the marchioness and dug into her pocket for a handkerchief. She gave a frustrated cry when she found she had none, but the marchioness thrust one in her hand before she could become more agitated. She took it gratefully, dabbed at her eyes, and then blew her nose noisily. She turned toward Lady Pemerton, though she was unable to meet her eye, and attempted to speak. "I am sorry," she said again, and then, continuing, hiccuped several times. "I should not have said such things to you. I have been so . . . so happy these last . . . few weeks. There is no cause to . . . drag up ancient history." She paused, trying to calm her breathing, ashamed of her lack of control.

The marchioness took her hand and held it gently. "Please do not apologize, my dear," she said in a soft, soothing voice. "And you have every right to speak of such things. *We* are to be your family, now. We want to know all about you—the good things and the bad." She paused, and Mary blew her nose again.

"I would like you to tell me what happened, Mary, if you can. Tell me about your father."

"Oh!" The word was stretched out into a mournful cry. "Please, no. I don't think . . . no, no . . . it does not matter. None of it matters anymore."

"It does matter, my dear," the marchioness said. "It is a part of you. It is important because you survived it—you rose above it somehow to become the sweet, delightful young woman you are today. Besides, it helps to talk about one's troubles. They become less burdensome when you share them."

Mary took a deep breath and looked hard at Lady Pemerton. Finally, she gave a ragged sigh and fell back against the sofa. She had already disgraced herself thoroughly. The full truth could do little additional harm at this point. It might even do some good, though she could not imagine how. But if the marchioness was willing to share this shameful burden, then it was certainly worth a try. She took another deep breath. "What do you want to know?" she asked.

"Tell me about your father."

"He was George Haviland, the fifth Earl of Assheton," Mary began in a singsong voice. "Both his father and mother, who died when he was a schoolboy, were Havilands, having been first cousins. He fell madly in love with Lady Honoria Beckwith and made her his countess." She paused and shook her head. When she continued, her tone was more even. "Besides being beautiful—I have seen her portraits, so I know it to be true—she had a sizable fortune left to her by her parents—she was an orphan, too, you see, and so I never had grandparents, either. Papa loved her to distraction. When she died . . . well, I have told you what happened." She paused and gazed through the huge gallery windows looking out onto the rear courtyard.

"You say he hated you," the marchioness said, "that he told you so."

"Yes."

"Did he . . . abuse you?"

"Did he beat me, you mean?" Mary, still gazing out the window, watched as young Lizzy, followed by her nanny and Charlotte, came skipping into view with a black-and-white spaniel at her side. Lizzy threw a ball that the hound chased after energetically while the little girl bounced and clapped her hands. "Yes," Mary said finally. "He beat me with some regularity." She rubbed a finger absently along the length of her nose as she watched Charlotte pick up Lizzy and swing the giggling child through the air.

"Why?"

"Why did he beat me?" She shrugged her shoulders and waved a hand in an indifferent gesture. "Usually, just for looking at him," she said. "He despised my ugliness. He said such an ugly, undersized runt of a child had no right to live while his beautiful wife lay dead in the ground. It was always the same litany, with minor variations."

"And what did you do?" the marchioness asked.

Mary was surprised by the question and turned to look at Lady

Pemerton. "What did I *do*? Well . . . when I was very small," she said, turning back toward the window to watch Lizzy tossing the ball back and forth between her nanny and her mama, "I shouted and screamed and kicked back. I soon learned; though, that such behavior only encouraged him. I discovered early on that it was to my advantage to submit quietly. He would soon become bored and leave me alone."

"How long did this go on?"

"Until I was seventeen," Mary said. "Papa had never allowed me out much, but he did take me to church every Sunday. The vicar had a large family, and some of the girls used to be allowed to play with me. Papa always disapproved, but was apparently reluctant to offend a man of the cloth, and so the vicar's daughters became my only friends." Mary paused, distracted by the simple game of ball taking place on the courtyard lawn.

"What happened when you were seventeen?" the marchioness prompted.

"A nephew of the vicar's wife came to visit," Mary said, wondering momentarily at the prudence of discussing this particular episode with her future mother-in-law. She brushed aside that concern—in for a penny, in for a pound—and continued. "Peter Morrison, his name was. He was three and twenty—a mature man of the world to a naive, sheltered girl of seventeen. He flirted with me shamelessly, although I understood nothing of flirtation. I had been told I was ugly for so long that I was overwhelmed by his flattery and attention. You can imagine how my head was turned."

"What happened?"

"I ran away with him." Despite her shame, Mary found it almost impossible to stop the flow of words, now that she had begun. "He had often teased me, saying we should run away together to some exotic place and be lovers. I took his words quite literally and saw an opportunity to escape my father. I confess to pleading with Peter to elope with me. He demurred at first, claiming he could not yet afford a wife. I assured him that I could expect a sizable inheritance as my father's only child. The castle was entailed, but I knew his fortune would come to me. And so Peter agreed."

As she spoke, it all sounded suddenly so obvious. How could she have ever believed that Peter loved her? His own words confirmed her father's subsequent taunts. "We fled early one dawn," she went on, "planning to go to Gretna Green. We never made it. My father caught up with us in Cheltenham the next day."

"What did he do?" the marchioness asked, when it seemed, after a few moments, that Mary would not continue.

"I have never known what he said to Peter," Mary said. "When he discovered us at an inn, he dragged me into a room and locked me inside. When he returned, almost two hours later, Peter had apparently disappeared, and I was to return to Somerset with my father. But not before he had vented his rage on me in the usual way. You see, Peter and I had . . . had spent one night together. Now, I was not only ugly, but ruined as well. For my father, I was completely useless."

The marchioness squeezed the hand Mary suddenly realized she had been holding the whole time. Mary turned toward her and met a look of such sympathy that she almost lost control again. She bit her lip and looked quickly away. Through the gallery windows she watched the tiny figure of Lizzy disappearing in the distance as she chased after the spaniel.

"What happened when you returned home?" the marchioness asked. "Did things change, or was it as unhappy as ever?"

"Oh, things changed all right," Mary said as her gaze followed the bouncing, running little girl. "I had to be punished for my insolence. Since I had no physical virtues with which to attract a man, only the prospect of Papa's fortune would ever entice a man to be my husband. That, he was to point out to me with vicious amusement almost daily for the rest of his life, was the only way I had managed to interest Peter. It was the only way I could possible interest *any* man. To punish me, he eliminated me entirely from his will."

The marchioness gasped.

"I was to get nothing," Mary continued. "After my father's death, I would be required to live on the sufferance of the distant cousin who would inherit—a man I had never met. But that was not my only punishment." Mary took a deep breath and considered how much to say about the next nine years. But then, there was really very little to say. "I was to be my father's prisoner," she said at last.

"My God!"

"I was never to leave the castle. I was never to go out of doors. I was never to speak to anyone save my maid—my jailer, I used to call her. I was never to see my friends again."

"Oh, Mary," the marchioness said, her voice tremulous and troubled. "How horrible. How . . . how long did—"

"Nine years," Mary said. "I was kept inside the castle for nine years, until he died. I never saw the sun or the moon except through a window. I never felt the wind or the rain on my face, except in my dreams."

"Good Lord. Good Lord, Mary. How did you bear it?"

"I created my own separate world in the castle," Mary said. "I escaped into books—some of my father's predecessors had amassed an extensive library. I read everything. I also escaped into music. He did not deny me that, at least."

"Were there no relatives to turn to?" the marchioness asked, her voice rising in a plaintive, almost querulous tone. "No sympathetic servants? What about the vicar? Was there *no one* to help you?"

Mary sighed and threw her head back against the sofa. "That is the pitiful part, is it not, that I did not fight to get out? I was so tired . . ." She paused, mortified with shame. The worst part of telling this story was not how badly it painted her father, but how badly it reflected on her. She had not fought back. She had submitted. She had allowed. She had accepted.

"But no," she continued, determined to finish what she had begun. "I have no close relatives and the servants were my father's agents. Any who showed signs of softness toward his insolent daughter were let go. I have no idea what was said to the vicar and his family. I have assumed they were told I was dead. I never saw them again."

"Tell me what happened when your father died," the marchioness said. "Did the new earl, in fact, treat you well? You are obviously not impoverished."

Mary laughed mirthlessly. " 'Tis an ironic tale, at the very least. Papa, who was generally in robust health, became ill very suddenly. An inflammation of the lungs caused him to decline rapidly and within days he was near death. The household was in somewhat of a turmoil over his impending demise and failed to watch me as closely as they ought. When Papa's solicitor came to meet with his dying client, I happened to be in the hallway and he asked to speak with me." Mary paused and shook her head, still amazed at what had transpired that day.

"The solicitor," she went on, "Mr. Fleming, was apparently surprised to find me unguarded. But he wanted to reassure me that, regardless of the lack of provisions in my father's will, that my own funds would be more than sufficient to my continued comfort."

"Your own funds?"

Mary chuckled. "That was my question, precisely. Mr. Fleming, disgusted with the whole sorry business, told me what he thought I should have known. It seems my mother—who had quite a bit of money of her own—had set up a trust fund for her unborn child. It had been administered all these years by Mr. Fleming. Papa had known about it at the time, of course, but had apparently forgotten about it—first, through grief and later through his increasing mental instability. Mr. Fleming had taken good care of it, nevertheless. He even hinted that he had deliberately failed to remind Papa of its existence, especially after he cut me out of his will. Anyway, it seems I had something of a fortune."

"Good heavens!"

"Imagine my astonishment," Mary said. "All that time I had had the means to live independently from my father and had not known it." She shook her head and smiled weakly. "But I was determined to waste no time in taking advantage of it. I requested Mr. Fleming's help in removing temporarily to Bath. He was extraordinarily sympathetic. He agreed to send his own carriage for me the next day. Papa died that night." She turned to look at the marchioness. "You will think me heartless, but the next morning I put on my brightest yellow dress, packed a few things, and left in Mr. Fleming's carriage. I left Assheton Castle for good. I have never returned. I did not mourn my father. It seemed . . . hypocritical. I hated him, you see."

The marchioness squeezed her hand again. "I understand, Mary," she said in a soft voice. "And I believe I would have done the same if I had suffered as you had. You have nothing to be ashamed of. All the shame lies at your father's door. He was the heartless one, Mary, not you. To have abused you all those years, to have lied to you about your looks and your prospects—"

"Oh, but that is just it, you see," Mary interrupted. "He never actually lied. He was brutally honest about my shortcomings. It is just that he took such cruel delight in pointing them out."

"No, Mary," the marchioness said in a stern voice, "he was not honest. You are not plain, as I am sure—as I hope—Jack has told you. And have never required a fortune to attract a husband. You are one of the most delightful, most personable young women I have ever met, my dear. That alone would pique any man's interest. Only look at Jack. He is besotted with you, my dear. And that has nothing to do with your fortune."

"It is true," Mary said, feeling suddenly shy and embarrassed. "I do not believe Jack ever knew of my fortune when he asked to marry me. I never speak of it, you see. Such wealth tends to alter people's perceptions of one. So I never mentioned it to Jack, although he surely knows now, having met with Mr. Fleming."

"Well, there you have it then," the marchioness said brightly. "You attracted a very fine, handsome man despite your father's belief that such a thing could not happen. You have proved him wrong, Mary. And if he was wrong on that count, you must necessarily suspect everything else he drilled into your head. Continue to turn your back on that unhappy part of your life, my dear, and look to all the wonders that lie ahead: your wedding, a new home, children, grandchildren . . ."

They both turned at that moment to look across the courtyard to the returning party of Charlotte, Lizzy, spaniel, and nanny. Charlotte was laughing as Lizzy skipped along energetically at her side.

"You see, Mary, there is always some small happiness ahead, regardless of what has gone before. Look at Charlotte," she said, nodding toward the happy domestic scene beyond the gallery windows. "She has lost Frederick, and Lizzy has lost her papa.

And yet they still find happiness with one another. You must look ahead as well, my dear, and put all that unhappiness behind you."

Mary blinked back tears as she turned to look at the marchioness, realizing how much more devastating it was to lose loved ones than never to have had any to begin with. Lady Pemerton was right. She *had* survived. And although she had always thought she had put her past behind her, she had never really let go of it. It colored her perception of the world, of herself, of other people, and their actions and reactions. But now she had a new frame of reference in which to view herself—as a woman soon to have a wonderful husband, a new and loving family, and a beautiful new home. Tears—of joy this time—stung her eyes as she felt the burden of the past slip from her shoulders like a tattered cloak, to be tossed aside and never worn again.

Suddenly, she threw her arms around her future mother-in-law and gave her a fierce hug. "Thank you, my lady . . . Mama. You are very good to listen to my poor history. I shall take your advice. I look forward—with gratitude . . . I cannot express how much gratitude—to a new life with my new family."

Chapter 16

"Pull up, Jack!" Edward Maitland shouted from his position bent low over the neck of his horse. He and Jack, having raced neck-or-nothing through the parklands of Pemworth, reined in their mounts as they neared the creek edge of the northern end of the estate. Panting slightly, Edward patted the horse's neck as he eased him in to a slow trot and waited for Jack. "This old bay ain't up to your stallion," he said when Jack had joined him.

"I wonder," Jack said in a breathless voice, "is it the old bay or the old uncle who has tired?" He laughed at Edward's outraged glare.

"I can outride you any day, boy, and don't you forget it," Edward said, equally breathless. "It is this second-rate horseflesh you have provided." He removed his hat and ran an arm across his damp brow. "Damnation, but it will be good to see a decent stable again at Pemworth. Your father kept only the best, you know."

"I do know," Jack said. "It is one of the things that nearly bankrupted the estate."

The men steered their horses to the bank of the narrow creek, which gradually widened and opened fanlike as it flowed into the cove and the sea beyond. When they reached the creek edge, they dismounted and let the horses cool themselves and drink from the fresh, clear stream. Jack removed his hat and jacket, hung both over the pommel of his saddle, and leaned against the trunk of an elm, grateful for its shade. He would not admit to his uncle, now shedding his own jacket, that he was indeed thoroughly exhausted. It was a pleasant sort of fatigue, though—almost exhilarating.

Edward perched himself on a large boulder and stretched his

legs out in front of him. "So," he said, "are the Pemworth stables among your list of improvements, I hope?"

"They are," Jack said, "but not at the top of the list. There is much to be done. *After* the wedding."

"The joyous occasion is only three days hence," Edward said, slanting a wary glance at his nephew. "Are you suffering any last-minute nerves?"

"None in the least," Jack said and then flashed his uncle a broad smile.

Edward gave Jack an assessing look. "I must admit," he said, "you appear decidedly self-assured and calm about the whole thing. If it were me, I would surely be trembling with trepidation and doubt. But then, I suppose you are pleased to have all this business settled at last."

"That I am." Jack leaned his head back against the tree and closed his eyes, enjoying the mingled scents unique to Pemworth: summer wild flowers and the sea, horse and leather, grass and mud.

"Still," Edward went on, "I sense . . . oh, I don't know . . . something else. It is just that I have never seen you so relaxed and contented. Certainly not in the last year."

Jack chuckled. "You are correct, sir," he said. "I have never felt more—how shall I put it?—satisfied."

"Ah. You have bedded her already, then?"

Jack's eyes snapped open and his head whirled around to face Edward. "Uncle!"

Edward tilted his head and raised his brows, as if to question such apparent outrage. Jack had to laugh, for who would have expected such sensitivity from Black Jack Raeburn? He would have to hang up that old soubriquet and coin a new one—something more suitable to his new attitude.

"No, Uncle," he said, still chuckling, "I regret to say that I have not yet bedded Mary, though I cannot see that it is any of your business."

Edward grinned sheepishly. "Sorry, my boy," he said. "I suppose, then, I must assign this new lazy contentment to some other cause."

"No," Jack said, "you may still lay the blame on Mary—but not in the way your sordid mind has imagined." He paused, considering precisely how it was that Mary had fostered such peace and contentment. "She has brought a new joy to this unhappy place, Uncle," he continued. "It is quite remarkable really. Have you ever noticed how everyone smiles when Mary enters a room? Well, it has been the same at Pemworth. She has Mama smiling again."

"I had noticed the difference, actually," Edward said, "but I suspected it was no more than prewedding excitement."

"No, it is Mary herself, not just the wedding, that has made the difference," Jack said. "She and Mama spend hours chatting and laughing together. She and Charlotte have become great friends, and she plays with the girls and makes them laugh. After all the grief this family has suffered, it does my heart glad to hear laughter once again."

The horses seemed to have drunk their fill and turned away from the water and were ambling lazily among the bushes and grasses along the creekside. Both men's eyes were drawn to the movements of the horses.

"I, too, am pleased to hear your mother's laughter again," Edward said, returning his gaze to Jack after his mount began to nibble at a clump of low grass. "I confess I had almost begun to despair for her health. Poor Lydia—she has lost so much. My heart breaks for her, but I had begun to believe she would never get over it. Thank God she still has you, Jack."

"Thank God for Mary, you should say. I tell you, *she* is responsible for Mama's good spirits. I am a lucky man, Uncle."

"So," Edward said as he cocked a brow, "it appears you chose wisely after all."

"More wisely than you, or I, could possibly have dreamed," Jack said. "I could not have found a more perfect partner if I had spent decades searching the globe. I do not know what twist of fate brought her to my side that night at Lady Pigeon's ball, but I shall be forever grateful."

Edward rose from his boulder, stretched, and moved to stand next to his horse. He grabbed his jacket and shook it out. "I take it, then," he said over his shoulder, "that it is more than the lady's fortune for which you are grateful."

Jack smiled and pushed himself away from the tree. "You are correct, Uncle." He directed a sheepish grin toward Edward. "Ironic, is it not, that I should have come to care so much for Mary after all? But I assure you, I have undergone a most dramatic change of heart."

"Well." Edward tugged on his jacket, never taking his eyes from Jack. His mouth twitched momentarily and finally formed itself into a roguish grin. "Well. I am speechless, my boy." His grin became a chuckle and he shook his head in disbelief. "You have taken me completely by surprise. I never thought to hear such words from the likes of you. After that business with that other girl—what was her name?"

"Suzanne, Miss Suzanne Willoughby."

"Yes, Miss Willoughby. After all that, it seemed you would never . . . I mean, I never expected . . . well, you know what I am trying to say. Something changed in you back then. That girl crushed your spirit. Oh, you survived well enough—"

"With your help."

"With my interference, your mother would say," Edward said. "In any case, I never expected to see you fall for another woman again. I always thought you invulnerable to such things. It is strangely reassuring to find that, after all, you are as vulnerable as any man. Ha! Listen to me!"

Jack shrugged into his own jacket and dusted off his hat with his sleeve. "I have surprised myself as well," he said. "I never expected to lose my heart again. And I certainly never expected to lose it to Mary. But you are right—Suzanne did crush me. I got over it years ago. I have often thanked God, in fact, for the good fortune of *not* being married to Suzanne. But I never got over the wariness, the mistrust, the fear. Mary has changed all that. She has taught me to trust again. And I cannot imagine life without her, now. I tell you, if I were to discover she had not a sou to her name, I would still marry her."

"Good heavens, my boy, you are well and truly lost!"

"I am," Jack said, smiling broadly. "I admit it."

Both men remounted their horses and pointed them back toward the Hall at a slow trot. After a few moments Edward gave Jack a slightly puzzled look and then returned his gaze to the parklands ahead. Jack watched as the corners of his uncle's mouth curled up slowly into a strange enigmatic smile. "You may not credit it," Edward said at last, "but I find this unexpectedly romantic turn of events quite . . . well, quite pleasant, actually. It warms the cockles of my old heart to see you so happy."

"Go on!"

"It is true, I tell you," Edward said and then heaved a gusty sigh. "I must be getting old, but do you know what? I find myself of late longing for the same sort of peaceful contentment you seem to have found."

"Really?" Jack bit back a grin. "With Olivia Bannister, perhaps?"

"Hmph!" was all the response he received as Edward urged his horse into a gallop and sped ahead.

The next afternoon Mary found herself in need of a few moments of privacy and decided on a stroll through the grounds. Her thoughts full of the excitement and anticipation of the wedding, she wandered alone in one of the side gardens. Well, not quite alone. One of the marchioness's spaniels toddled along beside her. Max, as he had been introduced to her by young Lizzy, had scampered up to her as she left the Hall, his liquid brown eyes and mournful whine begging her to take him outside.

"Come along, then," she had said, no match for such eyes.

The wedding guests had begun to arrive, and the Hall was bustling with activity. No doubt Max had craved a little peace and quiet as she did. Lord and Lady Bradleigh had arrived, much to Mary's delight. The countess's condition might have prevented their traveling, but she had insisted on coming, and Mary was glad for it. Emily and Robert were her only close friends, besides Olivia, among the wedding guests—the rest being Jack's friends or relations—and it gave Mary a sense of comfort to have familiar faces at hand. Robert had even agreed to escort her down the chapel aisle and give her away. He had seemed extremely touched by her request that he do so.

As she strolled aimlessly through the garden, under the shade of a jaunty parasol of blue shot silk with a deep Chinese fringe, Mary considered how her life would change in two days' time—

indeed, how much it had already changed. She felt happier than she had felt in all her life, happier than she had ever imagined she could be. Since her talk with the marchioness in the Long Gallery, when she had banished at last all her old demons, Mary had felt decidedly lighthearted, rejuvenated, invigorated.

"Is it not wonderful, Max?" The dog gave her a puzzled look, then proceeded ahead on his own. Mary laughed. "Don't worry, Max. I am not completely addled—only a little mad with happiness, perhaps."

In the three years since her father's death, she had known a great deal of contentment born of her new independence. But she had never considered how much the affection of a man—a man she loved—could add to her happiness. Whenever she thought of Jack, which was most of the time, she wanted to fling her arms wide and shout for joy.

At this particular moment, as she ambled contentedly through the gardens, she thought of her approaching wedding night, only two nights hence. Jack's kisses had become increasingly passionate since that day they had wandered along the smuggler's cove, and Mary found herself looking forward to the consummation of that passion with uninhibited desire. She could not wait to lie beside him, to feel his arms around her, to have him make love to her.

Although Jack had not made any declarations of love, he had more than once spoken very tenderly about his affection for her, about the happiness she brought him. It was enough. For now. If matters continued as they had, Mary was confident that in time he would love her. Perhaps when they had shared the intimacy of the marriage bed, it would be easier for him to speak his heart. She was perfectly prepared to speak hers.

Mary glanced about the garden and considered how perfectly content she was with the prospect of making Pemworth her home. She loved every inch of it: the grand Elizabethan exterior, the Tudor gates, the woodlands, the walkways, the headlands, the sheltered coves, the Great Hall, the Long Gallery, the music room—yes, definitely the music room—and the gardens. She stepped around a bit of hawthorn that had been allowed to grow unclipped, right onto the path. It reminded her of other signs of neglect she had noted at Pemworth. She had not wanted to mention anything, not wanting to insult the marchioness. It was likely that, during this last painful year, she had been less than conscientious about such things, allowing a certain laxity in the servants and staff.

"We shall have to have a word with Jack, won't we, Max? About taking things more firmly in hand, that is. Pemworth deserves better treatment."

Max, who had continued ahead while Mary had paused, turned and barked.

"Ha!" Mary said with a laugh. "You agree with me. Well, we shall see to it, then."

The garden path angled and took her close to the edge of the Hall. As she strolled along the path, admiring the fragrant lavender, verbena, and clematis hugging the pink stone walls, she heard voices from inside the Hall. Her heart leapt at the unmistakable familiarity of one of the voices. Smiling with anticipation, she closed her parasol and moved toward the open French doors of the library where she could now hear, very clearly, the voices of Jack and his friend, Lord Sedgewick, who had arrived earlier in the day.

"I believe she likes it here," she heard Jack say. "She and Mama have spent hours together going over the workings of the Hall. They seem to be getting along famously."

Mary stopped as she realized they were speaking of her. Pleased and embarrassed, she knew she ought to turn and walk away, or else walk straight through the French doors and make herself known. She ought not to eavesdrop. Nothing good ever came of eavesdropping. But some perversity, some imp of mischief, caused her to want to hear what Jack said. She stood back from the open doors and flattened herself against the stone wall, between two lavender bushes. She signaled for Max to stay.

"Mama adores her," Jack said, his voice trailing off as if he had walked across the room. Mary heard the clink of glass on glass.

"That makes it easier, then, don't it?" Lord Sedgewick said. "Imagine if they had hated one another on sight."

There was a brief pause before Jack burst into laughter.

"And you, Jack?" Lord Sedgewick continued. "Do you get along with her as well?"

"Oh, indeed," Jack said with some enthusiasm. There was another pause and another burst of laughter, this time from Lord Sedgewick.

"She certainly is a tiny little thing," Lord Sedgewick said, his voice slightly muffled.

"Yes," said Jack, "but you may have noticed that she is soft and round where it counts." Lord Sedgewick chuckled, and Mary felt herself blush. "I have taken to referring to her—not to her face, mind you—as my own little Pocket Venus."

As both men dissolved into bawdy laughter, Mary was unable to stifle her own giggle. *His Pocket Venus?* She wasn't sure whether she ought to be flattered or insulted. But she rather thought his lighthearted tone spoke more of affection than scorn.

She really ought to leave before she heard something even more embarrassing. She gently pushed aside one of the lavender bushes with her parasol and made a move to step forward; but she checked herself at once when she heard Lord Sedgewick speak again.

"You amaze me, Jack," he was saying. "I could never have imagined you would have chosen someone like Lady Mary. In fact, she is not at all what I expected."

"Indeed?" Jack said. "And what exactly did you expect?"

"Oh, you know . . ." Lord Sedgewick's voice trailed off, and there was another pause followed by some muffled sniggering during which Mary was rather glad she was unable to see what the two men might be doing.

"Since we last spoke at White's," Lord Sedgewick went on, "back in May, you recall, I have not been able to follow your career on the Marriage Mart. Had to rush off to Lincolnshire. M'mother was ill."

"I trust she has recovered?" Jack said.

"Fit as a fiddle," Lord Sedgewick replied. "But I missed the rest of the Season, so I don't know how you came to be with Lady Mary. I like her, but she ain't exactly your usual type."

"That's true," Jack said and then laughed.

She should leave. She really should leave. She did not want to hear this.

"Mary is as far removed from my *usual type*," Jack said, "as she could possibly be."

"Then she must be awfully rich."

Mary's breath caught in her throat.

"After all," Lord Sedgewick continued, "that was your main purpose in seeking out a bride, was it not?"

Her fist flew to her mouth to silence a gasp as her parasol fell to the ground and into the lavender bushes. *Oh, no. Please, no.*

"Of course it was," Jack replied.

Oh, my God.

"And, yes," he said, "she is in fact extremely wealthy. That is, of course, precisely why I offered for her."

Mary bit down hard on her fist to stifle an anguished scream, then turned and ran toward the front of the house.

Chapter 17

"And although her money was my original motive for wanting to marry her . . ." Jack paused, cocking his head toward the French doors.

"What is it?" Sedgewick asked.

Jack walked to the open doors and stuck his head out. He looked south toward the gardens, squinting toward the entrance to the rose garden. Suddenly, he was startled by a rustling in the bushes behind him. Spinning around, he found a small, furry, white face peeking out from the lavender, the soulful brown eyes regarding him with curiosity.

"Max? What are you doing in there?" Laughing, Jack reached down and scratched the dog's head. "It's not like you to be out on your own, old boy. Have you been abandoned by Lizzy again? Well, no matter. Come on in, then. Come on."

Max stepped out of the lavender, peeked through the French doors, then made a dash for the leather arm chair nearest the fireplace.

"I thought I heard someone outside," Jack said, turning to Sedgewick. "It was just this old fellow, after all." Jack walked to Max's chair and scratched him behind the ears.

"A bit skittish, ain't you, Jack?"

Jack shrugged. "It is just that . . . well, the topic of our conversation was a bit—"

"Ah," Sedgewick said. "Still keeping the financial difficulties under wraps, then? You haven't told anyone else?"

"No! Only you and Uncle Edward know the truth. But as I was saying, even though I most certainly became betrothed to Mary on account of her fortune, that is no longer the case." He grinned at Sedgewick, who was sprawled comfortably in a leather arm-chair near the open French doors, and watched in amusement as his friend's eyes widened slightly and his brows disappeared beneath his tousled blond hair. Jack was too full of energy to sit, and so he stood across from Sedgewick, one hand propped on his hip, the other holding a nearly empty glass of wine. "If you can believe it, my friend," he said, swinging the glass wide in an expansive gesture, "that sweet little woman has stolen my heart."

"Never say so!"

Sedgewick's wide-eyed look of astonishment as he sat bolt upright in his chair brought an involuntary crack of laughter from Jack. It really was extraordinary, Jack thought, how often he found himself laughing these days. Not the cynical, disdainful laughter that had once been second nature to him, but true, joyous, uninhibited laugher. *Ah, Mary.*

"It is true," he continued, unable to suppress a broad smile. "I adore her. I can no longer imagine life without her."

Sedgewick settled back once more in his chair and stretched his long legs out in front of him. "And the money, Jack?" he asked in a wary voice. "The money is no longer important?"

Jack walked toward the side table and poured himself another glass of wine. He cocked a brow at Sedge, nodding toward the decanter, but his friend shook his head. "Until my estates are in order," Jack said at last, "money will always be important. But that has nothing to do with Mary. Not anymore. Good God, I don't care if she is penniless or rich as Croesus. I adore her regardless. And would marry her regardless. Good Lord, Sedge, who would have thought I would ever be as besotted as Bradleigh? Ha!" He flung both arms wide and laughed again for pure joy.

Sedge ran his fingers through his hair and flashed one of his famous grins. "By Jove," he said, "I think you're serious. You've really gone and done it—you've fallen in love. I cannot believe it!" Sedgewick slapped his thigh and laughed loudly.

Jack's sheepish grin soon turned to laugher. The joke was on him, of course. The sheer irony of the situation was almost comical; that he should have set out in the most dishonest manner to find a rich wife, to have then betrothed himself to a very rich but otherwise extremely unlikely sort of female, and finally to have fallen in love with her after all. It was no wonder Sedgewick was doubled over with laughter. It was deliciously absurd. Jack Raeburn, in love!

"Hoist by your own petard!" Sedgewick said at last. "You shall never live this down, Jack. I, for one, will not let you. Ha!" He shook his head from side to side and laughed again. "But truthfully," he continued, "I *am* pleased for you. As improbable as the situation is, I can see you are contented. In fact, this is a side of you I've never seen, Jack. I have not heard a cynical cutting remark since I arrived. You must truly be happy."

"I am indeed, Sedge. More than I ever thought possible. My only regret," Jack said, his voice sobering, "is the deceitful manner in which this match began." He wandered toward the French doors, seeking the cooler fragrant air from the adjacent garden, and propped one arm against the doorjamb. "I cannot tell you," he continued, "how ashamed I am that I ever planned to use Mary in such a cold, calculated way. I could easily have proceeded in such a manner—without a single qualm—if it had been any of the other women I was considering. But with Mary, it seems an unspeakable, unthinkable insult."

"Does she know?"

"Good Go, no! I had known her a short while," Jack said, turning toward Sedgewick. "Even before you and I met that night at White's. If you can believe it, she had engaged herself as my champion, to help find me a proper bride. She knew I was in search of a wife, but she never knew my true motives, and I trust she never will. We had become good friends when I discovered—through Robert, though he does not know it—that she was wealthy. I immediately set out, God help me, to seduce her. She finally acquiesced to my proposal, and it was not long before I realized what a precious jewel I had stumbled upon. I have lost my heart to her completely here at Pemworth. She has brightened up the shabby old place so, and has brought a smile again to my poor mother's face."

Sedgewick uncurled his lanky frame, rose from the chair, and came to stand next to Jack in the open doorway. "She sounds wonderful, my friend," Sedge said, slapping Jack on the back. "I am happy for you. Truly, I am. Do not repine over the way things began if they ultimately end so well."

"Oh, I fully intend to appreciate my good fortune—and I do not mean the money—to its fullest extend," Jack said. "But I will do my best to protect Mary from ever knowing how dishonest a beginning we really had."

"Don't worry, Jack," Sedgewick said when Jack cast him a significant glance. "She will hear nothing from me."

"I never suspected she would," Jack said with a grin.

Mary ran blindly along the path that skirted the east wing. She had to get away, she had to get inside, but where was the blasted door? Realizing she should have gone the reverse direction and around the end of the wing toward the rear courtyard, she knew she would now be forced to swing around to the main entrance on the north front. If only there was some less conspicuous route to her suite in the west wing, but there was nothing for it now but to take the only route with which she was familiar.

But she must not think. Not yet. She must act. She would think later.

Mary slowed her pace as she reached the front drive, not wishing to draw undue attention. She paused on the steps to the entrance and took several deep breaths. She must not think. She must regain her composure in case she encountered one of the family members or guests. She clinched her jaw tightly, thrust her chin in the air, threw her shoulders back, and marched up the steps. A footman opened the door for her. She gave him a curt nod and entered the Great Hall. Her body sagged with relief when she saw that it was empty. Thank God for that. But she must not think. She must act. She would think later.

She turned left and through the doors beneath the Minstrel's Gallery until she found the great oak staircase. She slowly began the climb, eyes darting left and right and up, expecting at any moment to encounter one of the guests. She made it to the first-floor landing in grateful solitude, but was met there by one of Lady Pemerton's cousins—what was her name? She could not seem to remember her name.

She must not think. She must go on.

Mary nodded to the woman and mumbled some word of greeting, but attempted to indicate that she was in a hurry. The woman smiled hesitantly and let her pass. Mary charged up the next flight to the second floor without any additional encounters. Good Lord, her rooms were at the farthest end of the corridor, which seemed to stretch indefinitely before her.

She must not panic. She must not think. She must go on.

Mary had negotiated half the length of the corridor when a door opened on the right and Olivia came into the hall. *Oh, no. Please, not now.*

"Oh, hello, my dear," Olivia said brightly. "I was just coming to look for you. The marchioness would like . . . Mary! What on earth is wrong?"

Mary waved a dismissive hand. "Nothing is wrong," she said in a tight voice. "I just—"

"Good heavens, my dear. You look quite ill. Are you not feeling well?"

Mary quickly grabbed at that convenient excuse. "No, I am not," she replied, her jaw still clenched, her tone sharp. "I do not feel quite the thing just now, Olivia. I am going to lie down for a while."

She turned brusquely and headed back down the corridor.

Olivia followed close behind. "Oh, my poor dear," she said in a solicitous voice, "you have been overwrought by all the excitement of the wedding. I am not surprised you are feeling a bit out of curl."

"Yes," Mary said absently, "I am tired. So very tired. Please apologize to the marchioness. The dinner party tonight. I cannot be there. I am not feeling well. Tell her for me. I am tired. I will stay in my room tonight."

"A wise idea, my dear," Olivia said as they reached the door to Mary's bedchamber. "I know she will understand. You must be fresh for the wedding, after all." She put an arm around Mary's shoulder and led her into the room. "Here, let me take your bonnet. Shall I ring for Sally? If you'd like, I can prepare a cool cloth soaked in lavender water, to soothe your brow. Would you like a tisane? Or perhaps some laudanum? Shall I—"

"Please, Olivia!" Mary snapped as she roughly shrugged the

woman's arm off her shoulder. "Leave me alone! Just leave me alone. Please do not fuss. Leave me alone!" Her voice had become shrill and unrecognizable.

Olivia stepped back quickly as though she had been struck, her face pale and her eyes wide. "Mary? Are you sure you are—"

"Olivia! Do you not understand? I would like to be alone now. Please . . . please leave."

Olivia stared at Mary, her brows raised in helpless astonishment, her lower lip caught between her teeth.

"Go, Olivia. Please . . . just go."

Olivia's hand flew to her mouth and her face crumbled. She turned and walked away, closing the door behind her.

Mary fell back against the closed door and gazed about the room. When her eyes reached the large, curtained bed she was tempted to throw herself upon it and give in to the despair she had kept under tight restraint for the past half hour. But not yet. Not now. She must not think just now. She must act. She would think later.

She rang for her maid and began to pull dresses out of the wardrobe. If only she had not brought so many things! But then, she had packed enough to get her through a stay at Pemworth as well as a short bridal journey to the Lake Country. Well, she would just have to pack it all. She meant to leave nothing behind. When Sally arrived and saw what was going on, she gave a shriek and flew to Mary's side.

"What . . . what . . ."

"Help me, Sally. We must pack up everything. Quickly, now."

"B-but . . . I-I don't understand, my lady," Sally said, almost in tears. "Are we leaving Pemworth?"

"Yes. Now, please, help me."

"But the . . . the w-wedding?" Sally said, her voice tremulous and confused.

"There will be no wedding." Mary stopped her frantic activity, looked up, and placed a hand against her cheek, as if suddenly startled by the realization. It was true. There would be no wedding. But she must not think about that now. There was no time to think now. She suddenly felt very cold and began to shiver uncontrollably. She wrapped her arms tightly about her. "Sally," she said, fixing her maid with a steely glare, "you must say nothing about this to anyone. I find that I . . . that I cannot go through with the wedding."

"Oh, my lady!" Sally grabbed a woolen shawl that had been tossed on the bed and gently draped it around Mary's trembling shoulders.

"But I do not want to cause a scene," Mary said, gratefully accepting the shawl and pulling it tightly against her breast. "So we must be circumspect—quiet—about our plans. You must help me to pack, but somehow—I do not know how, but somehow—you must not let any of the other servants know what we are about. I want no gossip belowstairs that I am planning to leave. Do you understand?"

"Yes, my lady." Sally's voice was little more than a whisper, and she kept her eyes lowered.

"First, you must get a message—secretly, mind you—to John Coachman. He must have our carriage ready to depart before dawn. I know I can count on his, and your, discretion."

"Yes, my lady."

So the two women made plans to escape Pemworth without alerting the staff or the family. Sally and John Coachman, both loyal and trusted servants, were stoic but cooperative in organizing a quick and quiet departure. Sally had kept well-meaning family members away from Mary, carrying on with the story of her indisposition as she peeked her head through a crack in the door, or stepped outside in the corridor to speak softly with the visitor. Olivia had returned twice, the marchioness had stopped by, as had Charlotte. A footman had brought a dinner tray. There had even been a note from Jack, wrapped around one of the garden roses, which Mary had consigned to the fire, unread.

Somehow, she had gotten through the long evening. Sally had at first tried to get her to lie down and rest while she completed all the packing, but Mary needed activity to keep her mind blank. Sally seemed to understand, and they worked side by side, speaking only of inconsequential matters. The packing, which had taken days to organize two weeks before, was completed in hours. There was a hidden service stairway near Mary's suite at the far end of the west wing, so there was no need to carry trunks and bandboxes down the long corridor. Long after the family and guests had gone to bed, John Coachman carried all the baggage downstairs himself—thank God he was such a big, strong fellow—and loaded the carriage, which he had parked in a little used lane far away from the stables.

The carriage pulled away slowly and quietly an hour or so before dawn. Mary sat alone inside—she had allowed herself only a moment of guilt when she had asked Sally to sit up front with John—and watched Pemworth Hall, shimmering pink in the moonlight, disappear from her sight—forever. This beautiful place was not to be her home after all.

She jerked the heavy velvet curtain across the window and kicked at the opposite squab with such force that she yelped with pain. A single tear trickled down her cheek that she angrily brushed away. How could she have been so stupid? How could she have let her guard down so thoroughly? Her father had been right.

"Whatever made you imagine," he had said, "that you could hold a man's interest for any reason other than money?"

Of course, he was right. She had known all along that he had been right. How could she have forgotten the basic truth that had been drilled into her head for most of her life: she was ugly, worthless, and of no use to anyone. Damn Jack for making her forget that! And damn him for making a fool of her—or, more accurately, for allowing her to make a fool of herself. She pounded her fist against the velvet squab. *Damn, damn, damn!*

Mary began to untie the ribbon of her bonnet, but her fingers could not seem to function properly, and the ribbon became hopelessly tangled. Swearing with creative fluency, she tugged at the thing until it ripped apart, and she flung the bonnet onto the seat opposite. She knew her departure—her escape—would cause a momentary scandal. She regretted leaving the marchioness and Charlotte without a word, and harbored a terrible guilt for abandoning Olivia. But none of that mattered. The only thing that mattered at the moment was the need to get away—all right, to run away. However it was expressed, she had to leave. Knowing the truth of Jack's motives, how he had lied to her and manipulated her, made it impossible for her to remain at Pemworth. She could not and would not face him. There was no longer any question of marrying him. That was impossible now, despite what she had felt for him.

Had felt? Did she no longer love him? Against all her best intentions, she had opened the fortress she had carefully constructed around her heart—*stupid, stupid woman!*—and allowed him inside. Could she cast him out so easily and close the gates tightly once again? Mary angrily clawed at her cheeks to brush away the tears that now flowed freely. Yes, she could cast him out and she would, if it took her a lifetime to do so. She could never trust him again, so it should be easy never to love him.

How much blame, though, could she rightly assign to Jack? He had been honest with her from the start about his inability to offer love. He had never spoken to her of love. It was her own foolish imagination that had led her to believe that he might love her. His passionate kisses had been only that: physical passion—lust, even—but not *love*making. What a fool she had been!

He had promised her nothing but security and companionship, and she accepted him on those terms. She had never imagined, though, that her fortune had anything to do with it. She and Jack had never discussed money. How did he even know about her fortune, before speaking to Mr. Fleming?

But, wait a minute. Of course! No wonder he had rejected so many of the otherwise unexceptionable young women on Mary's list of candidates—like Miss Langley-Howe, or Lady Daphne Hewitt. They brought very unimpressive fortunes. Whereas others, like Miss Carstairs—the very rich Miss Carstairs—had been prime candidates. If he had gone to the trouble to investigate their circumstances, he must surely have investigated hers as well. No wonder he had so suddenly turned his attentions to her. The scoundrel! He had deliberately set out to make a fool of her, convincing her she wasn't plain and worthless, making her feel strong and confident—when all he really wanted was her fortune. Her damnable fortune. It was just like the last time, with Peter.

Her father was right.

How mortifying!

But it was her own fault. If she had not been so susceptible to Jack's charm, so willing to believe him, so quick to accept his offer, perhaps he would have sought out someone else—he might have renewed his attentions to Miss Carstairs, for example—and then she would not now be forced to endure her current humiliation. Mary rubbed at her eyes with the heels of her hands, trying to stop the tears that would not be stopped. She hated herself for such weakness—for her tears, for her shame, for her embarrassment, for letting herself forget who and what she was. Especially for that. She hated herself for forgetting.

She would not forget again.

Chapter 18

"Have you seen Mary this morning, Mrs. Bannister?" Jack loaded his plate with eggs, kippers, bread, and marmalade and then sat down at the breakfast table next to Emily, Lady Bradleigh. "I have been concerned about her," he said. "I hope she is feeling better today." He reached across Lord Sedgewick, on his left, for the salt cellar.

"No, my lord," Mrs. Bannister replied. "I have not seen her yet. I knocked early this morning, but there was no reply so I assumed she was still asleep. I did not wish to disturb her."

"Poor thing," his mother said from the other end of the table. "I fear we have overtaxed her these last weeks. We must indulge her today so she will be rested for the wedding tomorrow."

Emily pushed her plate away and looked at Jack. "Shall I go see if she is all right?"

Jack was about to speak when Mrs. Bannister interrupted. "No, please," she said. "Let me go." She stood up quickly and pushed her chair back into place. Nodding toward Emily, she said, "You should not be climbing up and down the stairs so often, my lady."

Emily gave a shy chuckle, and her husband put his arm gently around her shoulder. "Thank you, Mrs. Bannister," Lord Bradleigh said. He turned to smile warmly at his wife. "I am glad someone else is here to remind you to be careful, my dear."

"I'll just run up and see how she is feeling, my lord," Mrs. Bannister said to Jack.

"Be sure to ring if she would like a tray in her room," his mother called out as Mrs. Bannister left the breakfast room.

General conversation continued, the informal ball planned for that evening and the wedding on the following morning among the most popular topics of discussion. Soon, several of the earlier arrivals departed, leaving only a small group at table. During a momentary lull in the conversation, the marchioness turned her attention to Jack. "My dear," she said, "I believe you must have exhausted Mary with all those long walks along the headlands. I do not believe she is used to such exertion."

"She did not appear to be overexerted, Mama," Jack said. He cast an amused glance at Sedgewick, who was grinning broadly as he stared down at his plate.

"Nevertheless," his mother continued, ignoring the sniggering of the various gentlemen, "she has become overtired. I suspect she would not be willing to admit to you that she was not up to all that tramping about. She would not wish to appear . . . weak in your eyes."

"Really, Mama," Jack said, still smiling, "I cannot imagine that Mary is afraid to be honest with me on such a minor point. She is . . . Good Lord!"

Mrs. Bannister stood in the doorway in the breakfast room, white-faced and wide-eyed. *Oh, my God. Mary!* Jack jumped up, knocking his chair over, and moved quickly to the stricken woman's side. "What is it? What has happened?"

Mrs. Bannister stared at him mutely, her lips slightly parted and trembling. She seemed hesitant to speak. Finally, she tore her pleading eyes from him and glanced about the suddenly silent room, briefly meeting the anxious eyes of one after another of the assembled guests. It occurred to Jack that perhaps she wanted to speak to him privately, but he was too anxious to hear what she had to say to be concerned with the others. Besides, they were all family or friends, and if something had happened to Mary . . .

Jack wanted to shake the woman by the shoulders. "Mrs. Bannister?" he prompted in a tightly controlled voice.

When her eyes returned to his, he was reminded of a frightened rabbit. "She's gone," she said softly.

"What?" Jack said. "What do you mean she's gone? Out for an early walk, perhaps?"

"No, my lord," Mrs. Bannister replied, her lower lip quivering. "She has left Pemworth. She's gone." Suddenly, she buried her face in her hands as she dissolved into tears. The marchioness was quickly at her side, comforting the distraught woman while casting a puzzled look at Jack.

Jack stood immobilized with shock, gaping at Mrs. Bannister. No, it couldn't be true. He would not believe it. Mary had not left him. She would never betray him like that. Not Mary.

"Tell us what has happened," his mother said while leading Mrs. Bannister to a chair.

"I do not know what has happened!" Mrs. Bannister wailed. "All I know is that Mary's rooms are empty, her luggage is gone, and her maid is nowhere to be found." Realizing, apparently, that she had been almost shrieking, she lowered her voice when she continued. "She has gone. That is all I know."

Mrs. Bannister looked questioningly at Jack, but he looked away and said nothing. His stomach seized up into a knot. So, it was true. He did not want to believe it, but it appeared to be true. He clenched his back teeth tightly together to keep himself from shouting. She had left him after all. Mary had left him. *Bloody hell!*

Numb with fury, Jack watched as Edward Maitland rose from the table and signaled a footman to his side. "Check belowstairs," Edward told the young man, "and find out what is known about Lady Mary's departure. Did anyone speak with her maid? What about her coachman?" He turned to look at Mrs. Bannister. "She brought her own carriage, did she not?" When Mrs. Bannister nodded, he turned back to the footman. "Find out if her carriage is gone. And if so, when it left."

"Yes, sir." The footman, looking anxious and excited, quickly departed.

Jack had not stirred from his place near the door. He could not seem to move, his body stiff with suppressed emotion—anguish battling with rage for control. Though he saw and heard all the flurry of activity that went on about him, he was unable to focus on anything beyond a single thought. She had left him. She had actually left him. Mary had left him.

His hands slowly balled into fists.

"I do not understand," Emily said, shaking her head in disbelief. "Why would Mary have left Pemworth? You must have been the last to see her, Mrs. Bannister. Did she say anything to you? Was she—" she cast a quick glance at Jack—"unhappy?"

Mrs. Bannister, more composed now, looked at Emily and narrowed her eyes in thought. "She was certainly not herself when we spoke yesterday afternoon," she said. "She was sharp and . . . well, uncommonly rude. It was not at all like Mary. I suppose she might have been upset about something. I thought she might have been upset with me, for she had never spoken to me so harshly before. But she claimed to be unwell, and I assumed that accounted for her odd behavior."

The butler, Grimes, entered the breakfast room and stood before Jack, clearing his throat nervously. When Jack ignored him, Grimes turned to the marchioness. "Lady Mary's carriage and horses are not in the stables, my lady," he said. "Her coachman and his things are also gone. One of the stable boys heard a noise in the middle of the night, but did not investigate. Her maid has also disappeared. Her case and extra clothing are gone from the room she had shared with Betsy. No one can recall seeing her at all last evening."

"Thank you, Grimes," the marchioness said. She then signaled for him and the remaining footman to leave. She looked sharply at Jack when the servants had departed. "So," she said. "Mary has left. We must say something, Jack, to the other guests. I assume you are planning to go after her?" She breathed a ragged sigh. "I suppose we must postpone the wedding . . ."

"God damn it!" Jack exploded, no longer able to contain his fury. She had done it. She had really left him. It had happened again. "God damn it!" He tightened one fist, brought it up to his chest, then slammed it furiously against the wall. A small painting jumped from its hook to land with a loud crash upon the sideboard, knocking over the large coffee urn, which in turn sent serving dishes bobbling and smashing one after the other to the floor. "God damn it!" Jack shouted, oblivious to the damage as he pounded the wall again and again until it cracked, and bits of plaster began to crumble to the floor.

"Jack!"

Raising his fist for another blow, Jack was suddenly surrounded by Edward, Bradleigh, and Sedgewick, each trying to restrain him, immobilizing his arms, while the women scurried to the other side of the room, away from his uncontrolled rage. Jack stopped fighting his captors when he happened to catch his mother's eye, overwhelmed momentarily by the pain and fear he read there. Suddenly realizing he had made a spectacle of himself—and not much caring—Jack attempted to rein in his fury.

God damn her. She had taken him for a fool, just as Suzanne had. He had trusted her, and she had bolted. Probably discovered he was nearly bankrupt and no longer good enough for her. Probably even now seeking out a fatter goose to pluck. God damn her. God *damn* her!

He roughly shrugged off the restraining arms and hands of this friends and looked down with disgust at the mess of smashed porcelain, crumbled plaster, and food littering the floor. Coffee dribbled down the front of the sideboard from the overturned urn. "It's all right," he said. "It's all right. Let me go."

Sedgewick and Bradleigh backed away warily. His uncle stayed close at his side. Jack looked at the women, standing together at the other end of the room, and met the steely glare of Emily. Without unlocking her eyes from his, she strode forward slowly and somewhat awkwardly. Her eyes narrowed as she stood before him, her arms resting on her swollen belly.

"What did you *do* to Mary?" she said in an accusing tone. "What did you say to her? What did—"

"I?" Jack shouted. "What did *I* do? Dammit, Emily, I have done nothing but . . ." *But love her,* he had almost said. "Nothing but treat her with kindness and respect and, God help me, trust. I never—"

"But you *must* have done something! She was so happy. She wanted this marriage. She loved you—"

"Ha!" Jack exclaimed. "Loved me? Apparently not, my dear. She—"

"I don't care what you say, Jack!" Emily's voice had risen to a shout. "She was happy, I tell you, and something has happened. I don't know what, but—"

"Emily, please." Bradleigh had moved to his wife's side and placed an arm around her, frowning over her head at Jack. "Calm yourself, my love. Remember your condition."

"My condition? *My* condition? What about poor Mary's condition? Is there no one among you fine gentlemen willing to go after her? She might be in trouble. She might be injured. She might be—"

"Oh, yes, please," Mrs. Bannister interrupted. She moved forward toward the gentlemen, gripping her hands in front of her in a plaintive gesture. "*Please*. Someone must go after her. She may have—"

"She was *not* abducted, ladies," Jack said with a sneer. "She left in her own carriage with her own maid and her own luggage. And of her own free will. It was her decision. There is no need to go haring after her. And at the moment that is the last thing I intend to do. Frankly, I don't care if I never see the woman again."

"Jack!" his mother exclaimed.

"Oh, but you are a scoundrel after all," Emily said through her teeth. "Don't you know how fragile Mary is? How hard she worked to put all that unpleasantness behind her? Don't you realize how meticulous she has been in maintaining that mask of cheerfulness? And something . . . *something* happened to cause that careful mask to crack. But what? What is she running away from? Or whom? What did you do to her, Jack?" she shouted. "What did you say to her?"

"Emily, please," Bradleigh said, tightening his arm about her and scowling furiously at Jack. "I am taking you to our bedchamber. I won't have you upset like this. Come along, my love." He steered her toward the door, her determination to stay no match for his superior strength.

"Scoundrel!" she hissed over her shoulder as they left the room.

When the door had closed behind them, Jack spun angrily around. "Always the scoundrel, am I not?" he snapped. Meeting the confused yet incensed eyes of Mrs. Bannister, he fixed her with an irate gaze. "That is what you think as well, is it not, ma'am? It is all *my* fault. Dear, sweet Mary can do no wrong. *I* am the villain," he said as he stabbed a finger against his chest. "*I* am at fault. *I* am somehow to blame for Mary's unconscionable behavior, am I not?"

Mrs. Bannister chewed on her lower lip and said nothing.

"Well?" Jack shouted. "Is that not what you think, ma'am? Is that not what you *all* think? Well, to hell with you all. And to hell with Mary."

Mrs. Bannister turned and fled the room without a word.

Edward turned on Jack, an angry glare in his eyes, and grabbed him roughly by the arm. "Get ahold of yourself, boy!"

Jack shook off his uncle's firm grip and stared at him with undisguised anger.

"Damnation!" Edward said and then stormed out of the room.

"Et tu, Uncle?" Jack muttered. He turned toward his mother. Her face was pale, her shoulders slumped. "Well, Mama?"

"Oh, Jack!" she said, blinking back tears. She followed Edward out of the room.

God damn it!

"Well. What an unexpected development this is."

Jack turned toward Sedgewick, who had seated himself back at the table and was calmly slathering a muffin with jam.

"Go ahead, Sedge. Berate me just like the rest of them." Jack sank into a chair across from Sedgewick. He placed his elbows on the table and dropped his head into his hands. The fight had gone out of him. He felt drained, empty.

"I take leave to reserve judgment," Sedgewick said around a mouthful of muffin. "I met Lady Mary only yesterday, after all. Though I liked her, I have no knowledge of her character. I was encouraged, though, by your own words of affection. It sounded as though you had found happiness at last, that you had found someone to . . . to love."

"What a bloody fool I've been!" Jack did not lift his head from his hands, and his voice was soft and muffled. "I loved her, Sedge. I trusted her. I thought she was different. How could I have been so stupid?" He lifted his head and slumped back into his chair. "I learned years ago never to trust a woman. They are all heartless, faithless, fickle creatures. I should have known better. Mary is the same as all the rest."

"Are you so certain of that, Jack? She was different enough to have you singing her praises only yesterday."

"Don't remind me, please, of my own stupidity. She manipulated me into letting down my guard, that is all. Dammit, how could I have been such a fool?"

"Perhaps you were not so foolish," Sedgewick said. "Perhaps something *did* happen. Something beyond her control—"

"Sedge! She took everything. She sneaked out in the middle of the night without a word or a note . . . nothing. Nothing."

"It does look rather odd," Sedgewick said. "What do you suppose set her off?"

"I have no idea," Jack said, his voice rising with impatience. "She apparently changed her mind and bolted. Plain and simple. Bloody hell!"

A footman quietly entered the room and looked in horror at the mess on and in front of the sideboard. He walked toward it, hands outstretched as though to pick something up, when he turned and met Jack's angry gaze. Startled, he backed out of the room, mouthing apologies as he left.

Jack rose and began to pace the room. "I should have known better," he said. "I *did* know better. The question is, what made me forget? I was right to merely take my pleasure from women and never get involved. Well, by God, that is exactly what I will do from now on. I will never, *never* trust a woman again."

"What about her fortune?" Sedgewick asked. "You need to marry a fortune, or have you forgotten that minor point? What will you do now?"

Jack snorted. "Oh, I still need a fortune, to be sure," he said. "But I'll be damned if I will have it from a woman. No, sir. Never again. I will find some other way."

"And Lady Mary? What will you do about her? Do you not think you should at least try to find out what happened? Find out if—"

"No!" Jack shouted. "By God, she has done enough damage. She has humiliated me in front of my friends and family. I shall never forget that. Never. I want nothing more to do with her."

Standing near the sideboard, he eyed a piece of broken porcelain and kicked it hard across the room.

God damn it!

Chapter 19

Olivia fled the breakfast room and made her way toward the Great Hall. There was no particular reason for going there; she simply needed to get away from all those people. She found an oak settle in an alcove beneath the Minstrel's Gallery, sat down, and dropped her head into her hands.

My God, what am I going to do?

She had been abandoned by her employer, left among virtual strangers, with no transportation, save what she could beg, and no idea where she should go in any case. What in the world was she going to do? A tightening in her chest caused her to lift her head, sit up straight, and breath deeply. She was distraught beyond words, but the tears had stopped some time ago. She was still saddened by this strange turn of events, to be sure; but more than that, she was frightened. She was all at sixes and sevens, uncertain of what was expected of her, what Mary expected of her. Not since Martin had died had she felt so lost.

She had been upset—and hurt—by Mary's behavior yesterday afternoon, but had never dreamed anything like this would happen. But, then, what *had* happened? What had caused Mary to leave like that? Without a word? Without an explanation? To sneak off in the middle of the night like that? It was so unlike her—especially now. Olivia had not been unaware of Mary's increased attachment to Lord Pemerton, which was written plainly on her face for all the world to see, or of her great pleasure in his family and his home. Always cheerful, Mary had never seemed so happy as she had been at Pemworth. What, then, could have changed all that? What had happened?

Olivia heard a noise behind her. Not wishing to be caught

brooding in a dark corner of the Great Hall, she rose and turned toward the doorway in time to see Lord and Lady Bradleigh starting up the oak staircase.

"Excuse me, my lady," Olivia said without thinking. "But I wonder if I might have a word with you?"

Emily relinquished her husband's arm and turned toward Olivia.

"I was wondering," Olivia said, "if you . . . I mean, do you have any idea what . . ."

Emily smiled weakly. "What happened to Mary?" she said, finishing Olivia's thought.

Olivia nodded, embarrassed to have approached the countess in such a forward manner.

"I wish I knew, Mrs. Bannister," Emily said. "I am afraid I do not understand at all. I am frankly worried about her."

"Oh, so am I! I wish someone would go after her."

"I must agree with Jack on that point, Mrs. Bannister," Lord Bradleigh said. "I doubt Lady Mary wishes to be followed. She apparently made a conscious decision to leave—why, I cannot begin to say. But I suspect it was not an easy decision, and she probably wanted to be alone. That is most likely why, unfortunately, she left without you."

"Yes," Emily said. "Of all people, you must be closest to her, Mrs. Bannister. If she chose not to confide her plans even to you, then it must have been something very difficult for her to do. Poor Mary. What can have happened?"

Olivia stared at the countess hopelessly.

"We are all confused," Emily continued. "And hurt. But Mary must be feeling even more wretched than we are. I suppose we must simply accept her decision and continue on."

"Of course," Olivia said, "you are correct. I just wish I understood."

"Mrs. Bannister," Lord Bradleigh said, "you are welcome to share our carriage with us when we depart Pemworth—which I presume will be much earlier than we had planned. Tomorrow?" he asked his wife. She nodded. "We are traveling to Derbyshire, and in easy stages, I am afraid. I refuse to allow Emily to be jostled more than is necessary. But we would be happy to take you wherever you would like to go."

"Thank you, my lord," Olivia said. "Let me consider what I must do. Then I may well accept your kind offer."

The earl and countess continued their way, very slowly, up the stairs. Olivia appreciated the earl's offer more than she could say. But where would she have him take her? To Bath, she supposed. Most of her belongings were still at Mary's Queen's Square town house. She would have to retrieve them and look for new work, which, of course, she had planned to do in any case. Mary having no further need of a companion after her marriage. But now, with the wedding canceled, she was not sure if Mary would eventually want her back.

Good heavens, but her head was spinning over this new predicament. She needed fresh air. She turned back into the Great Hall to head out the front door when the marchioness entered from the opposite end. Olivia stopped to acknowledge her and watched as the woman ambled slowly across the tiled floor, her shoulders sagging, her head bent. When she reached Olivia, she looked up, and Olivia was stunned by the open despair in her eyes. She looked older, somehow.

"Mrs. Bannister," she said as she laid her hand on Olivia's arm, "do you understand this business at all? Mary's leaving, I mean."

"No, my lady. I am at a loss to understand it."

"She told me about herself, you know," the marchioness said. "About her father, her elopement . . . everything."

"Oh." Olivia was surprised to hear this information. Mary was normally very circumspect about her past. Olivia, more than anyone, knew how painful a subject it was for her.

"And because of what I know," the marchioness continued, "I am especially worried about her. I am convinced something happened to upset her . . . to reopen, somehow, those old wounds. I don't know." She shook her head in confusion. "But I'm afraid it must have something to do with Jack."

"You think he might have . . . said something to . . . to hurt her?"

"I do not know. But I can assure you he was as stunned as the rest of us. If he did say, or do, something, he was certainly unaware of it. This has hurt him badly, Mrs. Bannister. You cannot imagine. I am worried for him. For what he will do."

Olivia simply nodded, not knowing what to say. The raw sorrow on the other woman's face was agonizing to watch.

"I cannot stay and watch his self-destruction. Not again. I cannot bear it. If you will excuse me . . ." The marchioness turned away and walked toward the great staircase. Olivia watched as she dragged herself up the first few steps. Good Lord. What had Mary done?

Olivia pushed open the heavy oak doors and hurried outside. She stopped on the entry steps and took a deep breath to calm her nerves. The breeze came from the south, and the air was pungent with salt. Without thought, her steps took her toward the rear of the house, toward the sea.

As she followed the path along the east wing, her thoughts were all of Lord Pemerton and his mother, and the different ways Mary's departure had affected them, when she noticed something blue among the lavender bushes against the Hall. She stopped to idly investigate and was astonished to find a blue parasol, which she immediately recognized as Mary's. It was not among the newer items of her trousseau, but an old favorite brought from Bath. It lay half buried among the bushes near a set of French doors. Olivia peered cautiously through the doors and recognized the library. How odd, she thought. What on earth was Mary's parasol doing outside the library?

Ah, well, she thought, squinting into the bright morning sun. She could use a parasol just now. She held it out and shook it vigorously to remove the dirt, opened it, and perched it above her shoulder as she briskly wound her way through the various gardens stretching toward the sea. She found herself at last on the headlands path above the steep red cliffs and decided to visit the beautiful little pavilion at the highest point along the path. Mary had mentioned that it had been built by Jack's grandfather in imitation of some Greek temple or other. Perched precariously on the jutting edge of a rocky cliff, the small, round building was built of the same pink stone as the Hall. Simple fluted columns supported a domed roof topped by a glass lantern. Olivia paused a moment on the path to admire the graceful lines and simple beauty of the tiny building before proceeding.

She climbed the steps up to the open structure and walked inside where she found two curved stone benches, facing back to back in the center of the room to form a broken circle. She tossed the parasol and her bonnet on one of the benches and walked to the cliffside edge of the pavilion and leaned against one of the columns. She closed her eyes and threw back her head, letting the blustery wind sting her face, relishing the smell and taste of the salty sea air, which never failed to remind her of Martin. They had shared a small house near Plymouth during the ten years of her marriage, not far to the west along this same coastline.

Oh, Martin. What am I going to do?

"May I intrude?"

Olivia turned with a start to find Edward Maitland on the steps of the pavilion, smiling roguishly at her. Feeling the ubiquitous blush that always seemed to accompany his presence, Olivia looked down and made a great business of straightening her skirts, which had become ruffled by the wind. She felt somehow naked without her bonnet. "Of course," she said, not daring to look at him. "Please come in."

"You are a difficult woman to track down, Olivia."

Her head jerked up at the unexpected familiarity.

"You don't mind if I call you Olivia, do you?" He had entered the pavilion and now eased himself onto one of the benches, his arms stretched out negligently along the back rail. "In private, at least. After all, my dear, we are not such young pups that we need be overly concerned with the proprieties. Please, call me Edward." He patted the space on the bench beside him.

Olivia glared at him momentarily, instinctively retreating behind her stern paid-companion mask. But at the moment, she was no one's paid companion, and she was no match for that smile and those twinkling blue eyes. She soon abandoned her mask, smiled in return, and sat down next to him. "Edward," she said.

"Ah. We make progress." He chuckled and Olivia found herself watching him closely. Though he was a notorious rake, his face did not show the marks of dissipation one would expect. His skin was not mottled like a drunkard's, nor his features pinched like an habitual gambler's. Oh, his face was lined, to be sure, for he was not a young man. But the lines were most prominent when he smiled, which was often. He really was very attractive.

"Actually," he was saying, "I have come to apologize. For Jack, that is. His behavior toward you was shameful." His face sobered and his voice softened. "But I wish you would not hold it against him, Olivia. I regret his lack of control, but he was hurting and lashing out."

"I understand," she replied. She relaxed against the back rail, thinking how easy it was to talk with Edward. "It is just that I was in no condition to withstand his anger at that moment," she said. "I was hurting, too."

"She abandoned you as much as Jack, didn't she?"

"It is not quite the same, of course," she said, "but I have been feeling rather at loose ends. I still have not yet decided what I should do now."

"Will you follow her?"

"I have no idea where she has gone. If she is truly running away, I cannot imagine she would return to Bath. That is the first place one would look. But where else she might have gone, I simply do not know. Actually, I am quite worried about her."

"She is more vulnerable than she lets on, is she not?" Edward asked.

Olivia turned toward him abruptly. "Yes," she said. "How did you guess?"

"It was not so very difficult," he said. "I was listening, remember, when Lady Bradleigh railed at Jack this morning. She mentioned Lady Mary's fragile sensibilities. But then, I knew she had Assheton for a father. Any daughter of his would necessarily be fragile. She hid it well, though. She never appeared anything less than witty, vibrant, happy." A puzzled frown crossed his face, and he shook his head slowly back and forth.

"I have no idea what happened," Olivia said in response to his unasked question, "but to have left like that, without a word . . . well, it must have been serious, that is all. Poor Mary."

"And poor Olivia, stranded in the wilds of Devon."

Olivia laughed. "I am not precisely stranded," she said. "Lord Bradleigh has offered me a place in his carriage when he and the countess leave tomorrow. And besides, if I *was* stranded, I cannot think of a more beautiful place to be so." She turned her gaze to the sea and lifted her face again to the breeze. "I love the sea."

"Do you?" Edward cocked a brow when Olivia turned back to face him. "I . . . um, I have a small home by the sea, as it happens."

"Oh?"

"Yes. A bit more rugged setting than this," he said, making a sweeping gesture toward the cliffside. "Due north of here, along the Somerset coast on Bridgewater Bay. My small estate, Colfax Ghyll, is bordered by craggy cliffs on one side and wild, barren moors on the other. Rather gothic, I suppose. I am afraid I have not spent much time there. Tend to make London my home, most of the year. Though . . . well, I have been thinking, lately, that I should spend more time in the country. I have always enjoyed Pemworth, but this visit, in particular," he said, brushing his knuckles ever so lightly along Olivia's jaw, "has made me long to return to Colfax Ghyll."

His brief touch sent a tingle all the way down her spine, and she was very much afraid another blush had crept up her throat and cheeks. She tried, with little success, to keep her voice level. "I have never seen any of the more northern coasts," she said, keeping her eyes on the sea beyond. "I am only familiar with the southern shores. I lived in Plymouth for some years and have more recently traveled with Mary to Brighton and to Bognor Regis."

"And do you sail?"

"I used to," she said, turning to him with a smile. "My . . . my husband was in the navy, you see."

"Ah," said Edward, his own eyes now gazing ahead toward the sea. "And when did . . . that is, how long have you been widowed?"

"Martin was lost at Trafalgar."

Edward did not respond, but continued to stare ahead. Olivia did the same, wondering what had become of the comfortable ease between them. There was a kind of tension in the air that she could not quite describe, but which almost unnerved her.

"And you have been earning your living as a companion," Edward said at last, "all these years since your husband's death?"

"Yes."

"And is that what you intend to do now? Find another post, I mean?"

"Yes," she said, feeling suddenly shy and awkward, "assuming Mary has no further need of me. I have no other source of income, you see. I must work. I have no other choice."

"Yes, you do." With a movement so sudden that Olivia gave a squeal of alarm, Edward captured her in his arms. His face inches from hers, he did not move for a long moment. Finally, his head lowered so that only the space of a breath separated his lips from hers. "Yes, you do," he whispered before setting his mouth to hers and kissing her soundly.

When he raised his head and smiled at her, Olivia could do nothing but stare. She had not been kissed in almost ten years, and only ever by Martin. She had forgotten how pleasant it could be and found herself shamelessly hoping he would kiss her again.

"You do have choices, my dear," Edward said, still holding her, though not so tightly. "You can come with me to Colfax Ghyll."

Olivia pulled herself away from him, stood up, and walked stiffly toward the edge of the pavilion. Good Lord in heaven. The man actually had the nerve to offer her *carte blanche*. Her! Olivia Bannister! Who would have ever imagined that Olivia Bannister would ever be the object of such an offer? And at her age! She kept her back to Edward as a smile stole across her face. When she really thought about it, it *was* quite flattering, after all. To think that as a forty-five-year-old matron she still held some appeal to a gentleman so . . . worldly . . . as Edward Maitland, to think that he might find her desirable in that way . . . well, it really was most gratifying. Most gratifying, indeed.

She heard Edward move toward her. She bit back her smile with some difficulty and turned toward him. "I am sorry, Edward," she said, "but I cannot accept your offer. You know I cannot."

Edward's face fell, and Olivia felt a stab of guilt at refusing him. Did it really matter that much to him, then? Was it more than simply a frivolous spur-of-the-moment offer? No matter. She had to refuse him. She could not allow herself to feel guilty for refusing such an offer. But still . . .

She smiled warmly at him. "I very much appreciate your asking, though," she said. "It is very flattering, especially at my age, to receive such an offer, however improper."

"Improper!" Edward's eyes widened as a stunned expression crossed his face. Suddenly, his eyes twinkled with comprehension, and he threw back his head and laughed.

Olivia eyed him quizzically. Having no experience in these matters, she had no idea what she might have said or done wrong. She glared at him, uncertain how to react.

Still chuckling, Edward put his hands on her shoulders and drew her close. "My dear Olivia," he said softly, his blue eyes boring into hers. "I had no idea a marriage proposal was considered improper. But then I've never made one before, so I could be wrong."

Olivia stared at him in dumbfounded silence for a moment. This was an unexpected development, to be sure. When she was able speak, her voice came out in an unnatural squeak. "M-marriage proposal?"

"Of course, my dear," he said with a grin. "What else? All this business of weddings and such has made me quite the sentimental old fool. I find that, at last, after all these years, the notion of marriage has begun to appeal to me. Marriage with you, that is. I have become uncommonly fond of you, you know. I would be very honored if you would agree to be my wife, Olivia. But then"—his grin widened—"if you would prefer some less formal arrangement, I suppose I could oblige—"

Olivia stopped his words with her lips. "You would oblige me, sir," she said after a short but very satisfying interlude, "by repeating your offer."

"The slip on the shoulder?" He sighed in mock capitulation. "If you insist—"

"Not that offer, you oaf!"

"Ah." He pulled her closer. "The other, then. Will you marry me, Olivia Bannister?"

She breathed her answer into his ear before he captured her lips once again.

Chapter 20

Mary had arrived in Bath early that same afternoon. With no other idea but to go home, she realized it was not wise to remain there. If Jack took it in his head to follow her, she had no wish to be so easily found. During the journey north from Pemworth, she had determined not to remain in Bath longer than it took to accomplish a few essential errands of business. She was not yet ready to face Bath Society with all its insatiable curiosity and penchant for gossip. Somehow she knew she would have to regain her self-confidence, to once again find her own special strength to deal with the world. And she would do it. She had done it once before; she could do it again. But she needed time— time alone. She could not stay in Bath.

In fact, she had no intention of completely unloading the carriage. She would keep one trunk in the boot for a journey to . . . well, she had no idea to where, just yet. But she had devised a plan to seek help from one or two trusted friends.

Her arrival at Queen's Square, to the astonishment of Mrs. Bailey, the housekeeper, had generated scores of questions and curious looks. Mary ignored most of them, confident that Sally would satisfy the curiosity belowstairs. After a quick wash and change of dress, Mary retired to the library. She scribbled a few quick notes and rang for a footman to have them posted at once. She also left a letter for Olivia, knowing that her faithful companion would most likely return to Bath in search of her. Mary took some care with this note, attempting to assuage her guilt over abandoning the poor woman. She also left Olivia a draft for a year's salary along with a reference for future employment. Though she was very attached to Olivia after three years, and would be pleased to have her continue on as a paid companion, Mary did not believe she could face her just yet. Olivia had disapproved of Jack from the beginning. Though too well-bred and loyal to say "I told you so," Olivia's eyes would surely give her away.

No, Mary needed to get away from everyone, including her dearest Olivia.

She would soon need to hire a new companion, but for now she simply wanted to be alone. She wanted to disappear to someplace where no one knew her, as far away as possible.

But where?

She had decided to call on the dowager countess Bradleigh, Robert's grandmother, who had been a good friend to her in the last three years. She knew she could trust the old woman and prayed that she would be able to recommend a remote retreat somewhere to which Mary could disappear. Though the dowager resided in Bath almost year-round, she was known to be very wealthy and to own several other properties throughout Britain. It was primarily this knowledge that shamelessly drew Mary to her door in Laura Place later that afternoon.

The dowager, shocked to find Mary in her drawing room when she should be preparing to recite her wedding vows, did not mince words.

"What did that black-hearted scoundrel do," she asked, "to send you packing on the eve of your wedding?"

Mary should have known the dowager would waste no time getting to the point. She had prepared herself for the inevitable questions and had even mustered the courage to, at least, allude to the truth. Or so she had believed. Now, faced with the dowager's stern gaze and direct questions, she found it more difficult to be truthful than she had expected.

"I have simply decided we would not suit," she said at last.

"Nonsense. What happened, my dear?"

Mary stared at the hands in her lap for several moments. She must say *something*. She considered how much she should confide to the dowager. She had more or less determined not to reveal to anyone her true motives for jilting Jack. She had no wish to admit that she had been duped by a fortune hunter, seduced into believing she was something she was not. It was a very lowering confession, to say the least. And she was feeling low enough already and her nerves were on edge. She was not sure how much she could reveal without losing control.

But then, it would not really be fair to ask the dowager for help without telling her why she needed it. She looked at the old woman—whose sharp brown eyes, so often narrowed in contempt, were now full of kindness and compassion, inviting confidence—and made a decision. Before she could reconsider, she plunged ahead.

"I discovered that Lord Pemerton . . . that he had lied to me," Mary said. "About why he wanted to marry me, that is."

"Yes? Go on," the dowager said when Mary hesitated. "What did you find out?"

Go on with it. Finish what you've started.

"He wanted my money," she said. "Nothing more."

Upon deft questioning by the dowager, the whole story unfolded. When there was nothing left to tell, Mary reached for her reticule and retrieved a linen square to wipe her eyes. To her shame, she had been unable to hold back the tears.

"My poor lamb," the dowager said as she patted Mary's hand. "I can understand why you left. I always knew that young man was a blackguard. Never understood Robert's attachment to the fellow. He went up several notches in my estimation, though, when I heard of his betrothal to you. Perhaps I was wrong." She tilted her head back and glared at Mary down the length of her aristocratic nose. "Perhaps," she said as her eyes narrowed slightly. "But are you sure it would not have been better simply to have confronted Pemerton with what you had learned? What is he going to think, not knowing what you overheard?"

"I do not care what he thinks. And no, I could not confront him. I felt too much the fool. I had to leave."

"Of course," the dowager said in a solicitous tone. "But if he comes after you," she continued in a more stern voice, "and I am not so certain he will, by the way—I should think he will be more angry than hurt—he will surely seek you out here in Bath. Are you prepared to face him now?"

"No," Mary said, "I am not. And that is why . . . well, why I have come to you, my lady. I wanted to ask for your help."

"Anything, my dear. What may I do for you?"

"Well," Mary said, "I had hoped you might be able to recommend a place for me to go. I would like to disappear for a while, you see. I would like to be alone, to think. And I . . . well, I have nowhere to go." Mary cast her eyes back to her lap, uncomfortable making such a bold request.

"Let me think," the dowager said, her brow furrowed in concentration as she tapped a bony finger against her cheek. All at once her eyes lit up. "There is one place. Do you mind a deal of travel, my dear?"

"Oh no." Mary was suddenly seized with excitement. It was going to work, after all. "The farther away the better."

"Good girl. I have a smallish house in Scotland, given to me by my father. Glennoch was not a part of my marriage settlement, and still belongs to me."

"Scotland?" Mary had not actually considered anything quite *that* far away. "I have never been that far north."

"It is really very lovely. And in the south, in Galloway province, not too far from Kirkcudbright. My husband and I visited Glennoch several times in the early years of our marriage. He was fond of fishing. I have not been there in . . . oh, probably twenty-five years. But I keep in touch with the caretakers, a wonderful old couple named MacAdoo. Isn't that a marvelous name? Sounds rather like the call of some wild bird, does it not? MacAdoo. MacAdoo." She paused for a moment and chuckled softly. "The areas near Glennoch are full of people with the most amusing names. But I digress," she said. "I am sure the MacAdoos keep Glennoch in reasonably good condition. You are free to make use of it for as long as you like, my dear. I believe you will find it quiet and restful. Shall I write to Mrs. MacAdoo?"

"Oh yes, please," Mary said in a shaky, raspy voice. She reached over and planted a kiss on the dowager's cheek. "You are very kind, my lady. You are sure you do not mind?"

"Why should I mind? In fact, I would be glad for someone to have a look at the place for me. Just to reassure me that all is still in order. Stay as long as you like."

"Is there . . . is there by chance a pianoforte at Glennoch?"

"As a matter of fact," the dowager said with a smile, "there is, though it must be sadly out of tune, I fear."

"Then I shall go to Glennoch."

"Wonderful!"

"Oh, thank you, Lady Bradleigh. I am most grateful." Mary brushed away more tears, ever close to the surface and ready to fall. "I should like to leave at once. Oh, and, if it is all the same to you," she said, "I would prefer that no one know where I am just yet. I need some time alone."

"Of course, my dear," the dowager said. "No one shall hear of your whereabouts from me, I assure you."

The dowager wrote down directions to Glennoch for Mary's coachman and recommended several inns along the way. She also agreed to write a letter that afternoon to Mrs. McAdoo, hoping it would arrive before Mary. Just to be safe, she also scribbled a short note of introduction to the caretakers, in case Mary arrived before the letter.

They also discussed the inevitable issue of propriety. Mary was loathe to engage a complete stranger as a traveling companion. At the risk of her reputation, which was, after recent events, of little concern to her in any case, she convinced the dowager that her maid would be sufficient chaperone during the journey north, and that Mrs. McAdoo would do well enough at Glennoch.

Mary gave a quick hug to the dowager before leaving, thanking her again and extracting yet another reassurance of secrecy.

"Don't worry, Mary," the dowager said. "Be off with you, now, before anyone notices you've returned to town."

"Damnation!"

Jack crumpled the *Morning Post* and flung it across the breakfast room. How dare she make such a bald, public announcement? And so soon.

> Lady Mary Elizabeth Haviland regrets to announce the termination of her betrothal to John Malcolm Augustus Raeburn, Marquess of Pemerton.

How had she managed the thing so quickly. It had been only two days since his return to London. He had fled Pemworth the very day of Mary's departure, leaving behind, without a moment's remorse, a house full of wedding guests and concerned family members. He would return in a month or so to check on his mother. But he could not have stayed on at Pemworth just then to save his life. It had been impossible. The thought of listening politely to words of regret and sympathy from the gathered guests, to watch the pity in their faces as they made discreetly precipitous departures, had been more than enough to make him flee. He could not have borne it.

He had returned to Hanover Square only the night before last. He had considered, for a brief moment, the wisdom of placing such an announcement in the papers himself. But without having actually spoken to Mary, or in fact communicated with her in any way, he had felt it best to ignore the situation. There was always that tiny, niggling doubt lurking in the back of his mind that she had not actually meant to jilt him, that she perhaps simply needed more time and would eventually come back to him.

There were no longer any doubts.

But how had she done the thing so quickly? Had she come to London? Was she here even now? Or had she gone home to Bath? Where was she?

Lady Mary Elizabeth Haviland regrets to announce . . . The words taunted him, and he realized he no longer cared where she was. He hoped he never laid eyes on her again for he might not be able to refrain from wringing her little neck. And he sincerely hoped she did in fact regret the announcement. For if she did not now regret it, he would make sure that soon enough, she would.

Jack had returned to London because it was the only place where he could fully indulge in all the pleasures and debaucheries in which he intended to drown himself. He lost no time in doing so. He attempted to obliterate Mary's memory in the arms of a different woman every night. He drank heavily, frequented gaming hells more than he had in the past, and found himself in serious play more often than not. He was determined to make his fortune one way or another, so long as that way did not involve a woman. He completely discarded the notion of marrying an heiress. He would not make that mistake again. The idea of marriage at all made him sick to his stomach. So he played often and deep, won great amounts and lost greater amounts. And he drank to make it all more bearable.

Since it was clear that gambling was not the safest way to secure, and maintain, a fortune, Jack investigated alternative measures as well. He entered into a clandestine correspondence with a "gentleman" in Devon to arrange storage of certain goods on Pemworth property. Renewed use of the Lantern Pavilion could also result in a larger share of profits. Matters began to look brighter. If his luck held out, he might yet be able to save himself from drowning in the River Tick.

A few weeks after his return to London, Jack was surprised to find Sedgewick skulking in the doorway to the crowded green room of the Royal Opera House in Covent Garden. Jack had been dividing his time between Covent Garden, Drury Lane, Sadler's Wells, and other less reputable theaters in his constant and very public search for new women. He was able to boast of never bedding the same woman twice. It had become a kind of game among the women to predict whose favors he would pursue on a given evening. He had even captured the notice of several bored Society matrons out for sport. High-born or low, Jack cared not a fig. He meant only to use as many women as possible for his own pleasure and nothing more. He had even heard word of a wager in White's betting book regarding how many consecutive nights he would be able to sustain his reputation.

At the moment he was hovering over a prime little morsel who called herself Justine. She was pinned against the wall between his arms and giggled as she thrust her ample bosom against his chest. The scowling figure of Sedgewick, visible out of the corner of Jack's eye, kept interfering with his concentration until, finally, Jack dropped his arms, gave Justine a playful slap on the hip and walked, somewhat unsteadily, toward his friend.

"All right, Sedge. Why the big scowl?"

"Come with me to White's," Sedgewick said in a tight voice Jack had seldom heard him use. "I must speak with you."

"Not now, old man. Can't you see I'm busy?" Jack's arm swept the green room, indicating the collection of actresses and dancers in various stages of undress and provocative postures.

"You're making a fool of yourself," Sedgewick hissed between his teeth. "Come on. Let's get out of here."

"How dare you—"

"Come *on*, Jack. Let's go." Sedgewick turned and left the room.

Jack, furious at Sedgewick's interference, nevertheless followed him through the maze of corridors and prop rooms until they reached the back exit onto the street. Jack leaned against the outside wall and held his head between both hands. Sedgewick's furious pace had made his head spin, and his temples pounded against his hands.

Sedgewick hailed a hackney, jumped in, and held the door open for Jack, who pushed himself from the wall and made a rather ungainly entrance into the carriage. He plopped down next to Sedgewick, his head reeling from the noxious odors emanating from the grimy straw that covered the floor. He reached over and jerked open the window, and rested his cheek against its edge.

"Well, there is hope for you yet," Sedgewick said as the hackney lurched forward. "I wasn't sure you would come."

"I came to satisfy myself," Jack said, enunciating each word slowly and carefully, "that you truly had dared to call me a fool in public, to find out what possessed you to do so, and then to blacken one or both of your eyes."

"Oh, stubble it, Jack. You're in no condition to blacken anyone's eyes. You couldn't swat away a fly. And besides, it is not only *me* who is calling you a fool. I have just returned to Town and find that all the world is laughing behind your back. As your friend, it pained me to find you so often the butt of insulting jokes."

"What are you talking about?"

"Don't be so thick, Jack," Sedgewick said with an impatient wave of his hand. "You know exactly what I mean. Look at you! You look like you've been on a three-week binge. You look terrible."

"So, what if I do? It is no concern of yours."

"Jack, Jack. This is not the way to go about it. The gambling. The drinking. The women. Especially the women. Lord knows you have always been a tad loose in your dealings with females. But this"—he chopped the air with a vague gesture—"this indiscriminate, relentless pursuit of the flesh . . . well, it's too much. You have gone too far this time, Jack. Don't you think you ought to return to Pemworth and nurse your wounds somewhat less publicly?"

"Shut up, Sedge. I'll behave any damned way I see fit. It is none of your concern—"

"We have been friends for too many years, Jack, for it not to concern me. It makes me sick to watch you sink so low. Besides, your poor mother is still repining over your departure—"

"What do you know of my mother?" Jack interrupted sharply.

"I have just left her. I—"

"Just left Pemworth? You have been there this whole time?"

"Yes," Sedgewick said, "along with many of the other guests. Your Uncle Edward's wedding did perk up your mother's spirits for a while, but she—"

"Uncle Edward's what?"

"His wedding. Did you not know? No, of course you would not. I don't suppose there has been any announcement yet. But surely your mother wrote to you with the news?"

Jack stared slack-jawed at Sedgewick. The drink must have addled his brain. He could not have heard correctly. "Uncle Edward is married?"

"Yes," Sedgewick replied. Jack caught the gleam of white teeth in the moonlight as the famous grin slowly stole across his friend's face, crinkling up his eyes into slits. "He married Mrs. Bannister."

"Olivia Bannister? Good God!"

"Apparently they came to an understanding after," Sedgewick said, hesitating, "after Lady Mary left. By the time they came back to the house with their announcement, you had already bolted."

"Damnation. I had no idea."

Sedgewick laughed. "Neither did anyone else. Except, perhaps, for your mother. She was the only one who did not appear goggle-eyed with shock. Anyway, we all stayed put while your uncle hared off to Exeter to locate a bishop and a special license. Took some doing, apparently. They were finally married a week ago, and are off to someplace or other in Hertfordshire."

"My grandfather's hunting box at Datching."

"Aye, that's the place."

"Good Lord." Jack shook his sore head slowly back and forth. "I suppose I really ought to have read all those letters of Mother's. But I always assumed they were about . . ." He reached up to run a limp hand through his hair. "I cannot believe it. My dissolute, debauched, womanizing old roué of an uncle settling down with a respectable, middle-aged woman. It's incredible."

Sedgewick cocked a brow. "Yes, well that's why I stayed at Pemworth," he continued. "And as I said, the wedding cheered your mother for a time, but she still broods about you and . . . well, and about Mary. But, good Lord, if she hears how you have been carrying on—"

"It is none of her business, just as it is none of yours, my friend."

"Look, Jack. I know—more than most, I think—I *know* how you were hurt by Mary's departure. But you must see you are not handling it in the best way. You have made a bigger mess of the thing through your own outrageous behavior. Good God, Jack— all those women . . ."

"Leave off, Sedge."

"But—"

"I said, leave off." Jack knocked for the driver to stop. He opened the door and stepped out onto Piccadilly. "I do not need your advice on how to run my life, Sedge. And I would appreciate it if you would keep your nose out of my affairs. But thank you for the word on Uncle Edward. I shall write to Mama asking for all the news. Good night to you." He closed the door on Sedgewick's frowning face and signaled the driver to move on.

Jack watched the hackney continue toward St. James's Street, and then he turned and headed in the opposite direction. The news of Uncle Edward's marriage had an oddly unsettling effect on him. He considered how his own marriage might have transformed yet another aging roué into something more respectable. Aging, indeed. He suddenly felt very old and very tired. What he needed was a little rejuvenating activity.

He turned onto Princes Street and up the steps of a well-known establishment whose proprietress specialized in extremely young girls.

Chapter 21

Mary wrapped her heavy woolen shawl more tightly about her shoulders against the early autumn chill. The crisp air, fragrant of the sea and the mulch of dried leaves, felt good against her face. She had grown to love the dramatic scenery of this isolated stretch of the Scottish coast. She stood on a heavily wooded hill overlooking the bay and admired the view of a ruined abbey perched atop the opposite shore. This area of coastline was dotted with abbey and castle ruins, and she had done much exploring during the last month. But this particular view, with the ghostly black shapes of the ruin silhouetted against the orange and purple sky of early sunset, waves crashing against the savage rocky cliffs below, never failed to inspire awe. She wished she had a talent for drawing or painting, for such a sight ought to be captured for eternity.

She suddenly realized, with a small burst of pride, that she had not thought of Jack once all day. She had spent the day—the first day without rain this week—tramping along the countryside near Glennoch, and had become so immersed in the beauty and wonder of autumn in this part of Scotland that she had forgotten to think of Jack and all that had happened last month.

I shall conquer your memory yet, Lord Pemerton, she thought, a satisfied smile on her face.

Generally, every time she walked along the coastline, she was reminded of Pemworth and of Jack. Although the setting of Glennoch was more rugged and hilly, there were certain similarities between this shore and that of South Devon: the dramatic juxtaposition of woods and coast; the pattern of tiny bays, narrow inlets, and deep creeks leading into the woodlands; the steep, rocky cliffs interspersed with sandy coves.

All these things, though unique to this part of Scotland, nevertheless reminded her often enough of Devon. And of Jack.

The journey north and the following week or so had been difficult at best, with her emotions fragile and raw. Once at Glennoch, she had given into them, letting go of all inhibitions, allowing her despair to run its course. She had cried until she thought she would die. She had raged and sulked and fretted and lamented. Oh, she had known failure before, to be sure. This absurd tendency to allow overly charming gentlemen to convince her that she was something other than what she had always known herself to be was apparently a pattern she was doomed to repeat if she was not more cautious. But then, the failure of her elopement with Peter Morrison had not been entirely due to false expectations, but rather to underestimating her father. This time, with Jack, it had been all her own fault. She had allowed herself to be duped, seduced, and manipulated, all against her better judgment. And so she grieved the loss of the illusion of love and happiness.

The McAdoos had been wonderful. Mrs. McAdoo—a round apple-checked woman of indeterminate age, with wisps of wiry, gray-sprinkled red hair peeking out from beneath a huge mobcap—was a gregarious, cheerful sort, who had made Mary feel welcome and comfortable from the start. Mary had initially admitted to Mrs. McAdoo only that she was convalescing from a nervous condition—not entirely inaccurate, as it happened. But the wily Scottish woman was not fooled.

" 'Tis a man what sent ye runnin', I be willin' to bet," she had said.

When Mary had protested, Mrs. McAdoo had waved her hands, palms out, in a gesture of denial. "Now, my lady," she said, "ye canna hide that look in yer eyes. 'Tis yer heart what needs healin', not yer nerves." She had leaned closer and lowered her voice. "Ye're no increasin', are ye?"

"Heavens, no!" Mary replied.

"Weel, then," Mrs. McAdoo continued, "thank the gude Lord fer that, anyhow. Now, dinna be worritin' aboot a thing, milady. Ye just have yerself a gude cry and fergit the bleedin' rascal.

Ye'll be awright soon enou. Ye've a gude, sound head on yer shoulders and dinna need any man to tell ye how to go on."

And so Mrs. McAdoo, bless her heart, had left Mary alone to suffer in her own way. She seemed to know instinctively when Mary needed quiet and solitude or when she craved company and conversation. During the latter times, Mrs. McAdoo could become a regular magpie. She could go on for hours with tales of the history and people of Galloway that often held Mary spellbound. She was pleased, though, to learn of the rather insular, private nature of the local people. Rural and isolated, they were generally suspicious of outsiders and would therefore leave Mary alone.

She blessed the dowager daily for sending her to Glennoch. This time alone, away from anything or anyone familiar, had been exactly what she needed. Those tumultuous emotions of the first weeks, which had threatened to engulf her to the point of madness, had at last subsided. One morning she had caught a glimpse of herself in a mirror and had been stunned at the stranger's face staring back at her: cheeks pulled and gaunt from lack of food, vacant eyes bloodshot and surrounded by dark circles, hair wild and matted and hanging about her shoulders.

"Enough," she had told the unfamiliar reflection. "Enough self-pity. Enough obsession with pain. It is time to live again."

Using all the strength and resilience that had allowed her to make a life for herself after her father's death, she had begun the slow process of healing. She had begun to play again, the music acting as a balm to her soul, even though the instrument was old and harshly tuned. She could lose herself in the fury or the sorrow or the joy of the notes, but always returned to a kind of restful calm afterward. She had also begun to spend a lot of time outdoors, when it wasn't raining, and the sights and smells, sounds and color of nature had brought another sort of peace. She walked and walked and walked, until her muscles ached and her feet were blistered. And though everywhere she walked seemed to remind her in some way of Jack, the memories brought less pain these days. She still was not quite ready to face the world and all its questions, but she had reached a sort of acceptance within herself and felt stronger each day.

Congratulating herself again on the more than six hours without thinking of Jack every fifteen minutes or so, Mary turned away from the bay and began the walk back to Glennoch.

Perhaps tomorrow, my lord, I shall make it through the entire day.

Smiling and feeling more content than she had since leaving Pemworth, Mary wound her way through the woodlands, playfully kicking at piles of dried leaves as she followed the path back to the house.

As his carriage came to a stop at the graveled entrance to Pemworth, Jack could not help but remember the last time he had arrived, almost six weeks ago. He had been so pleased and proud to watch Mary's excitement and admiration as she caught her first glimpse of Pemworth. Today, all he saw was a shabby old pile of pink stone and unkempt, overgrown, neglected gardens. Memories of that last visit weighed heavily on him, and Jack found it difficult to drag himself out of the carriage.

Finally, heaving a resigned sigh, he jumped down, mounted the entry steps, and entered the Great Hall. It was empty and dark and quiet. Alicia, Charlotte, and their girls would have returned to their own homes after Uncle Edward's wedding. His mother was all alone in this big, empty house. He swallowed past an odd lump in his throat as he recalled how lively and happy this house had been while Mary had been here, bringing a new energy to the old place, and to his family, after all the grief of the previous year.

"Where is my mother, Grimes?" he asked as he removed his greatcoat and hat and handed them to the butler.

"I believe she is in her sitting room, my lord."

"Tell her of my arrival, if you would, Grimes. I will see her after I have had a bath and change of clothes. She would not appreciate receiving me in all my dirt."

"Yes, my lord."

Jack made his way to his rooms, where Jessop had already put things in order. He had sent Jessop ahead several days before, in order to finish preparations for the use of Pemworth's sheltered cove to receive the first shipment of smuggled goods. If all went according to plan, Jack was in line to make a tidy profit, which he desperately needed. His luck at the tables lately had been almost all bad.

Jessop appeared in the doorway, carrying Jack's portmanteau.

"Is this all you brought, my lord?"

"Yes. I intend to return to London as soon as possible."

Jessop's brows rose in surprise, but he said nothing as he entered the dressing room with Jack's luggage.

As Jessop unpacked Jack's things and carefully put them away, they discussed the plans for the shipment.

"All is in order for tomorrow evening, my lord," Jessop said. "The caverns are ready, and all the passages have been cleared."

"And the Pavilion?"

"The lantern has been repaired, and new wicks are in place," Jessop said. "The pully mechanism has been oiled and tested, so it should be a fast and easy job to bring the lantern down and light it."

"Well done," Jack said. "I knew I could rely on you, Jessop."

"Of course, my lord."

They reviewed the details of the operation while Jessop prepared a bath for Jack, careful to speak of other matters whenever footmen entered with cans of hot water. Jack suspected, however, that most of them were also involved in some way with the local "gentlemen." It was difficult to avoid the temptation in this part of Devon, where smuggling profits kept food on the table in most households.

Jack dismissed Jessop while he soaked in the copper tub near the fire. He needed time alone before facing his mother. He knew from her letters that she either suspected or knew for certain of his activities in London. It was doubtful she would confront him or reprimand him, however, for she had never done so in the past. But the look in her eyes would be enough to make him feel her disappointment.

And he did not need his mother's guilt to make him feel shame. He was already filled with shame in plenty. He was not proud of his hedonistic activities in London, but he had not been able to stop himself. He had been obsessed with the need to use and discard woman after woman in an attempt to forget that he had ever cared for one in any other way. It gave him no real pleasure, to be sure. Oh, the momentary pleasure of sexual release, certainly. But the loathing and disgust that followed obliterated all memory of pleasure. He hated what he was doing, though he seemed incapable of stopping.

He had intended to remain at Pemworth only long enough to ensure that all went well with the shipment from France. He had intended to return to London and all its pleasures as soon as possible. But having left all that behind during his few days on the road, the very thought of resuming his life of dissipation made him weary to the bone. He was getting too old to keep up that feverish pace. He was tired of making the effort. He was even tired of all those women, of the constant search for new skirts to tumble.

And, of course, the real irony was that he had not after all been able to blot out Mary's memory. Though he still harbored a fierce anger for her, for her abandonment, he nevertheless thought of her almost constantly. In moments of the worst despair, Jack had relived in his mind those last days at Pemworth, trying to pinpoint exactly when things had fallen apart so badly. And yet time after time, he failed to reach any kind of explanation. He could find nothing in his behavior toward Mary to cause her to bolt like that. It just didn't make sense, which did nothing to alleviate his despair, but did everything to feed his anger. Though he could not forgive her, neither could he seem to forget her. He fought to drive her out of his mind. It should have been easy enough to forget such a tiny little dab of a woman. And yet . . .

Every woman he used reminded him of Mary, if only by contrast. Whenever he heard a particularly delicious piece of gossip or amusing tale, he found himself almost instinctively turning to share it with her. But she was not there. Whenever he heard piano music, he followed it, expecting to find Mary at the keyboard. But she was not there. Whenever he went to the theater or drove through the Park, he found himself wanting to turn to her to point out something or someone of interest. But she was not there. She was never there.

He had not realized how much he had come to depend on her

presence, her conversation, her wit, her laughter. And nothing, or no one, seemed able to assuage that need.

He scrubbed himself until his skin was raw, attempting to remove the filth that had become his life.

When he joined his mother sometime later, he found her lounging on a silk chaise in her boudoir. She turned toward him as he entered and held out her hand to him.

"Mama," Jack said, taking her hand to his lips. "I trust you are well?"

"Tolerably."

Jack raised his brows at her cold reply, then relinquished her hand and sat in a nearby chair. Some of the peculiar languor of grief that had been so common with his mother during the last year seemed to have settled back in. A wave of sadness gripped Jack as he recognized the role he must have played in the return of her grief. When he thought of her smiling and laughing during Mary's visit, he felt almost sick.

But there was something else—something more tense and grim about the set of her mouth. She was unhappy, certainly, but it was not merely the maudlin sorrow of grief. She was angry.

"What is it, Mama?" he asked. "What has upset you?"

"Hmph!" she snorted. "You can ask such a question?"

"I *am* asking, Mama."

She turned away from him and tilted her chin up. "If this were not your home, I would ask you to leave. I have no desire to share a roof with such a wastrel."

"Oh, Lord."

"Yes, I know of your . . . activities in Town."

"Mama, please—"

"And I am not so stupid as to misunderstand your sudden appearance just at this time," she said. "I have not lived in Devon all these years and remained ignorant of what happens during a new moon. Oh, Jack, how could you!"

"Mama, I—"

"Oh, I realize it all has to do with Mary," she said. "But that does not excuse—"

"Lady Mary Haviland has nothing to do with anything, Mama,"

Jack interrupted in a sharp tone. "She walked out of my life, as you may recall."

"And you have been trying to get over it by behaving outrageously. You ought to be ashamed of yourself."

With a fierce grip on the arms of the chair, Jack held back his anger. "If it is any consolation, Mama," he said, "I *am* ashamed. But—"

"Good," she said with a flash of a smile. "I am glad to know I have not raised a son totally without conscience. Now, I want you to tell me what happened with Mary? You left Pemworth before we could speak about it. Did you ever hear from her? Did you ever discover why she left?"

"No to both questions," Jack said. "And I do not wish to speak of it in any case. Tell me about Uncle Edward and Mrs. Bannister."

"Later, my dear. I want to know about Mary first."

"I *said* I did not wish to speak of her."

"I am your mother, Jack Raeburn, and you will do as I ask."

Jack stared at her incredulously. He had never seen his mother so determined, particularly after last year's tragedy when she had shrunk into herself. All his life she had been calm, complacent, nurturing—never demanding. But here she was, glaring at him with the steely eye of the strictest schoolmistress, refusing to be denied. He was puzzled and did not know how to deal with this new side of her.

"We *will* speak of her, Jack," she said, "for, you see, I had grown very fond of Mary. I had already begun to think of her as my daughter. I miss her," she said, her voice softening. "I must understand what happened."

Jack slumped back in his chair and said nothing. This was the last sort of conversation he wanted to have with his mother, but there seemed to be no stopping her.

"Mama," he said with a frustrated shrug. "I know no more than you. I do not know what happened."

"All I know," his mother continued, seeming to ignore his words, "is that she would not have left without good reason—at least, what would have seemed a good reason to her. I know you do not wish to hear this, my dear, but I suspect it must have been something you said or did that scared her away."

Jack placed his elbows on his knees and dropped his head into his hands. "Don't you think I have considered that, Mama?" he said, throwing out the words in anguish. "Don't you think I have gone over and over every word spoken, every gesture, every nuance—but to no avail. The last I saw her was at breakfast the day before she left. She was as cheerful and radiant as ever."

Jack recollected that morning with vivid clarity. It was the last time he had seen Mary. When he and Bradleigh had risen from the table, announcing their intention to ride out to some of the tenant farms, she had smiled at him—that wide, brilliant smile that could light up an entire room—and their eyes had locked for a moment, a kind of spark passing between them as each seemed to recollect the particularly passionate embrace they had shared the previous evening. And then, quite unexpectedly, she had winked at him.

Surely, there had been nothing between them at that moment to suggest there might be a problem. For God's sake, she had winked at him!

"Nevertheless," his mother continued, "I am convinced it has something to do with you, my dear. She was still fairly vulnerable after all those years with her father. I am afraid her spirit was more fragile than we thought."

"Mama, what are you talking about? What fragile spirit? Mary was one of the most intrepid, most confident women I ever met. She was so unaffected and open, yet so vivacious and gay—well, that is why everyone in the *ton* adored her."

His mother gave him a quizzical look. "My God," she said, and her brow furrowed in concern. "You do not know."

"Know what?"

"About Mary."

"Know what about Mary?"

And so Jack listened while his mother told him everything she had learned from Mary about her life of physical and emotional abuse at the hands of her father.

Chapter 22

"I had finally convinced her," the marchioness said, "or so I thought, that her father had been wrong to suggest that no man would ever want her for herself alone. She was sure that you had not known of her fortune, and so she had reluctantly begun to believe that her father was wrong."

Oh my God. Jack brought a hand to his mouth. The thought of sweet little Mary brutalized by that madman caused the bile to rise in his throat. And to have bullied her into believing she was ugly and worthless, that only her fortune mattered—

Oh my God, Mary.

Thinking he might truly become ill, he took deep gulps of air.

His mother glared at him through narrowed eyes. "*Was* her father wrong, Jack?"

"No. Yes! Oh, God. What have I done?" He dropped his head into his hands. In a muffled, anguished voice he told his mother everything. He told her the truth about his finances, how he had determined to marry an heiress, how he discovered that Mary, a woman he knew well and liked, was worth a fortune, and how he had more or less seduced her into accepting his offer.

"And selfishly believing in my own irresistible charms, it did not seem such a bad bargain at the time," he said. "But then, after a time . . . then, dammit, the money no longer mattered. I had fallen in love with her."

And though he now recognized the depth of his love for her, the irony was that she probably felt nothing but hatred for him, for she must surely have discovered his original motives somehow.

He had loved only two women in his long, wicked life. The

first, a woman whose affections had been false and whose ultimate betrayal had taught him never to trust. The second, a woman who had taught him, briefly, to trust again, but who must now despise him for what he had done to her. The pain of Suzanne's disdain, though, was nothing compared to the agony of Mary's hatred. Was he destined forever to love women who did not want him?

"Why did you not tell me, Jack?" His mother's soft voice interrupted his reverie. "I had guessed there was somehow less money than before, but I had no idea . . ."

Jack reached across and took his mother's hand. "You had suffered enough, Mama. I did not wish to add to your grief."

"Oh, Jack." She pulled him onto the chaise and took him in her arms. "To save me from suffering, you took all this upon your own shoulders, without a word to anyone. All alone, with no one to help you. My poor boy. My poor, wonderful boy. But some good came out of it, after all. You found Mary and fell in love with her."

Jack pulled back from her embrace. "I did," he said. "How could I not? When I came back today, it almost broke my heart to see Pemworth again, to remember how joyful and happy it had been when Mary was here, and to think that it might never be so again. Oh, God. What am I going to do?"

Jack rose from the chaise and began to pace the room. Was it possible Mary had somehow, despite all his cautious circumspection, discovered that he was a fortune hunter? Had she convinced herself that he cared only for her money?

Oh, Mary.

But it seemed the only logical answer if what his mother told him was true. It appeared he had inadvertently wounded that sweet, lovable woman where she was most vulnerable.

Oh, Mary.

The further irony—and this whole situation was altogether too full of irony for his taste—was, of course, that she would be right. He *had* wanted her for her money. That was all he had wanted from her. At first. But not anymore. No, not anymore. And yet he had played straight into her most deep-rooted doubts and insecurities, unintentionally reinforcing them.

"Why didn't she tell me, Mama?" he asked in a choked voice as he continued pacing the room. "Why didn't she tell me about her father? I knew about her elopement—she felt obligated to tell me that, I suppose. But not the rest." He stopped pacing for a moment as a thought struck him. "Come to think of it, there were some hints of her unhappy past, if I had but paid attention. From Bradleigh and Emily and Uncle Edward. But I . . . I disregarded them as meaningless, believing Mary so bright and high-spirited that nothing really bad could have ever happened to her. Oh, God!"

His mother rose from the chaise and came to his side, placing a hand on his arm. "She did not tell you, I think, because she was ashamed. It was difficult enough for her to tell me. She seemed to think it reflected badly on her that she did not fight back, that she allowed her father's abuse. To admit such a thing to a man she cared for . . . well, that would have been unthinkable."

"But it was not her fault."

"Of course it was not," his mother said. "But she would not see it that way. I suspect most children of abusive parents must believe it is somehow their own fault, that they are deserving of such treatment. Mary must surely have felt that way. Having been so isolated and alone, she would have had none but her father to influence her behavior."

"Oh, my poor Mary," Jack said, blinking furiously against the moisture welling up in his eyes. "My poor, sweet Mary. I must go after her."

His mother threw her head back with a loud sigh. "Jack, my dear boy, I have waited six weeks to hear those words."

Jack gave his mother a quick hug and a kiss on the cheek and then bounded out of the room toward his own suite. He had to find her. He had to find Mary. He had to make it up to her, somehow. He had to make her believe him. He wanted more than anything to convince her that he loved her—for herself, not for her money. He should have known his Mary was not like Suzanne or all the rest. Blast it all! He should have gone after her right away. If only he hadn't spent the last six weeks wallowing in dissipation, she might even now be safely in his arms. And so now he had to present himself to her with an even more tarnished life. He could only hope that she would forgive him. If he could find her.

Jessop was dumbfounded to find that Jack was leaving before tomorrow's clandestine shipment was safely received and secreted in Pemworth's underground caverns.

"You stay and take care of it, Jessop. I have something much more important to do."

Jack had no idea where to begin his search. After six weeks she could be almost anywhere. He knew she had a home in Bath, so that was to be his first stop. But when he arrived at her Queen's Square house, he found the knocker off the door and no answer to his insistent pounding. He sought out Mary's man of business, but Mr. Fleming was either unable or unwilling to give out any information on his client.

Jack traveled from Bath to London, remembering her announcements in the London papers and thinking she might have been there all along. But the house she had let on Upper Brook Street was now occupied by a young baronet and his new family, and the lending agent had not heard from Mary since she had left for Pemworth.

Desperate, Jack dashed off notes to all those friends of Mary's he could recall, and called on those still in Town. He was received coolly in every case, which he supposed he deserved, but in the end no one knew where Mary was.

Jack kept thinking of the announcement in the newspaper. Perhaps she had not come to London, but had sent it from somewhere else. It was a long shot, but worth a try. He first visited the offices of the *Morning Post*. They were willing to admit that the announcement was legitimate and had been submitted by Lady Mary Haviland herself. Any further information was strictly confidential. However, after some judicious hints of potential lawsuits over misuse of fraudulent information, delivered in his best Superior Marquess manner, Jack was shown the original letter from Mary, still on file. It had been sent from Bath, on the same day they had discovered her missing from Pemworth.

So, she *had* been to Bath. Frantic and sick with worry over what might have become of her, he traveled once again to the famous spa. He would try to trace her trail from there. He returned to Mary's house on Queen's Square, where the knocker was still removed. He pounded on the front door, and this time it was opened by a housekeeper who eyed him warily. When he identified himself, her eyes widened and she stepped aside to let him in.

"Her ladyship is not here," the housekeeper said, "but perhaps you should speak to Mrs. Maitland, who is here just now. Wait here in the morning room, my lord, and I will send her to you."

Mrs. Maitland? Good lord, Olivia Bannister was here. Well, thank God for it, for perhaps she would know something of Mary's whereabouts. He paced impatiently as he awaited her arrival.

"Lord Pemerton!" The door swung open to admit a radiant and smiling Olivia. She offered her hand.

"Mrs. Bannister," Jack said, kissing the air above her fingers. "I beg your pardon. It is Mrs. Maitland now, is it not? Or perhaps I should simply call you Aunt Olivia?"

Olivia laughed. "Why not just call me Olivia?" She seated herself on a settee near the window overlooking the square. Jack followed suit and sat in an armchair across from her.

"I am sorry, Olivia, but I have not yet offered you my felicitations on your marriage. You are most welcome to the family."

"Thank you, my lord."

"I think you may be permitted to dispense with the 'my lords' and call your nephew Jack, my dear. Is Uncle Edward with you?"

"Yes, we are staying a few days at the White Hart," Olivia said. "I needed to return to Mary's house to pack those of my things that were still here."

"Olivia," Jack said in a quiet voice, "can you tell me where Mary is?"

She looked at him for a long moment, her head cocked to one side as if weighing what she should say. "I am afraid I do not know," she said at last.

Jack closed his eyes and breathed deeply. He had been so sure Olivia would know. "Are you certain?" he pressed. "She was here for a time, at least."

"Yes, I know," Olivia said. "She must have come here straight from Pemworth. She must have known I would return here eventually. She left a letter for me here, and . . . and a year's salary."

"She did not mention where she was going?"

"I am afraid not."

"What about the servants?" Jack asked in an almost frantic voice, his stomach in knots as he considered that he might never find her. "Might they not know where she has gone?"

"I have asked them myself," Olivia said in a patient tone, "and they have no more idea than you or I. She took her maid and coachman with her, but neither said anything belowstairs about where they were going. Perhaps they did not know. Anyway, they left after only one day and have been gone ever since."

Jack ran his fingers through his hair. He had never felt so helpless and frustrated in all his life. He was desperate to find Mary, but the only trail he had seemed to lead nowhere. Well, if Olivia could not help with Mary's whereabouts, perhaps she could at least shed some light on her departure.

"Olivia," he said, "you must have been the last person at Pemworth to see Mary. Can you tell me anything to help me understand why she . . . why she left like that?"

Olivia's eyes narrowed as she studied Jack. "You are in love with her, aren't you?"

"Yes."

Olivia sighed. "Edward told me as much," she said. "I must apologize for misjudging you at first. I had thought you a heartless cad and a shameless flirt, but at Pemworth I had begun to change my mind. I could see in the way you looked at her that you cared very much for Mary."

"Yes, I do."

"If you don't mind my asking, why have you waited until now to go after her?"

Jack let out a breath through puffed cheeks and leaned his head against the back of the chair. "Because I was an idiot. Because I was hurting. Because it took me this long to realize how much I want her."

"I hope you find her, then," Olivia said, her eyes softening, "for she deserves to be loved."

"Then help me decipher this mess. When did you last see her?"

"Let me think." Olivia's brow furrowed in thought. "It was late afternoon. She was heading down the corridor to her room and was very agitated. I asked if she was ill, and she said she was. I tried to help her, but she very curtly asked to be left alone and sent me away." She took a ragged breath. "I have not seen her since."

"Do you know where she had been when you saw her?" Jack asked.

"No," Olivia said, "but I suspect she had been outdoors for she was still wearing her bonnet. Although, because of her fair skin she usually carried a . . . Wait a moment. She must have been walking near the gardens along the east wing, for I found her parasol there the next day. She must have dropped it."

"Her parasol?"

"Yes," Olivia said, frowning in recollection. "I thought it odd at the time, but then . . . well, my thoughts were fairly well occupied with other things that afternoon. Anyway, I found her parasol in the bushes just outside the library doors."

"The library?" Suddenly, an image flashed through Jack's mind of the face of Max, the spaniel, in the lavender bushes. The dog, seldom one to prowl the estate alone, had looked lost and forlorn. There was something significant about all this, but it eluded him just now.

Think, Jack.

Mary must have been outside the library. He had been speaking with Sedgewick. They were interrupted. By the dog? No, by a noise. Jack had heard a noise, and it had alarmed him. But why? What had he and Sedgewick been saying?

A bit skittish, ain't you, Jack?

Oh, my God. It suddenly all came back to him. They had been speaking of his original mercenary purpose for offering for Mary, and he was worried for anyone to learn of his financial problems. He had been afraid someone would overhear them.

Apparently someone had.

Oh, Mary. My poor Mary.

Jack jumped to his feet. "I must find her."

"Have you thought of something? Did you remember—"

"I know now why she left," Jack said. "And now I must find

her." He opened the morning room door and shouted for the housekeeper.

"Yes, my lord?" she asked breathlessly when she appeared at the door.

"I wish to speak to all the servants," Jack told her. "All of them, at least, who were here when Lady Mary returned."

With some reluctance the housekeeper did as he asked. Because Lady Mary had not been in residence since early spring, there had been only three staff on hand when she arrived so unexpectedly: the housekeeper, the butler, and a footman. The footman could tell Jack nothing except that he had posted the letters to London for her. The housekeeper knew little else, save that she had been given the packet for Olivia.

"Did she leave the house at all?" Jack asked.

"Aye," the housekeeper replied, "she did leave for a short time but I can't say as I know where she went."

The footman also knew nothing of where she had gone. The butler might know something, but he had taken the afternoon off.

"When is he expected to return?" Jack asked with no little impatience.

"Oh, any time now," the housekeeper said. "We keep somewhat irregular hours when her ladyship is not in town."

"Hmph. I shall await his return, then," Jack said. "Send him to me at once."

And so Jack paced the morning room for the next two hour while he waited to speak with the butler. Olivia served him tea and told him of her wedding and the wedding trip to Datching doing her best to keep him distracted. Jack wandered aimlessly about the room—so obviously Mary's room—picking up object at random and putting them down again. He only half heard what Olivia said, immersed in his own thoughts—thoughts of Mary and how she must have felt when she overheard that blasted conversation in the library. If only she had stayed long enough to hear him confess his love for her to Sedgewick.

He wondered if he would ever be allowed the opportunity to confess his love to her directly.

When the butler calmly entered the morning room at last, Jack practically pounced upon him. Yes, he remembered Lady Mary leaving the house for a short time. He had called a chair for her, for she was only going a short distance.

"Where did she go?" Jack asked.

"She asked to be carried to Laura Place, my lord."

"Do you know whom she was visiting at Laura Place?"

"I cannot say for sure, my lord," the butler replied, "but she often used to visit the dowager countess Bradleigh, who lives there."

Robert's grandmother?

Muttering words of farewell to Olivia, Jack dashed out the front door and headed for Laura Place.

Chapter 23

Mary trod carefully up the stone steps of the sole remaining tower of a castle ruin near Glennoch. One of many ruins in the area, its standing tower still had an intact and reasonably safe looking stairway, and Mary had been unable to resist the climb. The small fortress had been built on the very edge of a rocky cliff that dropped off dramatically to a small cove below, and so when she reached the top and stood leaning out between the crumbled merlons, she felt as though she hovered above the sea like a gull.

She circled the tower, admiring the view from all sides: the sea ahead and the relatively high wooded hills behind. She saw the figure of a man walking on the path from Glennoch. She seldom saw any of the local people on her explorations of the area, so she wondered briefly at finding someone on that lonely path. She turned from him, though, more interested in the view of the cliff and the sea. She no longer feared meeting other people and would gladly chat with him if he came near the castle.

She stood facing the sea, her hair blowing loose in the strong breeze. Her eyes closed as she listened to the crash of waves against the rocks below. The sea was fierce and rough today, and the force of it smashing against the cliffside was strong enough so that, even this high above, the dissipated mist of each wave dusted her cheeks with moisture.

She felt each wave as if she were the cliff itself, strong and unimpeachable, able to withstand the mightiest assault, still standing tall and proud, changing ever so slowly and inexorably with time.

She had healed and was better for it and stronger than ever. She might never be able to stand literally tall, but she felt tall and strong and ready to face the world again.

Mary felt good enough that she had finally written a few letters to friends, informing them of her whereabouts, and the fact that she would probably not return to Bath until the spring. She had grown attached to this savage land and wanted to remain through the winter. By that time, when she finally returned home, she would have left all her problems behind her and would be pleased to join Society once again. People had always been kind to her. She had no doubt she would be made to feel comfortable once again among her friends, despite all that had happened.

Until this time she had corresponded only with the dowager countess in Bath, letting her know of her safe arrival and assuring her of the comfortable state of Glennoch. She had now written again to Olivia—in care of her own house in Bath, hoping someone in her household would know her friend's situation—apologizing for her abrupt and unexplained departure. She explained now, as best she could in a letter.

With more difficulty she had written to the marchioness, Jack's mother, thanking her for the kindness and hospitality she had shown Mary while at Pemworth. The subject of her departure had not been easy to explain, so she had simply stated that she had suffered from last-minute doubts and had decided she and Jack would not suit. She apologized for the trouble she no doubt had caused, but hoped that they would one day meet again as friends.

Once she had determined, finally, to give up her self-indulgent melodramatic despair, Mary had quickly come to grips with her own pain and humiliation. After all, she had spent most of her life learning to live with her shortcomings and failures, so often pointed out by her father. This latest incident had been simply another bump in the road, and though she had been thrown from the carriage this time, she had now picked herself up and was ready to move on once again.

But she had not escaped totally unscathed. Mary knew that she would never be quite the same. Jack had changed everything.

However false his displays of affection had been, for a brief time he had made her feel so special, so precious—it was a feeling she would keep close to her heart forever. For that, she could

forgive him anything, although, in fact, he did not require forgive
ness for he had never made false promises to her. More importan
she had forgiven herself, for the time she had spent with Jack ha
been too special to disregard. He had taught her how to love
However painful the aftermath, she could not regret it. At leas
now—finally, after twenty-nine years—she could at last say sh
knew how it felt to love.

Opening her eyes, Mary watched the waves crash against th
rocks below and was struck once again by the notion of her ow
resilience. Like the ancient rocks, she was a survivor. A bit wor
but a survivor nevertheless. Thanking the powers of the univers
for bringing her back to that realization, she spread her arms wid
and laughed for pure joy, glorying in the wind and the sea and th
sun.

Suddenly, she heard an indistinct shout from below. Lookir
down, she saw a man standing at the cliff's edge, motioning t
ward her. It must be the same man she had seen on the Glennoc
path. Although the tower was not terribly tall, she could not se
the man clearly as he stood in the shadow of the tower. Perha
he was concerned for her safety. Perhaps this old ruin was le
sturdy than she had hoped, and he meant to warn her of the da
ger. She waved down to him and turned to begin the descent.

She slowly made her way down, a hand anchored on each wa
of the narrow tower as she stepped carefully down the spiral
steps. She marveled that large, heavily armored men could ev
have maneuvered such a descent. Keeping her eyes on her feet
she gingerly moved from each narrow, triangular step to the ne
she did not see the man standing in the arched entrance to t
tower until she had bumped against his broad chest. Startled, sh
stepped back into the darkness of the tower.

"Hello, Mary."

The achingly familiar voice caused her breath to catch.

Jack.

He stood in the archway, a dark silhouette against the bri
sunlight beyond. But there was no mistaking him.

Jack. He is here. He is really here. Jack had come all the w
to Scotland. *Oh, my God.* All that renewed strength and con

dence she had been basking in only moments before now suddenly puddled at her feet.

When he shifted slightly so that he was partially bathed in the sunlight, Mary saw his face clearly for the first time and stifled a gasp at the sight of him. He looked awful. Always handsome, in a harsh, angular, swarthy sort of way, his face was now drawn and haggard, looking as though he hadn't slept for days. Dark circles hung beneath his eyes, and the lines between his nose and mouth and around his eyes seemed deeper and more pronounced. What on earth had happened to him?

They studied one another in silence for a moment before he spoke again.

"Why did you leave me like that, Mary, and break my heart in two?"

When he had first seen her standing on the tower, his heart had lurched in his chest at the mere sight of her. He had smiled as he watched her, standing with her arms outstretched, looking for all the world like a tiny eaglet ready to test her wings. When he heard her distinctive laugh float through the air, he almost wept with joy.

He had begun to despair of ever finding her, but the dowager had been most accommodating. She had protested ignorance at first, but it had been a deliberately poor display, as though she had meant for him to force her capitulation. The old woman was a romantic at heart and had finally admitted that Mary had been away long enough and should be more than ready to be rescued.

God, but she looked wonderful. Gone were the towering coils of hair she had always worn to increase the illusion of height. Her hair hung loose almost to her waist and was whipped wildly about by the wind like a flag. Her dress and pelisse were molded against her tiny curves as she faced proudly out to the sea. *Ah, my Pocket Venus,* he thought with a smile. God, how he had missed her.

He suspected she had not recognized him from atop the tower, and so the shock on her face after crashing into his chest was not totally unexpected. But when he spoke, he saw her stiffen. He watched as her face registered a series of emotions: surprise, confusion, fear, wariness. Somewhere in there he thought he detected delight as well; but if so, it was quickly extinguished. He thought for a moment that she was going to move toward him, and so he reached out for her; but she seemed to catch herself and did not move.

Pulling her shoulders back and standing as tall as she was able, she spoke at last. "I left because I decided we would not suit," she said as though repeating a memorized litany. Her voice was even huskier and more seductive than he remembered. "Besides," she continued, "I did not believe you had a heart to break."

Jack laughed. "Neither did I," he said. "In fact, I was convinced it had been shattered to bits fifteen years ago. But I was wrong, Mary. It must have healed while I wasn't watching, for it has surely been broken again."

The slightest frown flickered across her eyes before her expression settled into one of confusion. "Mary," he said softly, "I am so sorry. Can you ever forgive me?"

Mary's hand flew to her cheek. "Jack."

He took a step closer. "I know what you heard, Mary." At her incredulous look, he nodded. "Yes, I know that you overheard Sedgewick and me in the library. I cannot tell you how sorry I am you had to hear that. I only wish you had stayed to hear the rest of my little speech."

"W-what did you say, then?"

"I told Sedgewick that even though it was true that I had originally wanted to marry you for your fortune, I no longer cared about the money. It was you I wanted, Mary. You. Not your bloody fortune."

"You lied to me," she said in a trembly voice.

"I did," Jack said. "And I shall regret it for the rest of my life. I admit that I have been nothing less than a fortune hunter. It is not something I am proud of, but, understand, I was up to my eyeballs in debt. When you agreed to help me find a bride, I could not bring myself to tell you, or anyone, what sort of bride I truly needed."

A look of profound sadness gathered in her eyes, and he wanted to reach out to her, but knew it would be wrong to touch her just yet. His thoughts befuddled by the force of his feelings for her, by the nearness of her, he nevertheless stumbled ahead in the explanation he owed her.

"When I discovered," he continued, holding her gaze, "that you had a fortune . . . well, it seemed logical to offer for you. I was already quite fond of you. I thought we would rub along together well enough. But the more time I spent with you, the more I came to know how very special you are, and my affection for you grew. Suddenly, one day—shortly after we arrived at Pemworth I think—I realized that I no longer cared about your fortune. I wanted you. I wanted *you,* Mary, and your fortune be damned."

"Why have you come, Jack?"

"Because," he said taking another step toward her, "I have discovered that I cannot live without you. Because my life is empty and worthless if you are not a part of it. Because I could not bear the thought of your never knowing that."

Mary stared at him mutely, all the things he said racing through her mind. Was he serious? Or was this just another attempt at seduction? She watched his eyes, which appeared brilliant with contained emotion. Strangely, she saw none of the self-assured charm she had come to expect from Jack. He looked somehow nervous, almost boyishly uncertain.

Her own eyes must have softened as she regarded him, for he appeared to relax slightly. He took a step closer.

"And most of all," he said, his voice barely above a whisper, "because I am, in fact, hopelessly, desperately in love with you."

Mary hesitated only for an instant, and then, casting her fate to the winds, headed straight for his open arms. He clasped her against his chest, wrapping his arms tightly around her. She wound her arms around his waist and buried her head in his neckcloth. Sweet heaven, but he felt good. She had almost forgotten how wonderful it felt to be in his arms. She rejoiced in the feel of him, the shape of him, the smell of him. This was where she wanted to be. And she wanted to believe him. Good Lord, how she wanted to believe him. But it almost did not matter anymore. She did not think she would be able to walk away again.

He made no move to kiss her, but only held onto her as if he would never let go, crushing her so tightly she could barely breathe.

"Ah, Mary, Mary," he said at last, his breath tickling the top of her head. "If it wasn't clear to me before, it is certainly clear now. We belong together, Mary. Nothing has ever felt so right. Holding you in my arms again, I feel as if I have come home at last."

Mary moved her head away from his chest, wanting to see his face. The look in his eyes was her undoing. She knew at once that he spoke the truth. She reached up to touch his cheek and brushed away a tear. He grabbed her hand and kissed her palm.

"I love you, Mary. I love you." And suddenly, his lips captured hers in a ravenous kiss. She responded instantly with equal passion, reaching up to pull him down closer, threading her fingers through his soft, black hair. There was nothing else in the world in that moment but the softness of his lips moving hungrily against hers, the slight roughness of his tongue as it explored her mouth and circled her own tongue. She kneaded his back and shoulders with restless desire, wanting to meld with him, to merge completely with him. She was on fire for him.

His mouth left hers and she gave a small sigh of pleasure as he trailed butterfly-soft kisses along her brow and over her eyes, along her jawline and cheekbones, down the base of her throat and around her neck, and back again. She was lost to him. Gone were the fears of inadequacy and worthlessness. Gone were the doubts of her own attractiveness and desirability. Gone were the visions of a life of loneliness and emptiness. All that mattered now, all that she was conscious of, was that she was in the arms of the man she loved and he was enfolding her within his own passion.

Jack found her lips once again, and kissed her with an aching tenderness, slowly and gently, while his hands traced the curve of her waist and hips, bringing them into even more intimate contact. When he lifted his head at last, she moaned softly at the loss of him. He smiled sweetly down at her and held her face in his hands, stroking her jaw with his thumbs. "I hope," he said, "this means you have at least a little affection for me."

"More than a little," she replied in a husky whisper.

"I am glad to hear it, my love." He kissed her again lightly

"You can burn all your blasted money, you know," he said in a hoarse voice, "or give it away for all I care—so long as you come back to me. Forever this time. You see, I want to spend the rest of my life with you, Mary. I want to hold your sweet body naked in my arms and make love to you every night. I want to wake up each morning with you curled up all soft and warm at my side. I want to see your bright smile and beautiful eyes across the break-fast table each morning. I want to make babies with you and watch them grow and run wild over the shores of Pemworth. I want to grow old with you and die with my head cradled on your breast."

Overcome by the passion of his declaration, Mary buried her face against his shoulder. She had never dreamed to hear such words from Jack—from anyone. She knew in her heart that he was sincere, and the knowledge of his love was overwhelming to her. After weeks of despair and anguish, it was almost impossible to accept such joy. Almost. Too overcome for mere words, she simply held onto him tighter.

He reached down, tilted her head up, and kissed her eyes, lick-ing away the tears. "I will take care of you, Mary, for all the days of my life. No one will ever hurt you again." He feathered kisses lightly against her mouth again and again, as though he could not seem to get enough of her. Holding his mouth just above hers so that their lips still brushed as he spoke, he said, "Will you marry me?"

She opened her eyes, looked into his, and smiled. "Yes," she said in a firm, proud voice. "I will marry you, Jack. And this time," she said chuckling, "I promise not to run away."

"Mary, Mary," he said pulling her tighter against him, "I love you so much. But even those words don't seem adequate to ex-press how I feel. I wish I could say more. It is not enough, some-how."

"Stupid man," she said, pulling his mouth down to hers. "It is more than enough. It is everything."

It was sometime later when Mary nestled her head against Jack's shoulder as they sat leaning against a large boulder on the cliff's edge. Clothes disheveled and gaping, lips swollen, and hair

in wild disarray, they sat quietly watching the waves crash beneath them. Between moments of sweet passion, they talked and
talked and talked, at last opening completely to one another about
their mutual dreams and desires. Mary spoke, at last, of her father,
and Jack told her about Suzanne. There were no more secrets between them as they laughed and cried over what no longer
seemed important.

As the sun made its way west, they reluctantly decided it was
time to return to Glennoch. Mary straightened her bodice and retrieved her pelisse while Jack tried to make something presentable
out of his discarded cravat. Jack rose first and offered his hand to
Mary. He pulled her to her feet, grabbed her by the waist, and
swung her around and around.

"Put me down!" Mary squealed, laughing and out of breath.
"You're making me dizzy."

"Sorry, love," Jack said as he returned her to earth. "I was momentarily overwhelmed with joy at my good fortune."

"Good *fortune*?" Mary asked in a teasing tone. "Are we back to
that again?"

Jack shuddered. "I will have to think of another word," he said,
"for I will not be reminded of my initial mercenary motives."

"You know," Mary said, "I would be happy to hand over my
fortune to you. You are welcome to it. I can think of no better use
for it than to bring Pemworth to rights again. And your other estates as well. The money has never been that important to me. If
you had told me from the start, I would have gladly handed it
over."

"And we could have avoided all this heartache?" Jack said. "I
know. But I was too stupid and too proud to admit to you my
problems. I suppose each of us has a thing or two to learn about
too much pride." He put his arm around her waist and pulled her
close. "I will take your money, Mary, for I need it badly. But you
must promise me one thing."

"Anything."

"You must never, ever forget," he said, "that it is you I love,
and not your money."

She grinned up at him. "I may need reminding, now and then."

Jack pulled her into a passionate kiss. "Consider yourself reminded," he said breathlessly.

Taking Mary by the hand, intertwining his fingers with hers, he led her along the steep path toward Glennoch. "We must hurry," he said with a smile. "My mother is hoping to see us married before Christmas."

"Well then," Mary said with a playful gleam in her eye, "let us oblige her. We are, after all, in Scotland."

Jack stopped on the path and looked down at her, grinning rakishly. "So we are," he said. "Then let us find the nearest blacksmith."

"You're on," Mary said, and dashed ahead on the path, Jack close at her heels.